A Play of Piety

Margaret Frazer

BERKLEY PRIME CRIME, NEW YORK

THE BERKLEY PUBLISHING GROUP
Published by the Penguin Group
Penguin Group (USA) Inc.
375 Hudson Street, New York, New York 10014, USA
Penguin Group (Canada), 90 Eglinton Avenue East, Suite 700, Toronto, Ontario M4P 2Y3, Canada
(a division of Pearson Penguin Canada Inc.)
Penguin Books Ltd., 80 Strand, London WC2R 0RL, England
Penguin Group Ireland, 25 St. Stephen's Green, Dublin 2, Ireland (a division of Penguin Books Ltd.)
Penguin Group (Australia), 250 Camberwell Road, Camberwell, Victoria 3124, Australia
(a division of Pearson Australia Group Pty. Ltd.)
Penguin Books India Pvt. Ltd., 11 Community Centre, Panchsheel Park, New Delhi—110 017, India
Penguin Group (NZ), 67 Apollo Drive, Rosedale, North Shore 0632, New Zealand
(a division of Pearson New Zealand Ltd.)
Penguin Books (South Africa) (Pty.) Ltd., 24 Sturdee Avenue, Rosebank, Johannesburg 2196,
South Africa

Penguin Books Ltd., Registered Offices: 80 Strand, London WC2R 0RL, England

This book is an original publication of The Berkley Publishing Group.

FIRST EDITION: December 2010

Library of Congress Cataloging-in-Publication Data

Frazer, Margaret.
    A play of piety / Margaret Frazer. — 1st ed.
        p.   cm.
    ISBN 978-0-425-23709-0
    1. Medicine, Medieval—Fiction. 2. Great Britain—History—Lancaster and York, 1399–1485—Fiction.
I. Title.
    PS3556.R3586P555   2010
    813'.54—dc22   2010023083

PRINTED IN THE UNITED STATES OF AMERICA

10 9 8 7 6 5 4 3 2

To The Four
—Leslie H., Patty H., Carol M., and Cindy U.—
Excellent friends who have seen me through so much of the
Bad Times

Author's Foreword

My usual way has been to leave my authorial comments for the ends of my books.

I am adding this foreword because when I would tell people that I was writing a book set in a medieval hospital, as often as not their response was some expression of disgust that reflected the engrained, erroneous idea that medieval times were nothing but dirty, nasty, ignorant, and unremittingly brutal—a notion cheaply (and tediously) perpetuated in most novels and movies supposedly set in the Middle Ages. Therefore it seems a goodly notion to explain here at the beginning that the hospital in this story is imagined but *not* idealized. Its running is based on the recorded regulations of actual medieval English hospitals and reflects their expectations of cleanliness and care, as well as the charity and concern for souls with which they were founded.

Nor is a woman acting as a *medica* at the time an imagined possibility. Women could and did act as physicians in medieval times.

A Play of Piety

Chapter 1

It was the golden time of year, the wide fields of ripened grains standing tall under the hot August sky or already turned to golden stubble where the harvesters had passed with sickle and scythe, and soon the geese and cattle would be turned to graze, to fatten for Michaelmas and winter.

After three years of failed harvests and the dearth that followed, with hungry winters and starving springs, those golden fields under a cloudless sky would have been enough to raise Joliffe's heart high as he long-strided along the summer-dusty road, but besides the hope of a fat winter, he was free for the first time in more than half a year from lessons, from being taught and tested and then set to learning more. He had forgotten, in the years since he had been a boy and a scholar, how good it felt to be let out from school, but he was remembering it now. He had, in truth, enjoyed much of these past months' learning and some of the work that went with it, but this was better—to be on his way toward somewhere he had never been, with the sun warm on his back, coins in his belt pouch, and no one wanting him for anything.

Time was that he would have added, along with all else to the good, that no one in particular knew where he was, but anymore he had to doubt that was true, and somewhere far down in his mind he knew how little he liked that thought, but there was nothing he could do about it. Last year he had said certain words to a powerful man, and eight months ago, in answer to those words, he had been summoned out of his familiar life. Now, feeling crammed to the crop with new knowledge and new skills, he was on his way to rejoin the wandering company of players that had been his life and livelihood for years. There had been good times in those years, and some very bad times, and for the past two years—since the wealthy Lord Lovell had made the company his own and under his protection—increasingly good times. Through all of them, Joliffe had never been away from the company for any time long enough to be worth counting, until he was summoned away last winter. He had been told then that when time came for him to rejoin them, someone would know where they were. That had proved true enough, which was both a comfort and a discomfort. It was good to know where to find the players again, a discomfort to know some manner of watch was being kept on them at the order of someone whose heed they might well have been better without.

"Report is they're at a place called Barton, about three days' easy travel from here," Master Smith had said. Although Joliffe doubted "Smith" was truly his name.

"Any thought on where they'll be by the time I reach them?" Traveling players never being long in any one place.

But, "Likely still there. There's a hospital there. St. Giles. One of them is in it."

"Who?" Joliffe had demanded.

"The only word was 'one of them.' It'd not have been wise to ask too closely and maybe have someone wonder why the asking."

One of them, out of a company of five: Thomas Basset, the

master of the company; Ellis and Gil who shared the playing with him; Rose, his daughter who saw to keeping them fed and their garb ready; Piers, her half-grown son who played parts in their plays, too, when need be.

"What of the others?" Joliffe had asked.

"There, too. Working."

"At what?"

"That wasn't said."

So as Joliffe closed what had to be the last miles between him and this hospital of St. Giles, he was carrying worry with him as well as his canvas sack of belongings and walking faster than he might have otherwise in the afternoon's heat. Sweat was wet across his forehead and under his shirt, and he would have been glad of something to drink besides the warm water in the leather bottle hung from his belt. Still, he was better off than the men and women working at the harvest in the long open field he was presently passing. He had, one time and another, worked enough harvests to know how much the back was aching by this end of the day after the hours bent double, grasping the grain with one hand, swinging the sickle to cut it with the other, moving on. Grasping, cutting, moving on. Grasping, cutting, moving on. Binding what was cut. Moving on. Hour after hour under the hot sun, until the daylight faded. Then doing it again the next day. And the day after that. And the day after that until every field was cleared of its ripe-headed grain. Then on to the harvest of the peas and the beans rattling dry in their cods. Praying day and night that the weather would hold until everything was safely stored in the granary and barn, because a good harvest meant life for another year, where a poor harvest meant hunger for everyone and death for some. Or—if the dearth were bad enough—death for many.

It meant poor living for the players, too, because they were often paid in kind rather than in coin, and people could not give what they did not have, and even if the players were paid in coins, there might be little or no food to buy with them. They had always got by, one way and another and usually thanks to Basset's skill at leading them and Rose's skill at making the best of what was to be had.

They would be free of that trouble this year though. By everything Joliffe had seen on his way these few days on the road, this year was going to be one of plenty, making it maybe an easy year for the players, too, so far as being paid and able to eat went.

Unless whatever awaited him at this St. Giles was bad and an end to everything.

In the last village through which he had passed, he had asked his way, to be sure of it, and been told by the alewife, "That's some three miles on. If it's the hospital you're for, you'll come to it before you come to the church and all." So Joliffe supposed the squat stone tower he could see ahead of him now above the hedges was where he was going, and he was ready for it to be. In his worry for the other players, he had been walking maybe somewhat too fast, hurrying to learn just how worried he should be, and he was tired and willing to admit it, glad he did not have to keep on until the last daylight faded, the way the workers in the barley field he was presently passing would do. Another quarter mile and he would have shade and a chance to sit and surely be offered a cup of something to drink, even if only cold well water.

Come to it, cold well water sounded especially good, both to drink and to splash in his hot face.

A last long curve of the road brought him into full sight of the tower he thought would be the hospital, and he found he had been wrong. The tower was that of a small, stone-built church. An old one, to judge by the round-topped doorway facing the road and, to judge by the aged gray thatch of its roof, not a well-kept one, Joliffe noted without much thought about it. He immediately shifted guess of the hospital to the stretch of freshly white-washed wooden wall nearer to him along the road. Beyond it were the bright-thatched roofs of low buildings, and a sturdy timber-and-plastered-wattle gatehouse with a single, wagon-wide gate and a porter's room above it, making a short passageway into whose shade Joliffe went gratefully. The gate stood a little open, but Joliffe stopped there in the shade, slipped his sack from his shoulder, set it down, and gave a light pull to the bell rope hanging through a hole in the floor of the room above him. There was a muffled clank from overhead and a muffled voice saying something that might have been, "Coming."

Joliffe waited, hearing the uneven thud of someone limping down wooden steps, followed by a pause as whoever it was must have reached the bottom, before a stooped old man pulled the gate a little more open, looked out at him, and said in practiced greeting, "Welcome to this place. God have you in his keeping." And then more sharply, "You look hale enough. What do you want here? There's honest work to be had in the fields, if that's what you're after. If it isn't, best you be on your way."

Not an old man, Joliffe revised, having a longer look at him. Middle-aged at the most, his stoop not from age but because of a badly humped back that was probably part of whatever infirmity had likewise shriveled and stiffened his right arm into a crook at his side and given him the limp Joliffe had heard on the stairs. There would be no fieldwork for him, surely, nor much in the way of any craft he could do. He might have been made gatekeeper here out of plain charity, but the sharpness of both his judgment and his demand at Joliffe said he was good at his work, and Joliffe said as plainly back, "I was told a friend was here in hospital."

"His name would be?" the gatekeeper demanded, unyielding.

"Ah." Joliffe paused, awkward with lack of that. "We're a company of players. I was apart for a while, and all I've heard

is one of us is here, without the man who told me being able
to say who."

Instantly friendlier, the gatekeeper said with a smile,
"That will be Thomas the Player you mean," and stepped
back, drawing the gate wider open to let Joliffe into the yard
beyond it. The yard was a wide space, dusty in the August
heat, with various timber-and-plaster buildings around it. By
the glance Joliffe gave them, those at one end of the yard
looked to be a stable and storerooms. At the yard's other end
was a long, open-sided, empty shed, while facing the gateway
was the gable end of a high-roofed great hall and the long
side of a two-floored building with narrow windows above
and below. A wide doorway up a single step led into a foreporch, with presently the door at its far end standing open to
the warm day.

To Joliffe it looked much like any number of manor yards
into which he had come over the years, except that no one was
there save himself and the bent-backed gatekeeper. Such un-
natural quiet could only be because everyone was out to the
harvest, Joliffe supposed as the gatekeeper began to shuffle
toward the porch across the yard, saying, "I'll just see you to
him, to be sure he's the man you want."

And to see me right back out if he's not, Joliffe thought.

He would have been holding back a smile at the man's
busy assurance if his worry had not been keeping any smile
at bay as he picked up his sack and followed. He could have
hoped the gatekeeper's light mention of Basset meant there
was nothing greatly ill with him, but the thought was forestalled by knowing that Basset would not have been here
except he was too ill for Rose to care for him.

The door led not into any room but a passage that went
straight through the narrow building, with another door
standing open at its other end, giving glimpse of a roofed
walk, but there were two doors on the right as well, and another on the left, and it was through the latter that Joliffe

was led into what, from the outside, had seemed no more than a usual great hall. Inwardly, too, it partly matched that look, being broad and long, with a heavily beamed roof open to the high rafters, but where a usual hall would have been open from one end to the other for space to set up the trestle tables at mealtimes and for the gathering of the household for one thing and another at other times, this place was broken by posts and curtains into—he counted quickly as the gatekeeper led him into a middle aisle that ran the length of the hall to its far end—eight stalls, he supposed he could call them, four to each side, lined along the walls, their end to the aisle open but separated from one another by rough-woven, dark red-brown curtains hung on wooden rods just above head-height.

He had no time to note more just then as, ahead of him, the gatekeeper stopped at the first stall and said, "Is this someone you know?" to someone inside it.

Joliffe joined him, and there, stretched out on a wood-framed bed, was Basset. Enough propped up on two pillows that he need not raise his head to see who was come, he exclaimed, "Joliffe!" sat further up and swung his legs over the side of the bed. "How come you here?"

"On my own two feet, as always," Joliffe said.

The gatekeeper said, satisfied, "He knows you then. I'll leave you to it," and shuffled away as an old man's voice demanded from the next stall, "Who's there? Thomas Player, who's come?"

"One of my company. You hush and let me have his news. I'll tell it to you later."

"Have him push aside the curtain and speak up."

"Not until I know what he has to tell is fit for your chaste ears."

That brought a rasping, long-drawn chuckling from the curtain's other side but no more questions as Basset grasped Joliffe by the wrist and pulled him down to sit on the bed's edge with him. The booth was perhaps six feet across and mostly taken up with the narrow wooden bedstead standing with its head against the whitewashed wall, its foot toward the aisle between the booths. There was room enough—but only barely—on either side of the bed for a thin person to stand, and other than the bed and its bedclothes, there was nothing but a small, square wooden table beside the bed's head, set with a pottery pitcher, a wooden cup, and a partly unrolled scroll on which Joliffe recognized his own handwriting. A narrow window high up the wall—one of a row along the hall's length and matched by others on the hall's other side—let in afternoon sunlight strongly enough for Joliffe to see how cleanly kept everything was. Floor and bedding and Basset all had a scrubbed look to them, with no sign of illness on Basset at all, so that Joliffe said with mock indignation hiding his relief, "Why do you look so well? You're supposed to be ill."

Some of the delight went from Basset's face and what remained was forced. He lifted his bare legs. He was wearing under-braies and a loose, thigh-long shirt, sufficient clothing in the warm day. He nodded toward his bare legs and feet and said, "Those are still the worst. About Saint Mary Magdalene day the arthritics flared all through me like they've never done before. I couldn't walk."

He said it evenly, nearly no feeling in his voice, and the very blankness told Joliffe something of how bad it must have been. Quietly he asked, "How is it now?"

Basset circled his feet from the ankles and grimaced. "Those are still solid pain when I try to walk on them, but the hips are better, the knees bearable, the back no worse than it's usually been."

"So you're bettering."

"I'm bettering," Basset agreed. "When I first came in here, you'd not have seen me sit up the way I did just now. So, yes, I'm bettering." There was maybe a false note under his assurance, but he gave no time for Joliffe to be certain of it, going

on, "Their physician here is good." He lowered his voice
more. "And their *medica* is maybe even better, but it would be
a point of wisdom not to say so where Master Hewstere might
hear." Keeping his voice low, he added, "Now, how did it go
with you? Where've you been all this while?"

Since Basset wanted to change their talk's course, Joliffe
obliged, equally low-voiced, with, "These past few months
I've been in Northamptonshire." Where he had been before then was best unsaid. "Being taught like an over-sized
schoolboy." He tried to make it sound a lightsome pastime.
"All in all, they were satisfied with me, I think."

Leaving "they" vague, he looked for something he could
tell beyond that. That he was more skilled at riding than he
had been would be safe enough to say, but he would rather
pass over how far more skilled at dagger- and swordwork he
had become. Nor should he say anything about how much
he now knew about the reading and writing of ciphers and
of a powerful bishop's net of spies and "privy friends" spread
across England and beyond. Instead, groping quickly among
all the lessons he had been put through these past months,
he came up with, "My skill at lute and recorder are somewhat
more than they were, anyway."

In-held laughter creased the corners of Basset's eyes. "The
lute and recorder? That's what you were away to learn?"

"Among other things," Joliffe said, weighting the words
a little.

"Ah. Other things," Basset echoed and let them go, as
if understanding Joliffe was not going to tell him and that
probably he would be better not knowing. "Well, I'll leave
it to Piers and Ellis to make rude comment about your supposedly bettered skills that way. We can make use of them
anyway when we're back . . ." He fumbled, then recovered
control of his thoughts and voice. "When we're back on the
road again." His voice fell lower again. "Someone knew where
we were, to tell you."

Joliffe nodded agreement.

"Are we wanted for anything?" The company's skills had been called to the bishop's use last year, and there was nothing to say they would not be again.

"No," Joliffe said, glad that he could, but he in fairness had to add, "Not yet." Then he asked, "What reason do we have for my being gone from the company and now coming here? Or am I to be a full surprise to these folk?"

"They know one of our company had gone off on some private matter of his own, to do with family, we think. Now you've found us again. That's all."

Joliffe nodded approval of that. Tell enough but not too much and never more than need be—that had been one of the lessons in his just-past "schooling," but also one that the players had long since learned for themselves. Ever on the move from place to place, landless and for many years lordless, they were usually welcomed for their skills wherever they went, but were always suspect as folk who did not belong anywhere. That had changed for the better when Lord Lovell had made them his company, with the right to wear his colors and carry his letters of protection, but the old habits of wariness—of keeping themselves to themselves—were still with them and likely always would be, because they would go on being strangers, not belonging to anywhere through which they passed. Which raised questions about this place they could not leave until Basset was healed, and Joliffe asked, "How is it here? Any trouble?"

Basset, more than anyone, understood the levels of questioning behind those plain ones and answered, "This is a good place. We've been treated well." He shifted, stretching himself out on the bed again, a small groan betraying the effort's pain as he settled against the pillows before going on. "There's some better than others, just like anywhere, but on the whole, it's a good place."

A flicker of laughter behind Basset's words made Joliffe

wonder with light wariness what was not being said, but only said himself, jibing a little, "So here you are, Basset, sitting proud and prettily. What of the others?"

Basset settled himself more comfortably on the pillows and folded hands on his stomach in a way that Joliffe could only call self-satisfied. "Happily, it's harvest time. There's always need for more hands at harvest time. Ellis and Gil are doing fieldwork . . ."

"Ellis must be hating that," Joliffe said with a grin.

"Don't grin, my lad. You'll likely find yourself there tomorrow," Basset warned. "And don't think Piers will let you take over from him. He has Tisbe in charge. We've hired her out to pull one of the harvest wains, with him to lead her to make sure too much isn't asked of her."

Seeing that he indeed was unlikely to wrest that fairly easy work from Piers, Joliffe resigned himself to the likelihood he would be bent-backed under the hot sun in some field tomorrow. "And Rose?" he asked.

"In the kitchen here. Content enough, from all she says."

A little silence fell between them, full of much that neither of them wanted to say. To go past it, Joliffe reached out and took up the scroll that he saw now was one of the longer plays he had reworked for the company's use. "Planning for when we move on?" he asked.

With a startling fierceness, Basset said, "Always." Then he let go all pretense, his hands clenching into fists on the sheet beneath him as he added with deep and aching earnestness, "I'm truly doing all I can to get well and get us out of here. I truly am."

In a gesture not usual between them, Joliffe put a hand over Basset's near one. "I know," he said. "It's just a matter of waiting while you better. Then we'll be on the move again." He hoped. He very deeply hoped.

Chapter 2

rom somewhere along the line of stalls someone croaked loudly, " 'Ware sister!"

As if guilty of something, Joliffe stood sharply up. Basset laughed at him. From the far end of the line of stalls a woman said, friendliwise and for everyone to hear, "You mind your tongue, Deke, or there'll be gravel in your pottage next thing you know."

That brought a scattering of laughter and croaking chuckles along the hall, and the old man beyond the curtain beside Basset's bed called, "That'll clear your bowels for you, Deke."

Whoever was in the bed across from Basset's moaned and began to mumble, sounding confused, his voice rising.

"There now," the woman said in warning to everyone, yet kindly enough. Quiet-footed, she came hurriedly, with a soft rush of skirts, between the stalls to the moaning man's bedside. She set the basket she had been carrying on the small table there and was taking something from it even while she bent over the man, saying something to him in a low, questioning voice. His head thrashed weakly side to side on his pillow, not so much in answer, Joliffe thought, as keeping time with his moaning. Despite the day's warmth, he was covered to his naked upper chest by sheet and blanket. A white cloth wrapped around the crown of his head hid his hair. The woman laid a hand on his forehead, then along the side of his face, still talking to him, and he quieted a little. She took that for chance to unstopper the small vial she had taken from the basket. Using one hand under his chin to tilt his head a little back and then to draw his mouth open, she put the vial to his lips with her other hand and quickly tipped into him whatever it held, closed his mouth with her hand still under his chin and kept it closed, gentle but firm, to be sure of his swallowing whatever she had given him.

Watching her from across the way, seeing her from the back, Joliffe could nearly have thought her a well-grown girl, small-built as she was in height and all; but the deft, sure way she moved made him think she was a grown woman, and when she had settled the man against his pillows and smoothed the sheet and blanket over him, picked up her basket, and turned from the bed, Joliffe saw he was right. She wore a gray gown, plainly cut, with no excess of cloth, the sleeves straight, and the skirt somewhat short, leaving her plain-shoed feet clear. A white apron covered it from throat to below her knees, but she had neither wimple nor veil covering her neck and hair, only—like a servant—a long headkerchief over a close-fitted coif to hide her hair. But she was no servant, any more than she was a girl. She was a woman somewhere in her vigorous middle years, probably closer to Basset's age than Joliffe's, with brown, bright eyes sharp with confident intelligence as she took in Joliffe's presence, assessed him, and said even as he started a bow to her, "You're Thomas' friend. The one he said might come."

"I am, my lady."

"Sister," she said, putting aside the lady. "Sister Margaret."

"Sister Margaret," Joliffe repeated obediently, knowing that here "sister" meant not a nun but a nurse.

"And you?" she asked.

"Joliffe Norreys." Because "Norreys" was the name he had been called by for these past three months and it came first to mind.

"Joliffe Norreys," Sister Margaret repeated. "You are likely hungry and may want to wash off some of your travel and the day's heat. I'll be busy here in the hall this while, but if you go there"—she bent her head toward the hall's far end—"and turn rightward, you should find your way to the kitchen easily enough. Sister Ursula will see to you then."

"You'll likely find Rose there, too," said Basset.

Joliffe gave him a nod and Sister Margaret another bow and edged out of Basset's stall. She stood aside while he did, but then went forward, saying, brisk with business, "Now, Thomas, how does it go with you this afternoon?"

Keeping his smile inward, Joliffe went away up the hall, making no haste of his going, giving anyone there as alert as Basset's neighbor the chance to have sight of him if they wanted it. There were few enough pastimes here, he supposed, and he was used to diverting people in harder ways than this; but he also took the chance for a good look for himself to see in passing what there was to see. All the eight narrow beds had someone in them, all men, although no one else was sitting as up as Basset had been, and two were lying as flatly as the man just attended to by Sister Margaret and so maybe in as bad a case.

Joliffe wondered if there was a separate hall for women or if the place's founder had only seen fit to provide for men. Anyway, the place was as cleanly kept as he had first thought, with no more smell of sickness than there had to be among so many bedridden men—most of them old men, he thought from his glances at the them as he went. Men come to the worn-out end of their days and fortunate to be here. Which probably added to the reasons Basset must hate being here. For all he had put a good face to it, being daily reminded he might be come, early, to the worn-out end of his own days could hardly be welcome.

The far end of the hall where—in an ordinary hall of a household—there might be a door or even two leading to the lord's more private chambers, there was indeed a door toward one end of the wall, but in the wall's middle a wide arch had been made, opening into a small chapel. Because a hospital was meant to be a place of healing for souls as well as of bodies, a priest or priests were as surely part of one as physicians and nursing-sisters were, and a chapel at the end of a hospital's hall was the usual thing, its altar meant to be seen from every bed, as it would be here when the curtains beside each bed were pushed back, for every patient to see the priest at Mass for reminder that even if their bodies could not be saved, their souls might be.

The chapel was long for its width, windowless and flat-ceilinged, as if there might be a room above it, more evidence this place had not begun as a hospital but as someone's manor hall. Despite that, the chapel was lovely; in shadow now, but by the small lamp hung from the blue-painted ceiling beams above the altar Joliffe could see painted on the white-plastered wall behind the altar the Virgin in her blue cloak and Saint Giles with his deer and arrow, while the Seven Corporeal Acts of Mercy covered the side walls.

He did not take closer look at them, only paused to bow to the altar and give a short prayer of thanks that Basset had come to this safe harbor in his need, before he went in search of the kitchen and, hopefully, Rose. A doorway standing open near the last bed on the right side of the hall led him into a short passage with doors standing open at either end. To his right was the roofed walk he had seen from its other end when coming from the yard, so he went left instead of back toward the yard, and beyond another doorway came indeed into the kitchen, a broad, high room with a heavy wooden work table square in its middle, a wide-hearthed fireplace in the farther wall, and a tall louver in the roof. A use-blackened kettle big enough to cook the pottages and gruels that were likely the main food of the patients here was hung from a swinging iron arm over the low fire on the hearth, and Rose was stirring whatever was in it with a large iron spoon, her back to him. He circled the table toward her, was nearly to her as she finished her stirring and turned from the kettle, spoon still in hand. Not having heard him coming, she cried out with surprise and swung the spoon back, ready to hit with it. In a life spent traveling, she had learned not to be helpless. But then she knew him and her exclaim turned to delight as she flung her arms around him, still holding the spoon, crying, "You found us!"

Surprised both at her great gladness and at his own at seeing her again, he hugged her back. Only as they stepped apart, Rose smiling up at him, did he see the other woman, watching them from a doorway on the room's far end, eyebrows raised. She was maybe much the same age as Sister Margaret was and dressed likewise in a gray gown and white apron, plain coif and headkerchief. Another of the nursing-sisters then, Joliffe thought, with a pang that the gladness between him and Rose might be mistaken and Rose be in trouble for it, but as the woman came forward he saw the mischief twinkling in her dark eyes even before Rose said happily, "Sister Ursula! See who's here!"

"Your missing lamb, come back to the flock," Sister Ursula said, eyeing him up and down. "Certainly not the fatted calf. Are you hungry, fellow? There's bread and cheese and new ale." Even as she asked, she was fetching a loaf from one of the shelves along the wall where a line of other loaves waited, and she added with a nod of her head toward the bench beside the table, "Sit down. How long have you been on the road? Rose, bring him a cup."

Joliffe sat. "Four days," he said. Which was not quite true but would do.

"Nor eating well on the way?" Sister Ursula asked as she took up a knife lying ready to her hand on the table.

"Not so well," Joliffe granted, although he had never gone hungry.

Sister Ursula deftly cut a thick slice from the bread and flipped it toward him from the knife's blade, asking, "Name?"

"Joliffe Norreys," he answered, catching the slice and not glancing at Rose, depending on her to show no more surprise at the name than Basset had.

"Are you willing to work?" Sister Ursula demanded as she returned the bread to its shelf.

Behind Sister Ursula's back, he slid a look toward Rose, questioning what this was about as he answered, "Yes."

Also behind Sister Ursula's back, Rose gave him a shrug and a smile, while saying aloud, "Sister Ursula is huswife here in St. Giles. She sees to everything and everybody being as they should be."

Now bringing a cloth-covered cheese on a cutting board to the table, Sister Ursula said, "I *try* to see to it, though there are times I think herding cats would be an easier task. Just now there's Ivo gone off when he shouldn't have, and I'm in need of someone to take his place." She paused in cutting a large wedge from the cheese and gave Joliffe an assessing look. "You seem fit enough, but are you willing?"

Joliffe looked rapidly back and forth between her and Rose. "To work, yes," he said. "At what? What did Ivo do?"

"Everything." Sister Ursula impaled the cut of cheese with the knife and held it out to Joliffe. He took it from the knife point as she went on, "He was the extra pair of hands that's always needed around a place. Someone to lift, shift, fetch, and carry. He's gone off to seek his fortune somewhere, may he have a plague of boils, and there's no one else to be had, they're all at the harvest."

She was returning the cheese to its place on a shelf, and Joliffe took the chance behind her back to question Rose with a look, asking whether this was a good offer or not. She gave him a quick, single nod, and when Sister Ursula turned back to him, he held off from the bread and cheese long enough to ask, "You mean I'd be working here around the hospital, not at the harvest?"

"Here, yes, and stay here, too, rather than with your fellows, because you'll be needed in the night sometimes. So a bed and your food and drink come with the work. And a penny a day."

"I'll only be here so long as we have to be," Joliffe said. "I'm away when the rest of them go."

"Better to have you a while than not at all," Sister Ursula answered with firm practicality. "Maybe Ivo will have shifted himself back here by the time you all leave. Or the harvest will be done and there'll be someone else to hire."

Harvesting would pay better in coin, Joliffe thought, but hurt more in body. Better, what with one consideration and another, to work around here than sweating at the harvest— with the added benefit that Ellis would be irked he was not breaking his back with the rest of them.

"Done, then," he said. "I'm yours for the while."

"Good. Rose will show you where to bed and all. Tomorrow you can start. You've no horse we need see to, do you?"

"No horse."

"Good." She nodded at the bread and cheese he held. "Eat up. Rose, everything's in hand here?"

"All's well," Rose said.

"Bless you. Time I was away to Mistress Thorncoffyn then."

And she was gone out of the kitchen and away. Gazing at the doorway through which she had vanished, Joliffe asked somewhat wonderingly, "Is she always so brisk?"

"Always," Rose assured him. "Always brisk, always definite, always generous-hearted. Mind you"—Rose raised the spoon to emphasize her warning—"she doesn't suffer fools gladly."

Joliffe sat down on a stool beside the table. "Fortunate then that I'm not a fool."

"Um," said Rose, not committing herself to that one way or the other but smiling at him before she turned back to the pot over the fire.

Joliffe chewed through a mouthful of bread and cheese, then asked very quietly, "How is it with Basset? How is it truly?"

Rose swung the pot to the edge of the fire and hung the spoon on a waiting hook before she faced him, to answer gravely, "He's far better than he was. When it was at the worst, he could barely bear to move. The pains in his hips and knees and even the bones of his feet were terrible, but if he didn't move, his joints stiffened, and then he could hardly move even when he had to, and that was worse. So he had to move but was in barely bearable pain when he did. It was beyond anything I could do to ease or better it. We were fortunate to come on this place when we did. They've helped him as I never could."

"How long, at a guess, until he's fit to leave?"

Rose took too long to answer that. If she had not been strong of will and mind and brave-hearted into the bargain, she would not have lasted in the life the players led, but still she took too long to say anything, and Joliffe stood up, leaving the bread and cheese, and went around the table to her, just in time to put his arms around her as her tears spilled over. She leaned her forehead against his shoulder, letting herself be held, but only for a moment before she drew a trembling breath and straightened away from him, swept tears from her cheeks with firm fingers and said, "I'm sorry."

"Rose," Joliffe said gently. "Just how bad is it? Worse than he told me, yes?"

"We don't know." Her voice was steady, the tears gone. "That's the trouble. No one can say how far better he's going to be. How he is now—this may be the best he'll ever be."

And that was not good enough for him to go on as a player. If he could hardly walk, that was the end of playing for him and the end of the company.

"I've given you nothing to drink," Rose said suddenly and made a bustle of fetching a cup of what proved to be good new ale, setting it on the table beside him, and going to put the kettle over the fire again, asking as she went, "It went well? Your business?"

"It did," Joliffe said.

"You're not needed . . . somewhere else sometime soon?"

"Not that anyone's said. That smells good. They eat well here?"

Understanding he had told her all he was going to tell just then, she answered, "They do," and went on to talk of where the players had been after he left them and where they had been going when Basset's necessity had stopped them here. "It being harvest time and workers always needed, they're as grateful for us just now as we are for them. Father told you what the others and even Tisbe are doing?"

"He did. What happened to this Ivo whose place I'm taking?"

"Oh, it seems he tired of being paid his penny a day here when fieldwork would earn him more. So he took himself off to elsewhere. Sister Ursula says he'll likely be back sometime. He does this almost every year." And in despite of the statutes there were forbidding workers wandering in search of better pay when they could get work where they were, he could be sure of finding work somewhere at better pay than a penny a day, because at harvest time no one ever had enough workers. Rose looked at Joliffe. "How did you come from wherever you were without being set to work somewhere?"

Joliffe patted the leather purse hanging from his belt. "A signed, sealed permission from Lord Lovell giving me leave, as his man, to go as I must, without let or hindrance."

"Very useful," Rose said, with plain memory of times before they were Lord Lovell's players when such a thing would have greatly eased their lives. She swung the pot altogether away from the fire. "There. That's done, I think. Now let me show you where you'll sleep and warn you of a few things."

Chapter 3

Where he would sleep proved to be a small room off the short passageway between the kitchen and the roofed walk—and small was the only word for it, with just distance enough to fully open the door between the doorway and the narrow bed along the far wall and no space for anything else except a little wooden chest against the wall beside the bedfoot, with a wall-pole above it for hanging clothing. Joliffe slid his bag from his shoulder yet again, this time to the wooden floor beside the little chest, and said, "I hope Ivo wasn't a large man." He nodded toward the wall beyond the bed and asked, "What's there?"

"The stairway to the storeroom that's above here," Rose said from outside the doorway, there being hardly space for them both at once in the room. "Beyond the stairs is the scullery. You'll be seeing enough of that soon."

"Will I?" he asked, suddenly wary. "Washing dishes was part of this Ivo's duties?"

"Everything was part of his duties," Rose said with a serenity suspiciously underlain with laughter. She looked at the bare mattress on the roped bedstead. "I'll bring you sheets, a blanket, and a pillow." She stepped backward from the doorway, inviting him to come out, adding, "We stripped and scrubbed the room and aired the mattress after he went. That only leaves doing the same to you."

"Pardon?" he said, following her back toward the kitchen.

"Cleanliness of body and soul. Those are the lights that lead us here." She sounded as if she were quoting—and maybe a little mocking—someone.

"I note that cleanliness of body comes first," Joliffe said dryly. "I suppose because it's easier to be sure a body is clean than a soul."

"Only too true," Rose agreed, crossing the kitchen toward a far doorway. "So, as with anyone newly come here, we'll begin with your body."

Still following her but his voice rising more strongly, Joliffe repeated, "Pardon?"

"And hope for the best with your soul," Rose said as she went out the door.

Joliffe followed her into a small, stone-paved yard enclosed on either side by low, long buildings and at the far side by a waist-high wall of willow-woven hurdles and a broad gateway to what looked a larger yard with varied buildings that Joliffe supposed were the place's byre, haystore, and granary as well as a poultry yard somewhere, to guess by the many multi-colored chickens scattered and scratching about the dusty yard.

Here in the smaller yard Rose pointed at the buildings on the left and said, "The bakehouse and woodstore." Then to the right and, "The brewhouse and laundry. That's where you're bound for."

"The brewhouse?" Joliffe said with pretended hope.

"The laundry," Rose said with the same ruthlessness she used toward Piers when he was going to be given no choice about something. "It's also the bathhouse, it being the rule

that no one is admitted here without they be thoroughly
bathed—soaped and scrubbed from hair to toenails. Patients
and all," she added as they reached the doorway, then saying
as she went in, "Emme, I've someone needs a bath."

Plainly, the place had been built with the thought of how
it would be used. The roof was held up on stout wooden posts,
but on two sides the walls stopped a foot short of the eaves, the
better to let out the smoke and some of the heat from the two
fires burning in the long, low-walled hearth in the middle of
the room. Two cauldrons sat on short-legged gridirons above
the coals, the steam of hot water rising from their depths,
while just inside the door was a well with a long-roped bucket
sitting beside it to keep those cauldrons filled. The round,
high-sided wooden tub standing in a far corner was the bath,
Joliffe guessed, and the tall woman coming toward him and
Rose from beyond the cauldrons had to be Emme, the laun-
dress. Lean as a coursing hound, she was gowned in the same
gray gown and white apron as Sister Margaret and Sister Ursula, but her sleeves were pushed above her elbows, the gown
was unlaced at her neck, and her hair was bound in a headcloth wrapped to leave her neck clear, to be as cool as might
be in the place's heavy, wet heat. She was red of face and red
of arms, and Joliffe noted that those arms were as sinewed as
any fieldworker's. But the face was friendly, her eyes merry as
she looked the length of him while saying to Rose, "He looks
somewhat too healthy to be one of ours."

"He's taking Ivo's place for the while," Rose said.

"Nor a moment too soon," Emme said, then turned her
head to add. "Amice, hear that? We've someone for the firewood again."

On the farther side of one of the cauldrons a woman stood
up from where she had been kneeling, probably feeding firewood into the fire there. She was younger than Emme and not
yet worn to such leanness, with a pretty plumpness to her and
a curl of dark hair escaping the forehead edge of her headcloth

that was wrapped, like Emme's, to leave her neck clear. And a very pretty neck it was, too, Joliffe thought, smiling back to the smile she was giving him before it crossed his mind that her pleasure might be not so much at him for himself as for his ability to carry firewood.

That did not change her prettiness, however. Since they were all servants together, no bow was needed among them, and he simply nodded to her, still smiling, before Emme caught his heed back to her by saying, "Let's have him clean, then. Amice, start filling the tub. You—"

She paused, waiting for his name, and he gave the one he had already given Sister Ursula.

"Joliffe, then," she went on. "Strip off and get into the tub. Do you have fleas or suchlike, that we need to deal with your clothing, too?"

"No fleas or anything," he said.

"Clean shirt and hosen and braies?"

"In my bag. In my room."

"I'll fetch them," Rose said and left him to Emme's firm ordering, beginning with telling him in no uncertain terms, when he was rid of doublet, hosen, and shirt and down to only his short braies, that he need not stop there. "We've seen too many men's bodies to take much interest in them beyond whether they're clean or not. Those off, too, and into the tub with you."

Which would have been well enough, if Amice had not added, a little laughing, "Still, his is a better body than most we see."

"It is that," Emme had agreed, openly approving.

In his life Joliffe had not had much chance or use for shyness over nakedness, his own or other people's, and the women's laughter made it easy to finish stripping while Emme went on, "Most men we bathe are on their way to a sick bed, see you. Dirt in a hurt makes the hurt harder to heal, and even if it's not an outright hurt they have but sickness, there's the thought there's evil little creatures that carry sickness, too small to see, and the less of them a sick man takes to his bed with him, the better his chances of living to leave that bed. That's what we're told, anyway, and whoever cast the rules for St. Giles put into them that everyone, whether they're here to be tended or to work, has to start out clean. So into the tub with you."

There was nothing new to Joliffe in any of that. He knew the scholarly thoughts on the possible existence of some sort of life so small as to be invisible and yet a cause of diseases. Knew, too, that—scholarly thoughts or no—any good hospital lent heavily toward cleanliness and that after his warm days on dusty roads he was more than willing to a bath now it was offered to him. Only the suddenness of it all was disconcerting him. Hardly an hour ago he had been trudging along a road, hot and dusty and alone. Now he had not only found Basset and Rose but had work, a promise of meals, a room to himself, and was about to sink into pleasantly warm water and be clean.

"Besides," Amice added, quite cheerfully as he put himself into the tub, "there's the stink that goes with sickness. That's always good to wash away, too. Not that you smell bad, just of honest sweat."

As good-humoured at it as they were, Joliffe settled himself into the bathing tub, hip-deep into warm water, his knees drawn up so he would fit, and while Amice went to scoop another bucketful from one of the cauldrons, Emme set a bowl of soap in his reach and said, "Wash everything. Your hair, too."

He washed. His shirt and hosen and braies went into a pile of laundry after Emme had a look at them sufficient to be sure he had been right about no fleas or lice. Rose came back with his clean shirt and braies, told him he would find her in the kitchen when he had done here, and went away again. He finished his scrubbing, helped Amice tip the tub so the dirtied, soap-scummed water flowed into an open stone gutter and away under the wall, then stood in the tub while Emme and Amice poured clean, warm water from the rinse-tub over him. Having dumped the tub again, he dressed, thanked both women, found Rose in the kitchen, and was told he should keep himself out of the way if he did not want to be put to work before his time.

"I won't be free to take you to the others until supper is done with here," Rose said.

"You do it alone?" Joliffe asked.

"The rest of the women will be here any moment, and unless you want to face us all at once, best you go to your room. Lie down for a while. You look tired."

"But clean," he pointed out brightly.

But she was right about him being tired, too. Not just the few days' walking but the several months before them had him worn out more than he could deny to himself, and he went to his room, found Rose had made the bed with clean sheets and blanket and a pillow slip that smelled of lavender when he settled his head against it. He sighed contentedly, folded his hands on his chest, and slept.

It was a light sleep, though. For better air in the warm afternoon, he had left the door slightly ajar, and while he drowsed in and out of sleep, he was aware of women's busy voices from the kitchen on the other side of the lathe-and-plaster wall at his bedfoot. Heard, too, for a while, a man's voice raised in probably prayer to judge by the patterning of it. That would be someone saying Vespers in the chapel, he thought. The full Offices of prayer and psalms would not be kept here—this was no monastery—but some would be, and this was Vespers' time of day. The voice was not a strong one, but it prayed firmly and without haste, and Joliffe rolled onto his side and slid into another drowse that broke when something large went suddenly lumbering past the door, accompanied by the clack of a wooden staff hitting the stone

floor and the quick pattering of very many feet that was so
ill-suited to the bulk of the other that he jerked full awake,
confused at what he was hearing. He was struggling up on
one elbow when the door moved, was pushed slightly more
open to let in, at somewhat less than knee-height, a white,
long-muzzled face, bright of eye and pricked-eared with interest at him. For a startled moment—startled on Joliffe's
side, at least—he and the dog stared at one another until a
woman's voice demanded, "Kydd! Here!" and the bright-eyed
little face disappeared, followed by a quick pattering away
of feet, not as many feet as there had first been but, "Dogs,"
Joliffe thought as he sank onto the pillow again. It had been
a pack of small dogs going past his door. He frowned at the
ceiling. Small dogs and someone large. Assuredly not anyone
he had yet met here.

Dull in the way that sleep in a warm afternoon was apt
to make anyone, he was admitting to himself that he was
not sufficiently curious to bother getting up about it when
the same voice that had called to Kydd demanded from the
kitchen, loud with indignation, booming through the lathes
and plaster as if they were parchment, "If you know how it's
supposed to be, *why wasn't it?*"

Whatever answer was made to that demand was too quiet
for Joliffe to make out. At least he supposed an answer was
made, but it must have been an unsatisfactory one because
the strong-voiced woman declared, "You may say so. But I
expect better. I will *have* better or else Master Soule will hear
of it. Be sure of that!"

Not one of the patients, *that* was certain. First, because it
was a woman, and Rose had confirmed only men were tended
here. Second, because whatever was the matter, that was not
the voice of anyone sickly.

Someone must have made another answer to the woman
because now she ordered, "See to it then! Children, come!"

Joliffe rolled back to his side in time to see, through the

slightly wider door-gap the dog Kydd had made, the surging
past of a very large red gown, followed by a low seethe of
white dogs, too many for him even to guess at their number
in the instant before they were past, too, the wild pattering
of their feet going with them.

A silence followed, ended by something flat and metal—
Joliffe guessed a pot or pan—being slammed down on a hard
surface in the kitchen.

Joliffe willingly stayed where he was, glad to be no part of
whatever all that had been about. Westering sunlight came
through the small, high-set window above the bed's head,
slanting down the wall at the bedfoot, and he guessed that
whatever work was being done in the kitchen was end-of-day
work, to be done while there was sun enough to need no
lamps, for the saving of candles or lamp oil, and Rose would
likely soon be free to take him to the other players. All he
need do was lie here until she fetched him, he thought. So he
did and, to his later surprise, slept again, not knowing he was
that tired. Slept deeply enough that he dreamed that he was
on the practice field where he had lately spent so many days,
standing bare-handed while a bear on horseback charged at
him with an upraised sword he knew he had to avoid while
closing with the bear to pull it from the saddle. The part with
the bear was wrong. So were the moor-topped hills beyond
the field. It had usually been Hede on the horse, sometimes
Therry, never a bear, and those moor-topped hills were from
another place and time in his life altogether.

But the rest was real enough, and in the dream he did
as he had finally learned to do when awake without taking
a whack from the wooden practice sword, which was good
because in the dream it was a great blade of shining steel the
bear had in its paw. But as he pulled the bear from the saddle
he did not know what he would do next because somehow he
seemed to have no weapon on him and the bear's sword had
disappeared and . . .

He was awake. That instantly awake he had also been learning in these past weeks, with one hand shifting to draw the dagger hidden along his forearm even as his mind caught up to where he was and that his dagger was not there, was not needed here, that it was only a tap at the door that had awakened him.

The tap came again. He opened his eyes and sat up, shaking his head to clear it while swinging his legs off the bed and saying, "Come."

Players lived a wary life, never belonging wherever they were and therefore never quite trusted—or ever quite trusting. For their own company, very warily had been the only way to live in the years they had been lordless, before Lord Lovell had taken them for his players. That had lessened—not ended—the need for wariness, but all that had been a familiar wariness. This reaching for a dagger was another matter, and it troubled him. He was not surprised by how deep the past weeks of learning had gone in him, but he was not at ease yet with the wary someone who was come to live inside himself. It was as if—weaponed with skills he had never thought to have—he was now standing knife-edged to the world. He had always had a sideways way of looking at the world that had sometimes made him uncomfortable with who and where he was—had sometimes made uncomfortable the people around him, too. Among the players it had not mattered so much, since players always lived somewhat sideways to the world, belonging nowhere as they did and spending so much time and skill on pretending to be other than they were. It was his skill at that that had helped make him valuable enough to Bishop Beaufort he was come to where he was. He did not like that it was now a skill he must needs use to hide himself from his fellow players.

And nonetheless as Rose looked around the door's edge, he smiled at her easily while stretching his arms out mightily to show he was just awakening, and asked, "Time we went?"

Chapter 4

He went with Rose to the kitchen where she picked up a cloth-wrapped bundle and tucked it under one arm without explaining it, then led him out the rear door again. This time, though, rather than crossing the yard, she led him rightward into a narrow alleyway between the kitchen wall and the laundry. At its far end a wide wooden plank took them across a narrow, deep, stone-lined runnel, flowing with water from somewhere to carry away waste from the hospital's jakes, kitchen, and laundry. Beyond it, they passed through a gap in a line of thorny berry bushes and came into what could only be the hospital's kitchen garden, wide and stretching well away to both sides, in one direction behind the kitchen, the other way behind the laundry and one of the long byres Joliffe had glimpsed from the yard, and ending at both ends in high wicker fences.

Its beds were held in by weathered boards; the paths were graveled; and judging from the flourishing greens of everything growing there, someone more than a little capable saw to its care. Joliffe guessed that someone was a nearby woman in the now-familiar gray gown and white apron, small shears in one hand, a spray of some green plant in the other, straightened from beyond a bed of enthusiastically growing herbs to see who had come. Her eyes were deeply dark in a smooth face that was round rather than long and momentarily austere and without welcome as she stared at them. Then, as if her thoughts had been so far away that it took that long moment to come back from wherever they had been, Joliffe saw her know Rose, and the warmth of the smile that came changed everything about her as she said happily, "Rose. And this must be your Joliffe."

Joliffe bowed to her as Rose answered, "He is. Joliffe, this is Sister Letice. She oversees our cooking and is our herbalist. You'll likely find yourself helping her here when you're not needed elsewhere."

"We're come to that time of year when more hands are welcome," Sister Letice agreed. "Can you tell one plant from another? Do you know any herbs?"

He pointed at the plants beside them. "Basil," he declared confidently.

"Marjoram," she corrected with dry resignation. She nodded at the bundle under Rose's arm. "You remembered the peas?"

"Yes. Thank you."

Sister Letice looked sideways at the sun. "Best you be on then, if you're to have their supper cooked for them."

She nodded farewell to Joliffe, friendly enough but already bending back to her herbs before he had finished his answering slight bow, a woman intent on her own business and little interested in anyone else's, he guessed as he went on with Rose across the garden.

Its farther side was bounded by a wide, free-flowing stream with an orchard on its other side. They crossed dry-footed by a plank whose each end rested on a single large stone, into the orchard where Rose turned to the left to follow a well-walked path between the trees heavy-hung with apples. Joliffe, ducking past one low, laden branch, said, "It looks to be a good year for fruit as well as all else."

"There'll be cider-making in plenty," Rose said. "We're looking forward to the change from ale."

The "we" in that disconcerted Joliffe. The company had sometimes helped at harvests, for the extra coin the work brought in, but there had always been a strong line between "we"—the players who would move on when the time came—and the "them" who belonged to the fields and would stay. This easy "we" from Rose said something else. He might have counted it as merely a word, but he had made his daily living by words for enough years to know there was nothing "mere" about words. Whether their user thought closely about them or not, they carried a power that was sometimes the more powerful for not being forethought by whoever spoke them, and Rose had used "we" as if "we" belonged with the fields and the harvest, instead of merely pausing here.

Was she betraying an unspoken understanding that Basset would not be sufficiently better any time soon? That the players would all be held here for weeks upon weeks more, no certain end in sight?

Joliffe stopped his mind going that way. There was use in a wary watching forward, but too much dwelling in trouble-maybe-to-come could waste a great deal of effort better used otherwise; and to take himself elsewhere, he asked, "So. The large woman with dogs. Who is that?"

"You weren't sleeping then?" Rose asked.

"Something large going past my door woke me, and then a dog looked in. Then I heard her in the kitchen, and she and the dogs came past again. Not another of the sisters, is she?"

Rose made a sound that caught somewhere between a laugh and scorn and said with feeling, "She assuredly is not.

That is Mistress Cisily Thorncoffyn. Her father founded St. Giles as a thanks-offering for having survived a sickness he had thought would kill him. He gave this manor for it and paid for changing the buildings to a hospital's needs."

"Very laudable," Joliffe said.

"To a point. He included in his provisions for it that anyone of the family could stay in certain chambers provided for them when and as they wished, for their better health and refreshment of soul."

"Ah. And Mistress Cisily Thorncoffyn is taking advantage of that provision."

"She is."

"With her dogs."

"With her dogs."

"Her very many dogs," he ventured.

"Her very many dogs," Rose grimly agreed.

"For how long?"

"For as long as she wants. She's been here a week. From what Sister Ursula says, we can expect her to stay until at least Michaelmas. This is a yearly thing. Here we are."

Where they were was the orchard's edge and the deep-worn cart track that ran along it, bounded on the other side by a high hedge with a field beyond it. Drawn up on the track's grassy verge and partly under the trees was the players' familiar cart, its weather-daunted red and yellow painted canvas tilt muted among the leaf-shadows. His heart's lift at seeing it again surprised Joliffe as he held back from patting its wooden side like he might have patted a familiar horse as he and Rose circled it to where a firepit had been dug into the turf. Setting on the grass the bundle she had carried, Rose said, "If you'll open the cart and get out the kitchen box, I'll bring up the fire."

From there, no more time than yesterday might have passed since they last made camp together. While she lifted off the turfs that had banked the fire through the day, Joliffe untied the rear flaps of the cart and retied them out of the way, pulled out the wooden kitchen box and took it to the firepit where Rose was now carefully feeding dry twigs into the lingering coals to rouse them to a proper fire.

"More wood?" Joliffe asked.

"Whatever you can gather," Rose said with a nod around at the trees.

All the near deadwood had been gleaned already. He had to go fairly far among the trees to find enough, bringing it back to Rose in small batches as she built up the fire, then gathering more until there was a small stack waiting to see them through the evening and maybe start tomorrow's fire. By then Rose had the tripod standing over the flames and a pot set on the tripod and had opened the bundle she had brought from the kitchen to reveal two large, round bread loaves, a fat wedge of yellow cheese, several small onions still with their long green leaves, and a cloth bag that likely had the peas Sister Letice had mentioned.

"I take my daily wage in food," Rose said, seeing him look at all of that.

"They pay well."

"Sister Letice adds what she calls 'alms' to what I earn. Thus the peas." She prodded the bag. It gave a dry rattle. "Last year's but still a kind gift."

"Water?" Joliffe asked, because that would be needed to cook the peas.

"Under the front of the cart. Piers fetched a full bucket this morning."

"From where?"

"There's a well in the rear-yard beyond the laundry," Rose answered.

"You're sure he went that far?" Joliffe asked, bringing the bucket.

"I'm sure," Rose said, soft laughter at him behind the words. "Nor it isn't that far." She nodded sideways. "We're nearly at the corner of the orchard, with the garden just beyond it and then the rear-yard."

"No one's troubled the cart?" Joliffe asked. That was always a worry, there being no way to secure the cart beyond tying closed the flaps at front and back, so that usually one or another of the company was left to guard it, which was not possible here.

"None. With hayward and reeve and bailiff all prowling to be sure everyone is where they're supposed to be and working hard at the harvest, anyone troubling things here would likely be easily found out."

Having poured sufficient water into the pot for her, he sat down on his heels out of her way while she busied herself with stirring the peas into it and asked, his voice very low, "The money? Still safe?"

Her voice equally low, she answered, not pausing in her work, "Still safe."

Years ago a secret place had been made in the cart for the keeping of the scant coins the company had been able to spare from daily needs. Of late there were a comfortable number of them there, but sometimes they had been very scant indeed and sometimes the only thing between the players and dire need. The secret place had been made by Rose's husband. After he had deserted her and their son and the company, never to be heard from or of since in the years afterward, only Rose had known where the secret place was, with her father's willing agreement because she, being the most careful of any of the company, was least likely to be foolish with the money. Only eventually had she shared the secret with Joliffe, that if anything untoward happened, someone besides herself would know. That *he* knew of it remained secret between them.

Now he asked, "Should you tell someone besides me?"

"No," she said. She swung away to find something in the

kitchen box. "You've come back. There's no need to tell anyone else." She turned back to the pot and added, not looking
at him, "Is there?"

"No," he said in his turn.

"You're staying in the company?"

"Yes."

"Until he wants you elsewhere."

"He doesn't want me elsewhere." Neither of them saying
the powerful bishop's name.

"Where does he want us?"

"I don't know. Wherever we want to be for now, I
suppose."

Rose sighed. "Well, here is where we have to be for now,
want or not."

The weight of that worry came down immediately on
both of them, and Joliffe, to go a more cheerful way, forced
though it might be, said, "And here is none so bad. Basset is
bettering. You seem content. Ellis, Gil, and Piers are earning
money. Tomorrow I'll be. We've done worse."

"We have done." Rose matched his cheerfulness without
he could tell how forced her own was. "Why don't you fetch
the cushions now?"

He did and sat himself down on one. The well-westered
sun was striking long, golden light through the orchard,
pooling deep green shadows among the trees. Supper was
cooking. Tonight and probably tomorrow were taken care of.
All in all, he had no complaints about the world at just that
moment and after a comfortable stretch of silence he said easily, "So. Tell me about this place, these people."

"Um." Rose hesitated. "Ah."

It seemed a more difficult question than Joliffe had intended. "Good? Bad? Mixed lot?" he prompted.

"Good," Rose said immediately. "On the whole, good."

"Mixed lot, then."

Rose laughed at him. "Mixed lot. But none of them so bad. Or so I'd have said before Mistress Thorncoffyn came. She's unsettled everything."

"A cat come into a dovecote," Joliffe suggested.

"If you grant the cat doesn't want to make a kill, only keep everyone's feathers ruffled. And that the cat brought dogs with it. Master Soule has all but disappeared from sight since she came." Her tone suggested "fortunate man."

"Master Soule?"

"Master of the hospital. And please don't make any jests about his name," she added, although she had not been looking at Joliffe and could not have seen he had opened his mouth to do just that. As he closed his mouth, she went on, "He and Father Richard are our priests, with Father Richard priest at St. George's across the road, too. Then there's Master Hewstere. He's our physician. He sees to the men's bodily care, while Master Soule and Father Richard see to their spiritual."

"I'd begun to wonder if I was the only man here besides the patients." Although he had not truly wondered that, because every hospital had its priest or priests, they being necessary to the patients' longer well-being than anything a physician could do for them.

"You saw Jack at the gate," Rose reminded him.

"I'd forgotten. Yes."

Rose spooned one of the peas from the boiling water, tried it for how cooked it was, and was turning to the kitchen box again as she went on, "Best you ready yourself for Mistress Thorncoffyn, though. She'll want to know all about you." Having taken the cloth bag of oatmeal from the box and opened the drawstring, she took out a handful of meal and let it flow into the bubbling water with one hand, spoon-stirring with her other hand while going on, "Besides Master Soule and Father Richard and Master Hewstere, there's who you've already met. Sister Margaret knows as much of medicines as

Master Hewstere does, I think, though it won't do to say so. She and Sister Letice together know as much about herbs and what purposes they best serve as anyone is likely to. Then there's Sister Ursula."

"Who hired me."

"And will be watching to see you earn your keep, never doubt it," Rose assured him. "You've still to meet Sister Petronilla. She mostly sees to the children."

"The children?"

"The children. Mistress Thorncoffyn's father made this hospital for the care of aged and ill men, with 'four discreet men of the town' and the master to govern it, but with the provision that his heir of the next generation and the three generations after that have right of say and stay."

"The right not only to stay here when they choose, but a right to a say in the hospital's governing, you mean."

"Just so," Rose agreed.

"And when the four generations of heirs have passed?"

"Then all reverts to the next heir who will be free to continue the hospital or take all back into his own hands."

"And the children?" Because a hospital was not the usual place for children. Ill children were cared for at home. Unwanted, orphaned children, if they were fortunate, went most often into the care of a nunnery or monastery.

"The older at least is Mistress Thorncoffyn's doing," Rose said. She was now slicing the onions, leaves and all, into the pot.

"It's Mistress Thorncoffyn's child?" Joliffe said incredulously.

Rose scorned that with, "No. I've never made out whether he's the son of someone among the gentry she knows or of one of her servants she decided to favor, only that he's the child of someone she knows who couldn't or wouldn't keep him. He's twisted of body and was thought to maybe be slight in his wits, which he isn't, as it's turned out. By rights, there's no provision in the hospital's statutes for children to be here, but Mistress Thorncoffyn wanted it and she—" Rose paused, seemingly searching for a word.

"Forced?" Joliffe suggested.

"Persuaded," Rose said quellingly. "She persuaded the others with say in the place to accept the boy. So I've gathered from the talk. Maybe it's thought he'll take over from Jack at the gate when the time comes. Anyway, since he was already here, that made it easier to let in the other boy when that was the only way to have Sister Petronilla here. She's a widow, you see, and he's her son and not at all right in the head, poor little thing. Sister Margaret and Sister Ursula are widows, too, come to that."

Widows were preferred for work in hospitals and almshouses, and the older they were the better, to put them beyond the temptations of the flesh. The trouble with that, Joliffe had always thought, was that someone old enough to be beyond the temptations of the flesh was likely to be too feeble for the necessary work. Certainly, the women he had seen here were not in the blushings of youth—save for Amice in the laundry perhaps—but equally certainly they were far from old and assuredly far from feeble.

"Then there are Emme and Amice in the laundry, but they're not sisters here, only hired like me, with Emme having her gown and apron as part of her wages. That's all of us. Not that anyone except Emme and Amice have any one set of tasks all and only her own. We all set our hands to whatever needs doing. The cooking. Tending to the men. The garden. Anything."

There it was again, that including herself in this place as if she belonged. This time Joliffe might have taken her up about it, but she said, peering into the pot that she was stirring again, "And now there's you, and I'm going to lie down for a time before Ellis and the others come." She handed him the spoon. "Tend the pot. If supper burns, you'll go hungry and no one will be glad you're here."

Pretending injured dignity, Joliffe said, "I think I can stir a pot of pease pottage to everyone's satisfaction."

"Um," said Rose, admitting to nothing except her doubt, and went away with one of the cushions to an apple tree's deepest shade.

Chapter 5

Having taken off her headkerchief, folded it, and carefully set it aside, Rose lay down with a self-betraying sigh of weariness and, by her breathing, was very soon asleep, her head on the cushion and one arm over her eyes, her other resting across her waist. Joliffe settled himself beside the fire with his back to her for what little privacy that gave.

The orchard was in early evening quiet, warm with the day's gathered heat, no slightest breeze stirring among the trees, the shadows thickening toward darkness as, somewhere beyond sight, the sun must be nearly set. Unseen birds were twittering as they settled for their night, and Joliffe was contented to be alone in the peacefulness for a time, to catch his thoughts up. The long day had gone ways that, looking ahead to it, he would never have thought it would. Not that any of them were bad in themselves. He wanted more time to talk with Basset to judge for himself how he did, that was certain, but if Basset had been helped as much as he and Rose said he had been, surely he could be helped the rest of the way.

Surely.

Except Joliffe knew there was no "surely" about anything in the world except death. Even taxes could be out run if you weren't tied down to place and property or were poor enough. Until lately the players had managed all three of those *and* avoided death into the bargain. Thus far, thus good, he thought. Nor was Basset going to die of the arthritics. But if he did not heal more than he was at present, the company was finished.

Joliffe circled that thought, unable to keep away from it. In a company like theirs, everyone had their share of work and everyone had to do it or the whole fell to pieces. Along with his skill in directing their plays and the parts he took in them, Basset's sharp choosing where they would go and what they would play had kept the company going through the worst times. As much as the company needed his wits, though, they also needed his body upright and performing. True, until Gil joined them two years ago they had done with one less player—had done so again these past months with Joliffe gone, their plays changed back to how they had been before Gil joined them and parts been shifted around. Without Basset, there would be another shifting of parts, and any plays they could no longer do could be dropped. That was straightforward enough, but it still left the plain problem of travel. Their cart was loaded right to the edge of what Tisbe could draw. If Basset was going to have to ride from here onward, they would either have to abandon some of the things by which they made their living or go to the cost of changing their cart to a two-horse draw and getting another horse. Leaving behind any of the hard-bought necessities of their trade was hardly to be thought on, while the laughable part of it was that, with their wealthy bishop now in some sort— for the use he hoped to make of them—secretly their patron behind the front of Lord Lovell, there was surely money to be had to keep their company together and going onward. The trouble there was that if their company became so openly

prosperous beyond the ordinary, would questions be asked
about their prosperity? That would not be to the good. Their
value to the bishop lay in no one thinking twice about them
being other than they were.

Joliffe, having been sitting with the long-handled spoon
idle in his hands, remembered to stir the pottage just before
it would have begun to burn at the bottom.

He told himself that was reminder not to lose heed of the
immediate moment in brooding about what had not, might
not come to pass. Why should he worry overmuch just yet?
Basset might altogether better and then the worry would be
all a waste. If Basset did not altogether better, *then* would be
the time to set to worrying.

The trick there, Joliffe knew too well, was to follow his
own wise advice. And knew himself too well to believe he
was likely to. But why shouldn't he? Let things be as they
were for a while. For the time being, Basset was bettering,
Rose was content, the others were earning money. Beginning
tomorrow he had easy work for himself, and if he had read
her smiles at him a-right, Amice of the laundry had possibilities. What was there to be discontented about?

He was saved from following through on that thought by
hearing voices calling good-nights and other things from the
far side of the orchard where another field track must run.
That would be folk coming home from the fields. Since there
was never any saying when the weather would turn, harvest
work began as soon as might be in the mornings and went
on until it had to stop for darkness, everyone kept at it by the
constant spur of knowing that what was not harvested now
would not be there to feed them in the winter. Ellis, Gil, and
Piers were going to be tired—ready for their supper and more
than ready to sit down, Joliffe thought.

He found he had forgotten to stop stirring the pottage
once he had started. He stopped now, took a taste from the
spoon, and found it good. As always, Rose had made a plain

pottage into something savory by whatever herbs she had added.

Rose sat up and said, "Take it from the fire, if you would, please."

While Joliffe used a cloth she kept for pot-handling to shift the heavy pot from the tripod onto the trampled grass beside the firepit, she stretched and got slowly to her feet. "It's done, isn't it?" she asked.

"Done and delicious."

"Lid it, please." Rather than covering her hair, braided and coiled at the back of her head, again, she went to the cart to put her headkerchief safely away in her own small box of belongings such as they all had for what little was possible to carry with them in their life as players.

Several familiar voices were coming along the cart-path, accompanied by a soft thud of hooves. Joliffe, having put the spoon aside and the lid on the pot, went to meet them, glad to see as they turned from the track into the orchard that Tisbe had been rid of her harness somewhere, had only her halter and rope still on her. Ellis, Gil, and Piers were all stripped down to their shirts and short braies, with their hosen rolled down below their knees. They were sweat-marked by the day's heat and probably twice as tired as they looked but had plainly paused along the way to wash something of the day's sweat and dust from them—their heads had been lately ducked deep into water or had buckets poured over them—but they were all of them walking with the heavy tread of one-foot-in-front-of-another tiredness, and Joliffe was pleased all over again that he would not join them in the fields tomorrow.

Gil saw him first and called out, "Hai! Look who has come wandering back!"

"Look who's been doing honest work for a change!" Joliffe returned.

"Not you, that's sure," Ellis growled.

"Here," Piers said, thrusting Tisbe's lead-rope at him. "Your turn."

It was all so familiar that Joliffe wanted to laugh aloud, but instead scowled at him while taking the rope and demanded, "Have you been growing?"

"Like the proverbial weed, and just as useful," Ellis said.

That Piers made no fast answer to that showed just how very tired he must be. Nor did he run ahead to see what his mother had ready for supper but continued to trudge on Tisbe's other side. She rubbed her head against Joliffe's shoulder to show she was pleased he was there, and he rubbed her on the hard bone between her eyes, letting her know he was pleased, too.

At the cart, Ellis, Gil, and Piers dropped down onto the waiting cushions. Joliffe, leading Tisbe to the cart to get out her hobbles so he could let her free to graze the long orchard grass, caught Rose's worried look around at all of them, to judge how tired they were and make sure they were none of them hurt or in need of anything but food and sleep. The food they got immediately, Rose ladling pottage into wooden bowls and handing them around while Joliffe saw to Tisbe, wiping her down with a dry cloth, brushing her some—meaning to do more later—and putting tansy ointment around her eyes to keep the flies away, then giving her a portion of oats from the bag they kept for her. By the time he finished and joined the others, Ellis, Gil, and Piers were to their second bowlfuls, with large pieces of bread to go with it, but the first headlong thrust of hunger was gone, and as Joliffe sat down and took the bowl Rose held out to him, Ellis said, "No fatted calf for you, I fear."

"We could make do with your fat head," Piers suggested around a mouthful of bread.

"Isn't it pity," Joliffe said to Rose, "how his mouth has grown bigger along with the rest of him?" He fixed a glare of feigned threat on Piers and added, "We might have to cut you down by a few inches all around. That would save your mother the trouble of making you new clothes."

"Ha!" said Piers widely around the half-chewed bread.

That earned him, "Don't talk with a full mouth," from Rose, sitting now to her own meal between him and Ellis. "Nor half-full neither," she added, seeing him shift some to his cheek and swallow the rest.

Grinning, Piers leaned sideways to bump his shoulder against her arm friendliwise and, for a wonder, kept his mouth shut while Gil said to Joliffe, "You're not in hope you can hide here in the orchard, are you? The reeve is keen. He'll find you out and invoke the statute. You'll be at the barley with us by noon tomorrow."

"He's already been caught," Rose said. "Sister Ursula saw him first. She's hired him to replace that Ivo for the while."

"I'm even to have a room there, and a bed, and my meals," Joliffe said grandly.

"You and your life of ease," Ellis grumbled. "We spend the year walking our feet flat on the road, then get stuck here working the fields, while you take your ease at some bishop's palace, hardly stirring a sweat, I'll warrant."

"When it's my wits that are wanted rather than your brawn, what can I do?" Joliffe protested sweetly.

Ellis suggested, unsweetly, what he could do.

Joliffe kept to himself that he had not spent the past months in anything like a life of ease, and especially the past weeks at a plain manor in an out-of-the-way corner of nowhere in particular where the lessoning had been unceasing, including—all too often—alarums in the night when he was supposed to be awake on the instant and knowing what to do. He likewise kept to himself the paling scar across his upper left arm from a dagger wound five months ago and the yellowing remains of a bruise under his left ribs where, a week ago, he had failed to block the thrust from the padded end of a wooden practice dagger. The fight-master had stepped back from him, saying, "See the angle I had the dagger? Up into the heart is where it would have gone. If this had been steel and me in earnest, you'd be dead by now," then had set to making him block that manner of thrust over and over again, and afterward shown him how to give a thrust unlikely to be blocked.

Gil asked, "Have you seen Basset yet?"

"Seen him and had a goodly talk with him," Joliffe answered. "He's pleased with how much better he is but can't say when he'll be ready to be away."

"Not until harvest is well and truly done, would be my guess," said Ellis. "The reeve has likely given word there that he wants us to the end. It was so the reeve could have our bodies for the harvest that Basset got taken into the hospital at all. I swear it."

"Nah," protested Gil, reaching for more bread. "It was for our playing the day before. He can't bear to part with us after that." He explained to Joliffe, "The village was mostly in the fields when we came into town that day. So Basset asked at the hospital if they'd like us to do some holy saint's play for the men there. The master was willing, only he said maybe something to make them laugh would be best. So we did *Saint Uncumber and the Bad Husband* to give them both."

The play, where the determinedly virginal Uncumber, after fending off her new, unwanted husband's attentions in various laughable ways, prayed to be made ugly to keep him away from her and was promptly blessed with a thick beard, to her delight and her husband's dismay, always set folk to laughter.

"Then we did *Robin Hood and Maid Marian* for the village in the evening," Gil said.

"Short and sweet," added Ellis. "Before full dark came on."

That made them note that while they had eaten and

talked, today's dark had come on in its turn. With the fire in low coals in the firepit, their eyes had grown used to the thickening shadows around them without their thought about it until now. The year was something like two months past mid-summer, so the nights were lengthening but still not long enough after a long day's work in the fields: it was time and past to be to bed, and Ellis finished, "Then the next morning Basset was so stiff and pained there was nothing for it but to ask help at the hospital, and here we are."

Rose stood up, asking as she gathered the empty bowls out of everyone's hands, "Does anyone want to finish the pot?"

Gil and Piers both quickly scooped out and ate what little pottage was left, leaving it to Ellis and Joliffe to take bedding and straw-stuffed pads and pillows from the cart. With the nights warm and dry, there was no need for the tent. They simply laid everything out on the grass, Ellis asking of Joliffe, "You're here for tonight?"

Joliffe, holding back from pointing out that was why he was laying out a bed for himself, simply said, "Saves me from the walk back." He did not add how he had been sleeping under roofs and inside walls for weeks now and was ready to have the sky over him again. Or, presently, sky and apple branches.

Gil and Piers had finished with the pottage. Rose put the bowls and spoons in the pot and sloshed water from the bucket over them, sufficient to soak them overnight but leaving water enough in the bucket for face-washing come the morning. Necessities were done away among the trees, most clothing was taken off, and everyone lay down to their sleep, Joliffe no less readily than the others. He was maybe awake the longest, listening to their breathing go even around him and watching a bright star straight overhead appear and disappear with the gentle sway of apple boughs. Somewhere away in the darkness, Tisbe was tearing grass, and now that talk had stopped, he was aware of the unconsidered sounds of night-insects in trees and grass. Not for the first time in these past weeks, he wondered what had led him to be fool enough to accept Bishop Beaufort's offer. A player's life was a hard one, but in all the different ways of living there were, what life in its own way was not? You chose the hard one that had the most about it that you liked, and he had chosen to be a player and still loved the life that had come with that choice. Given that, why was he imperiling it all?

He did not know. Except that he had wanted not only the life he had been living but more. Not other, and not instead, but more. Bishop Beaufort had offered that more.

He realized he was not seeing the star anymore because his eyes had closed. His lids were too heavy to open again, nor did he want to. Sleep was a good place to go. He welcomed it.

So long as the dreams kept away.

Chapter 6

The day was in its first easing from night toward the promise of a clear dawn when Joliffe left the other players and Rose to their breakfast of bread and cheese and returned on his own through the orchard and kitchen garden and passageway to the rear-yard, all still shadowy gray in half darkness. In the kitchen, though, a stub of candle burned on the middle of the worktable, casting its soft yellow glow across the faces of the four women gathered there. Only one of them was not familiar from yesterday, and as they all looked toward him with a mingling of welcome and curiosity he made a flourished bow to them with, "Good morrow, my ladies."

They all smiled at that, and Sister Letice a little laughed, friendliwise, before Sister Margaret said crisply, " 'Sister' is sufficient here," and added to the others, "Someone wake me after Prime, please, if I'm not awake before."

The others nodded and she left toward the passage past Joliffe's room, to wherever the sisters' dorter was, Joliffe presumed, while Sister Letice explained to him, "She was up much of the night. One of our men was in pain again."

"Have you eaten yet this morning?" Sister Ursula asked.

When he willingly said he had not, she pushed a pottery pitcher and a wooden cup toward him along the table, and the woman not yet named to him drew a wooden platter with thick slices of bread, a wedge of cheese, and a bowl of butter from the middle of the table into his reach, giving him reason to look full at her for the first time as he thanked her. She was a broad woman with clever eyes and answered his thanks with a smiling nod as Sister Ursula said, "Sister Petronilla. Joliffe."

He acknowledged her with a bow of his head that she returned before he took up a knife lying to hand and cut a piece from the cheese while Sister Ursula, apparently going back to what they had been saying, asked Sister Letice, "How much longer does Master Hewstere think it will be?"

"There's no knowing. Whatever the fever is in him, it's kept its hold longer than Master Hewstere thought it would. He says all that can be done now is to let the thing run its course."

"And to pray," Sister Petronilla suggested.

A little silence fell, maybe for that prayer. For the seemliness of it, Joliffe paused his eating and only began again on what proved to be day-old bread and dry cheese when Sister Ursula said, taking up the day's business, "There now. So you know, Master Soule will do Prime this morning, but Father Richard will take the rest of the Offices and Mass again today."

Joliffe did not see why that brought smiles and some smothered laughter around the table, and in answer to his puzzled look Sister Petronilla said to him, "It's safer for Master Soule that way."

That widened Sister Letice's and Sister Ursula's smiles, although the latter made obvious effort to curb hers as she said, "Enough. It's time we were on with things."

The women, done with breaking their fast, bowed their heads, each making her own murmured prayer of thanks. Joliffe again paused his eating until they had done. Then, as Sister Petronilla and Sister Letice left the table, Sister Ursula said to him, "I'll show you your duties today."

Mouth full, he nodded to that, washed down his last mouthful of bread and cheese with the ale that was strong enough but not of the best—these women assuredly did not keep themselves in ease here—set his cup down with the others left on the table, bent his head in a quickly muttered grace, and raised his head to let Sister Ursula know he was ready for whatever came next.

What came next proved to be bed-pots.

As Sister Ursula explained while leading him to the hall, emptying and washing and returning the bed-pots to each man's bed would be his first task every day.

"Now, you must understand that some of the men can rise to use their own. Others will call for you to help when the need comes on them, be it day or in the night. Don't delay about it, or you'll have to explain to Emme why there are extra sheets to wash. Today, the way their sleep was broken last night by Adam Morys' trouble, the men may be troublesome in their turn. You'll be patient with them, nonetheless, I know."

That was pleasantly said, but left Joliffe without doubt that what Sister Ursula meant was that he had *best* be patient with them. There was a crisp certainty to Sister Ursula that left no doubt why she was huswife here, with all the overseeing of the place's daily needs put in her hands. Joliffe judged that if he did exactly as she told him in his duties, he would do well enough. At the same time, there was nothing unfriendly about her, and he gave way to his curiosity and asked, "Why is it safer for Master Soule to do Prime today?"

Quite steadily but with something of the same laughter under the words as there had been in kitchen, Sister Ursula said, "Because Mistress Thorncoffyn will not be up this early."

That again was no sufficient answer but it was all she gave. They were in the hall now. There was enough gray dawnlight through the windows that Sister Ursula paused beside a low-standing table just inside the hall's door to put out the fat candle burning there. Several smaller, unlighted candles in holders waited beside it. "For use in the night, when you have to go to someone," she explained.

She went to the nearest bed, said quietly, "Deke Credy, good morning," and pushed back the curtain. "Wooden rings," she said to Joliffe, nodding upward. "They make less of a noise than metal would." As not really an after-thought, she added, "And are less costly."

"More to spend on m'comforts," mumbled the toothless old man grinning up from the bed. "Um'll have roast pork for my dinner today, Sister."

"You'll have pains in your belly all the rest of the day and all tomorrow if you do," Sister Ursula said back as if it were an old jibing between them. "This is Joliffe who's taken Ivo's place for the while." And to Joliffe, "Deke is here nearest the altar because he's more in need of blessing than most."

"Um that," Deke agreed cheerily. "Bad man all my days."

"Leave the pot a moment," Sister Ursula bade Joliffe who had bent to draw the cloth-covered pottery pot from under the bed. "You can meet the others while I set back their curtains to the day and gather up the cups from their night-time drink."

Joliffe willingly put off the first bed-pot in favor of following her as she made her way back and forth and down the ward, opening the curtains beside each bed with cheersome good-mornings and sharing some talk with each man that told Joliffe a little about them. Only Deke and three others were decrepit with years. Another man was in hale middle-age save for a broken leg that had him bedfast and grumbling, his summer-brown skin beginning to pale from being away from the sun too long.

"Let a hay wain roll over him, did our Adam," Sister Ursula told Joliffe, and added sternly to the bedfast man, "You're lucky it wasn't your head, drunk as you were, stumbling about like that."

"I wasn't drunk and you know it!" he shot back. "Nor don't think I don't hear the wild times and drinking goes on in that kitchen among you women, neither." But he grinned as he said it, and Sister Ursula returned a smile of her own.

In another bed a hollow-chested young man much about Joliffe's own age was lying quiet and pain-eyed, too taken up with the effort of his breathing to strain at talk. Sister Ursula spoke quietly to him, calling him Iankyn, and gentled him a little higher on his several pillows. As they left him, Joliffe asked softly, "Lung-sickness?"

"Of a kind, yes. It's asthma, and sometimes he's quite well, but some times of the year are worse for him than others, and at its worst there's nothing but here for him, for us to do what we can."

The man they came to now lay with his eyes half-closed, twisting his head back and forth on his pillow, clutching and unclutching at the sheet over him and muttering, seeming hardly aware of Sister Ursula as she bent over him to feel his forehead and say firmly, "John. It's morning, John. There'll be Prime soon. Master Soule will soon be saying Prime." She looked over her shoulder at Joliffe to add, "He always quiets during the Offices." A basin of water with a cloth in it sat on the floor under the table beside his bed. "If it's set on the table, he's likely to tip it off when he thrashes," she explained, bending to wring out the cloth.

While she gently bathed his forehead and cheeks, Joliffe asked, "What manner of fever is it?"

"A cotidian, given the particular way it comes and goes in him daily. If it weren't harvest time, he'd be cared for at home, but there's only his wife and a half-grown son. They both have to be in the fields, so he's here for the while." She put the cloth back into the basin, briefly touched the man's shoulder, and said again to him, "There'll be Prime soon now," before moving across the aisle to Basset who was wide awake. He laughed when Sister Ursula said they would begin taking up the bed-pots now and said to Joliffe, "Found your right place in the world at last, eh?"

With a great, grave dignity that did not go with the pot he was picking up, Joliffe said, "Humility and service will win me the better place in Heaven."

Basset laughed again, and Sister Ursula said, benignly enough, "It's to the good when a man is well enough to laugh," but Joliffe suspicioned that she was laughing, too, if only inwardly.

While they collected the pots, Sister Ursula told him, "Usually, this will be your task alone in the mornings. It's best if you can have it done before Prime, to be out of the way." And she showed him how they were to be emptied in the necessarium at the far end of the kitchen and scullery but reached along one arm of the roofed walk that he now saw ran not only along the side of the hospital's hall but also down the inner sides of the kitchen wing and the range of rooms facing it, across a square of greensward surrounded on three sides by the walk and presently being kept short by a tethered nanny goat. At its far end the greensward was closed in by a hip-high latticed fence beyond which he could see the orchard, so presumably the stone-lined drain and stream were there, too.

"We call this the cloister," Sister Ursula said as they went along the walk. "Such as it is. Those of our men who aren't bedridden can come out to sit on the benches here when the days are warm. Now, about these pots," she went on as she led him into the necessarium. It was a narrow room. A stone bench with two suitably sized holes through it and low enough for comfortable sitting ran along its outer side, with the gurgle of water below it telling how waste was carried off along the stone-lined runnel. At the far end of the bench was a tub kept there for cleaning the bed-pots.

"You'll do well to fill the tub the evening before, to make one less thing to do in the morning," Sister Ursula said.

This morning, she helped him, probably for the sake of making sure he understood how to scrub a pot clean, but she talked while they worked, and not idly, telling him more of the men who would be in his care, beginning with, "Adam Morys, the man who has the broken leg. He was never drunk when he fell. He was grabbing Jack Denton's grandson out of the wain's way and slipped in mud and went under himself. He's fretted with losing all the summer's work his fields need. He needn't be, though. His folk and Denton's and others are taking it up for him. He'll be back on his leg well before All Hallows. This being the first summer's work he's missed since he could toddle, you'd think he'd not mind the chance to rest, but he does. Keep something of an eye on him, that he doesn't get restless and try to walk ere he should. They do that—not use their good sense. Not that Iankyn Tanner is likely to be up until he's allowed. He tends to be too weak to be other than sensible. The old men don't move about much, but they're allowed if they want to. You'll find them sitting in the sun in the cloister, as I said. Ned Knolles sometimes makes it as far as the foreyard, although when he does, Jack at the gate usually has to help him back."

As they were fetching the last pair of bed-pots back to the hall, a bell began to be rung from somewhere outside the hospital.

"There's Father Richard at St. George's across the way," Sister Ursula said. "The parish's church. That will be for Prime. He's ever prompt to prayers."

Working to remember what he had heard so far, Joliffe

said, "This Father Richard, he's parish priest as well as the priest for here? Is that the way of it?"

"It is."

"But he and Master Soule don't take prayers and Mass turn and turn about here."

"Since there's no knowing when Father Richard will be needed somewhere in the parish, he and Master Soule have never tried to settle any pattern between them. They just do as choice and chance allow."

Joliffe added that to all the other pieces he was gathering about St. Giles. Master Soule was master of the hospital and a priest. Father Richard served here but also for the parish, and they shared the Offices and, presumably, other priestly duties here in the hospital, while the sisters worked at keeping everyone clean and fed and tended to. And his own job was bed-pots and . . .

As they were putting the last of the pots back under beds, Sister Ursula said, "Dick Leek's needs emptying again. I'll leave you to it. If you hurry, you can have it back and be out of the way before Master Soule begins Prime. We're not asked to be at the Offices, only at Mass. Unless you want to attend?" Sister Ursula added, delicately questioning.

Joliffe had had his fill of prayerful hours before he became a player. Given a choice, he was not minded to have more if he could help it, so taking up the bed-pot, he said simply, "No," and hurried to be done with it.

Chapter 7

Although Joliffe made as quick work as he could with the bed-pot, by the time he returned Master Soule had already begun Prime, but since the master was facing the altar, his back to the hall, Joliffe made bold to slip to Dick Leek's bed and slide the bed-pot silently under it, taking only a single quick look into the chapel as he slipped out again. All he saw of Master Soule was a narrow back, a floor-long black gown, and a tonsured head. The only other thing he could tell about the man was that his voice was somewhat thin but that he sounded as if he were giving actual heed to the words he was saying, which was to the good, Joliffe thought. With all the praying there should be here, it would be a shame to waste the effort by giving the prayers too little heed.

In the kitchen, he found Sister Petronilla and Sister Ursula gone but Sister Letice still there and that Rose had arrived and Sister Margaret come back. The latter surely had not slept enough to set her up for the day, but she was busy with the others, readying what Joliffe presumed were the men's breakfasts, with something warming in the pot on the fire, bread being sliced at the table, and wooden cups being set out on waiting trays—flats of wood lap-wide and slightly hollowed in the center. Rose promptly sent him to fetch clean wooden bowls and spoons from the scullery. He brought them with the discomfortable thought that the next time those bowls and spoons were scrubbed, he would be doing it.

He had just set them on the table when Sister Petronilla came in, shepherding a small boy ahead of her and leading a slightly older boy by the hand. Joliffe supposed they were the children Rose had talked of earlier. As she had said, the younger was not right in his head. He shuffled forward as if uncertain where either his feet or the floor were, despite his head was deeply bowed toward them, leaving him unlikely to see anything else. Joliffe suspected only Sister Petronilla's gentle hand on his back kept him moving at all.

The older boy was more aware of where he was, despite a lop-sided, rolling walk, his left leg seeming to follow his right only with especial effort, while his head and shoulders seemed set in a twist to the side that must be unrestful, but unlike the other boy, he was altogether aware around himself, and stopped when he saw Joliffe, immediately knowing him for a stranger.

"Daveth," Sister Petronilla said quietly. "That's Joliffe. Remember I told you he would be here."

She touched the boy's shoulder lightly, and he came on and climbed by himself onto a stool at the table, keeping a wary watch on Joliffe the while. Sister Petronilla lifted the other boy onto another stool, gave a single stroke of her hand to his fair hair, and moved away, to take up two of the bowls and go toward the hearth where Sister Letice was swinging the pot clear of the fire. After that, while Sister Petronilla saw to feeding the boys, Joliffe became busy with helping ready the bowls of oatmeal pottage, slices of buttered bread, and cups of ale that would be the men's breakfast until Sister Petronilla said, "Daveth, go see if Master Soule is done in the chapel, please." The boys had had cups of milk with their oatmeal and bread. Daveth wiped the back of his hand across his mouth, slid from his stool, and lopped away toward the hall. Sister Petronilla, catching Joliffe's eyes as he looked back from watching the boy leave, said simply, "He's a good child. They're both good children."

From lack of anything useful to say but feeling the need to say something, Joliffe offered, "Quiet, too."

Again, she gave a single stroke to the other boy's hair. "Most of the time. Daveth can speak when he wants to. Heinrich, I think, is mute."

Joliffe echoed with surprise, "Heinrich?"

"I was married to a merchant of the Hanse. We lived in Danzig. When he died and there was no reason for me to stay there, Heinrich and I came home." She said it with the simplicity of having long since accepted that was how things were with her. And with her son.

Daveth came limping back.

"Is he done?" Sister Margaret asked.

Daveth nodded.

Sister Petronilla said, gentle and firm together, "Say it aloud, Daveth."

Just above a whisper, Daveth said, "He's done."

Sister Petronilla prompted, "Who is done?"

Daveth gave a small sigh, sounding disconcertingly like Piers when much put upon, and granted softly, "Master Soule is done."

"Thank you, Daveth," Sister Margaret said.

Daveth started back for the door. "Daveth," Sister Petronilla said. He turned back, grudged toward the floor, "You're welcome, Sister," and continued on his way. Behind him, Sister Petronilla shook her head while the other women traded smiles. Then they all became busy taking the breakfasts to the men. With Joliffe able to carry two trays at a time, the task went quickly, except for Sister Letice who sat down to persuade John Oxyn, the fevered man, into eating even a little something. "Or at least drink," Joliffe heard her saying gently as she raised him from the pillow and held a cup to his mouth.

Even Deke Credy in the bed by the door was more interested in eating than in talk, but Bassett took the chance as he took his tray from Joliffe to say, "Not made a break for it yet, I see."

"Not yet. I'm waiting to see what comes next."

"Mass. Then bedsheets," Bassett said with the authority of someone who knew only too well.

But when Joliffe returned to the kitchen, just behind Sister Ursula and Sister Margaret, a woman—tall and thin, gray of hair and grim of bony face—turned from poking a doubtful spoon at what pottage was left in the pot and said sharply at them, "There you are," as if they were remiss in being somewhere else when she wanted them here. "My lady wants that cooked for her." She pointed to a perhaps half-pound slab of meat on the table, lying on the oiled cloth in which it had been wrapped.

Just as sharply, Sister Ursula said back, "This is early for her to be up. Didn't she sleep well?"

No love lost there, Joliffe thought. Neither between Sister Ursula and this woman here, nor between Sister Ursula and whoever "my lady" was. Certainly the woman did not bother to reply. It was Sister Margaret who said, moderately, "Sister Letice will make a stronger sleeping draught for her."

"She'll have Master Hewstere's or no one's," the woman snapped. "She wants to see him when he comes today."

"She always does," Sister Ursula said, well above a mutter but away as she headed for the pantry, so that the woman could ignore her and did, while Sister Margaret answered, "He'll come to her, of course."

The woman gave a sharp nod, acknowledging that, then

turned gimlet eyes on Joliffe. "Let *him* bring her breakfast. She wants to see him."

Sister Margaret responded with a wordless nod. The woman looked around as if wanting to find something else to snap about, but had to satisfy herself with a disparaging sniff and stalked out. When it seemed she was safely gone, Joliffe asked, "And that was?"

"Idany," Sister Margaret said. "Handmaid to Mistress Thorncoffyn."

Sister Ursula, taking up a broad knife and advancing on the meat, said, "I know she pays the butcher well for seeing she gets the first and best whenever he slaughters, but a meal this heavy at this hour of the day—" She shook her head. "We'll suffer right along with her after she's downed this."

Sister Margaret, going to set a three-legged fry-pan over the fire, said, "She'll eat as she chooses. Master Hewstere might as well say nothing at all to her."

Rose came in through the rear door.

"Cleared out, did you?" Sister Ursula said. She had begun to slice the meat into small pieces.

"I heard her tread in the passageway and fled."

"Well done," Sister Margaret approved.

Rose came to take over the slicing from Sister Ursula, who gave way willingly and sat down on one of the stools. Joliffe cleared the children's dishes away to the scullery and scrubbed them. By the time he returned, the meat was sizzling in the pan and Rose was setting a tray—larger and better made than the men's—with a pewter pitcher and several thick slices of bread, some buttered, some not. Sister Margaret, despite the meat could hardly be more than browned by now, asked for "the bowl," and Rose pointed Joliffe toward a high shelf where a broad pewter bowl sat by itself. He realized he had seen the pewter pitcher there, too. Mistress Thorncoffyn's own, they must be. He fetched the bowl to Sister Margaret who said, "Nor does she like her meat too cooked, either," and shifted the reddish meat into the bowl while Joliffe went on holding it. Then she lifted the fry-pan with both hands and poured the drippings into the bowl, too.

"There. That should hold her for an hour or so," she said and set the fry-pan down on the hearthstone, clear of the fire, with somewhat more force than might have been necessary.

Joliffe, adding the bowl to the tray, asked Sister Ursula as she laid a white cloth over everything, "Where do I go with this?"

"Along the walk and to the first door on your left. Just go in. She'll be in the farther chamber. Guard your back and watch your tongue," she added as he took up the tray.

She did not seem to be altogether jesting. Or maybe was not jesting at all, because if the maid Idany was only the guard of the dragon, the dragon could be presumed worse and, from what he had overheard yesterday in the kitchen, probably was. But he went. As he had to. The morning was promising a day as warm and rainless as yesterday, excellent for the harvest, and he would not have minded lingering along the roofed walk along the small garth where the dew was still on the shadowed grass, but Mistress Thorncoffyn was all too likely to take note if her meat had too much cooled, and he kept going, passing from the walk into the passageway toward the foreporch and turning left as Sister Ursula had directed him.

The chamber there suited with the rest of the hospital, was plain, with white-plastered walls and cleanly kept, with a bed at one wall, possibly for when a patient could not be kept in the hall for one reason or another. What did not suit were the two wooden traveling chests and four woven hampers set at seeming-random in the chamber's middle. Mistress Thorncoffyn's, he supposed, as he passed them. If they were, she did not travel lightly; he had seen small households shift from one where to another with less.

Despite Sister Ursula having said he could simply go in, he

chose wariness as his better part and scratched at the chamber's opposite, closed door. The immediate response was a torrent of barking and many pattering feet coming his way. The woman's bold voice of yesterday ordered, "Dogs! Here! Quiet!" and, for a wonder, the patter of feet went back the way they had come and the barking ceased except for a few yips from someone too excited to hold them in.

The maid Idany opened the door. She looked no more delighted to see him than she had in the kitchen but widened the door and stood aside as she said, "It's him. The new one. With your breakfast."

Joliffe went in, still wary but curious. Despite all that curiosity had done to him of late, he still could not curb it. Mistress Thorncoffyn and her dogs were something he wanted to see.

See them he did. The chamber was larger than the outer one, and he guessed it had sometime been someone's good parlor. The floor was of green glazed tiles, and its windows looked onto the garth's greensward and south to the orchard so that sunlight would fill the room most of the day. From the corner of his eye, he noted a curtained bed, but what he mostly saw was a pack of smooth-haired small hounds scrabbling toward him, nails clicking and slipping on the tiled floor. That they were no higher than his knees did not lessen the startlement of so many dogs coming at him at once but, to the good, they were bright-eyed and ear-pricked with friendliness and not barking now. As they surged around his ankles Joliffe found himself smiling down at their sharp-muzzled faces.

"Fawn. Fox. Kydd. Swan. Falcon. Here!" the same voice ordered.

As vastly enthused as they had surged toward Joliffe, they surged away, back to the woman in the chair in the middle of the room, and Joliffe saw Mistress Thorncoffyn for the first, full time.

There was much of her to see.

In truth, there was more of her to see than he had ever seen of any one person. There was enough of her to make at least two other people and not very slender ones, either. Or maybe three others if they *were* slender. Besides that, Joliffe guessed that if she had been standing, she would have been near to six feet tall. Presently, though, she was seated in a chair that had to have been made particularly for her; the wide bulge of her hips in her red gown filled it from side to side. Joliffe could not help wondering whether the gown had been made as tightly fitted to her as it was, or if she had simply continued fattening until she was as crammed into it as a sausage into its skin. A bulging, malformed sausage. The huge, falling mounds of her breasts rested on the top of the broad swell of her belly, and her neck was almost as wide as her head. She was not yet wearing a wimple and veil for the day nor even had her hair bound up; it was spread wide over her shoulders and of a red too even and unlikely to be anything but dyed, which was a strange vanity in a woman so distorted in every other way. Her face was smoothed to an undoubtedly false youthfulness by its fat. Did the maid Idany hold up a mirror to show her only her face, and Mistress Thorncoffyn, seeing that, ignore the rest?

At any rate, her dogs were happy to have so much of her. Two of them, come at her summons, leaped from the floor to where her lap would have been if her belly had not reached nearly to her knees and scaled her outward bulges as if they were a steep hillside, to lick happily at her chin and cheeks while the other three—there were only five of them, Joliffe could see now—stood with their forepaws on her knees, hoping for their turn.

Idany pointed to a small-topped table near to Mistress Thorncoffyn's right side and ordered, "Set it there, boy."

Joliffe, who had left boyhood behind him a few years ago, obeyed with a servant's properly downcast gaze.

"Now," Mistress Thorncoffyn ordered, "come here, to in front of me." She had pulled the two dogs away from her face, one to either side, was cuddling them against her in the crooks of her arms, leaving her able to give her full heed to Joliffe even before her meal.

Obediently he came to stand in front of her, eyes still down.

"Look at me," she ordered.

He did and was disconcerted at how sharp and bright were her eyes looking out from the ample flesh, as if maybe the mind there had not gone doughy, fat, and slack like the rest of her. Whether it was a mind he was going to like, he fully doubted as she demanded at him, "Where are you come from?"

If he had paused, he might have answered otherwise, but the demand grated, and with face and voice both bland, he said, "From somewhere else."

"That's no answer," she snapped.

"It's an answer," he pointed out mildly. "Just not the sort you wanted."

"Respect my lady, you good-for-nothing vagabond," Idany said and slapped the back of his head.

Joliffe's last weeks of training had taught him instant and harsh response to any attack, but what he could have done to her was uncalled for here, and he clamped down on his first urge, kept his face frozen in its blandness, turned his head and upper half of his body until he was looking at her, and only then, with only her to see it, used his player's skill to very deliberately let rage show in the narrowing of his eyes, the twist and tightening of his mouth. In truth, he felt only severe irk, not rage, but he doubted irk would trouble this Idany at all. The mime of rage did, though. She did not show fright—maybe she lacked sense enough—but she did show sufficiently startled that he thought she would not try striking him again. Satisfied with that, he turned back to Mistress Thorncoffyn, bland-faced again, and said, even-voiced, "Except for present matters concerning my ill master, patient here in St. Giles, I'm a travelling player. I'm always from somewhere else. Nor am I or any of our company vaga-bonds. We're licensed players to Lord Lovell of Minster Lovell in Oxfordshire."

"Are you indeed?" Mistress Thorncoffyn said, making it halfway to a challenge that Joliffe chose not to meet. He might be required to give her service; he was not required to account for his life to her; and still even-voiced he answered, "I am—and we are—indeed." He bowed a servant's bow to her, since servant he was supposed to be—but the hospital's, not hers—and said, "Now, by your leave, I'm needed else-where." And without waiting for her leave, turned and left.

The three little dogs not in their mistress' arms followed him to the door with a busy flurry of clicking toenails on the tiles but no barking, and when he looked down at them as he closed the door after himself, they were all three looking up at him with friendly, dog-laughing faces, more as if merely seeing him to the door than hurrying him on his way. On the whole, they had far more charm than did their mistress, he thought as he shut the door and heard them go clicking back to her.

Chapter 8

Rather than back to the kitchen, he went into the hall, finding he was in time to help Sister Letice with clearing the men's breakfast trays away to the kitchen. Basset, handing over his own, gave him a grin and asked, "Been to see Mistress Thorncoffyn, I understand. You behaved yourself?"

"As well as she did."

Understanding that a-right, Bassett pulled a false-dismayed face and said, "Oh, my."

"And her maid slapped the back of my head for me."

Both Bassett and Tom Lyttle in the next bed laughed outright at that, and Lyttle said, "The old toad and her sour-apple maid will chew you over all day, spit you out, and want you to come back for more."

"I can hardly bear the waiting," Joliffe said, returning their grins. Trying to keep up with brisk Sister Letice, he stacked their cups and trays and moved up the hall. As he and she reached the chapel end of the hall together with their gathered trays and cups, a half-grown boy bolted in at the hall's other end and skidded in a turn past Basset's bed. Then, seeing Sister Letice, he nearly fell over himself coming to a stop.

"Good morrow, Will," she said. "You're *running* late."

Looking past her into the chapel, he said breathlessly, "He's not down yet? I'm not late then?"

"You're late enough. Best you keep on hurrying. I think I hear him on the stairs."

"Oh, saints!" Will exclaimed and bolted forward again, to disappear through a doorway at the far side of the chapel.

"That was one of our grammar boys," Sister Letice said. "Master Soule keeps the school and the boys take turns, week and week around, helping at the Mass. Not that there's school now, with everyone to the harvest."

"There's a school here, too, then," Joliffe said as they went along the short passage to the kitchen.

"In season. In a room in the outer range, not to disturb our men."

Somewhere inside the hospital a sweet-toned bell rang three times, paused, and rang once more. Sister Letice said, "We'll put these in the scullery. Scrubbing them will have to wait. We all go to Mass."

Indeed they did—not only the sisters but Rose, and Emme and Amice from the laundry, bringing a pile of folded sheets that Amice set on the foot of Basset's bed, and Sister Petronilla and the two boys, and Jack from the gatehouse. They gathered at the hall's lower end, to leave the bedded men with a clear view of the chapel, altar, and priest. Only as Master Soule, now in a priest's Mass robes, was coming through the far doorway beside the chapel, followed by a suitably gowned and subdued Will, did Mistress Thorncoffyn come lumbering in, thudding her staff on the floor to support herself. Her dogs were not with her, just Idany carrying what looked to be—if it was intended for Mistress Thorncoffyn—a wholly unsuitable three-legged stool.

The women, boys, and Joliffe drew back and aside. Idany set the stool down firmly where her mistress would have open sight of the length of the hall to the chapel, and Joliffe watched with interest as Mistress Thorncoffyn lowered and settled herself on it. Great portions of her over-hung on all sides, but the stool held. Idany took her place behind it, and Master Soule, who had not looked around but had known how long to wait, began the Mass.

It went the usual way of Mass, with nothing required of the onlookers but to look and listen until the showing of the host. For that, in usual places, all were supposed to be standing. Here that was not required of the patients, and everyone else was already standing, save for Mistress Thorncoffyn who was helped to heave to her feet by Idany on one side and Sister Ursula on the other. To see the host was the important part of the Mass for the onlookers, giving safety to the soul for the rest of the day. Mistress Thorncoffyn, having seen it, apparently felt no need for more in the way of prayers. Her soul apparently sufficiently seen to for the while and not bothering to wait while Master Soule finished, she lumbered out of the hall, Idany carrying the stool after her. As Master Soule brought the Mass to its end, her dogs could be heard greeting her at the door across the passageway, with after that the tiny thunder of their feet as they ran out into the foreyard.

With the Mass done, Master Soule and the boy Will left the hall the way they had come, presumably into the sacristy. Talk started up among the men. The women readied to go back to their work. Joliffe, for his part, was given no chance for uncertainty over what he did next because Sister Ursula said to him, "Now is when we change sheets."

He found that "we" meant now was when he and she changed sheets. "Four of the beds today. Four of them tomorrow. Turn and turn about," she told him while Basset shifted to the stool beside his bed, out of their way. "Unless there's need to do it oftener," she added.

Since the making of beds was not a skill Joliffe had ever learned, he immediately proved unsatisfactory at it, but Sister Ursula crisply corrected his insufficiencies. By the third bed, working straight down the hall, he was becoming adept, but those were the beds of the men who could get up on their own. Joliffe suspected that tomorrow the beds of the bed-bound men along the hall's other side—John Oxyn of the fever, Adam Morys of the broken leg, and perhaps Iankyn Tanner with his labored breathing—would be different matters. But a sooner, unexpected challenge came with Deke Credy in the last bed on this side of the hall.

For all his quick mouth, it turned out he was wasted away from the waist down, hardly able to shift his legs at all. He could manage some, but with him Joliffe learned how a bed was made while someone was still in it. It was a finer art than he would have supposed, supposing he had ever thought about it at all, which he had not. Even so, by Deke's silence and the set of his jaw, Joliffe suspected there was some pain for him in the business, and was therefore untowardly pleased at the end when Deke gave a sharp nod at him and said to Sister Ursula, "He's not so ham-fisted as Ivo. See if you can keep him."

"I'll do what I can," she promised.

While they had been at their changing of beds, Sister Margaret had been going from bed to bed, back and forth across the hall behind them, feeling foreheads and wrists and talking quietly with each man. Sister Ursula had said, "She's seeing how they do, to tell Master Hewstere when he comes later in the morning," and Joliffe would have liked to ask Basset what she had told him, but had no chance, Sister Ursula saying now, "Now you take the used sheets to the laundry. While you're there, Emme will have you shift firewood if she needs it and draw water if Amice has not. Then you'd best get to the scullery, to see to the breakfast dishes."

Emme did indeed want firewood shifted from the wood-

store, and Amice gladly let him haul up bucketful after
bucketful of water and pour them into the wash-kettles while
she and Emme got the washing of the sheets and other linens
under way. At Emme's suggestion, he likewise took a bucket
of water away with him for the scullery, saving himself a return to the yard.

In the kitchen the smell of new-baked bread was warm in
the air, and Rose and Sister Ursula and Sister Petronilla were
busy with cooking. Mute little Heinrich was sitting cross-
legged under the table, lightly whapping a small wooden
spoon on one knee with the air of having done so for a long
time and the likelihood of going on for a long time more.
Daveth was not to be seen. Joliffe and the bucket of water
went into the scullery where the wooden cups and bowls and
spoons, the morning pottage pot, and other kitchen things
all awaited him. Rose had more water heated by the fire for
him, too, which helped at the work, but he soon began to
find himself in deep sympathy with the vanished Ivo's wish
to be away, especially when he found he had finished with the
washing of the cups and bowls and spoons just in time for
them to be used to serve the men's dinners, setting the cycle
going all over again.

It was while taking the trays around to the beds that he
first saw the oft-mentioned Master Hewstere, the hospital's
physician. He was standing beside John Oxyn, saying something across the bed to Sister Margaret on its other side. He
was a hale-looking man, somewhere in his middle years and
soberly dressed in a three-quarter-long gown of dark gray
cloth with wide sleeves that gave him somewhere to tuck his
hands in the way physicians often favored, their knowledge
setting them, much of the time, above such base necessities
as touching of the ill. Usually that was for the lesser learned
to do. It was a physician's place to view and question and give
judgment on what was reported to them.

Presently, Sister Margaret was nodding and nodding to

whatever he was saying. Once she shook her head and said something. With a shake of his head and a stern look, he answered her, and she went back to nodding. Joliffe would have liked to hear what they were saying, but it was Sister Letice who went to John Oxyn's bed with his cool broth and ale—less and lighter fare than the other men were having, a fever being something to starve out of a man, not feed and make stronger. Joliffe had also seen Sister Letice put a powder of well-ground herbs into the broth, less as if for a seasoning, more as if medicine. Against the fever, he supposed.

Sister Margaret and Master Hewstere moved away from the bed, the physician ignoring the slight curtsy Sister Letice gave him. While she sat down and set to spooning broth to John Oxyn and gently urging him to eat, Master Hewstere, on his way out of the hall, likewise ignored Sister Ursula's curtsy and Joliffe's bow as he passed them, and behind his back as he left the hall by the same door as Master Soule had after Mass, Sister Ursula and Sister Margaret caught each other's eye and shrugged, a little mocking, seemingly dismissing Master Hewstere's careless way.

Joliffe, expecting to have little to do with the man, did not care. He was looking forward to his own dinner that he understood he and the women would have while the men ate theirs; but at the end of taking trays around he found one more tray waiting in the kitchen. It was a large tray like Mistress Thorncoffyn's, its dishes covered by a white cloth, but Rose said, "It's for Master Soule and Master Hewstere. They often dine together in Master Soule's chamber at mid-day."

Willing to indulge his curiosity before his hunger, Joliffe took the tray readily and went the way he had seen both Master Soule and Master Hewstere leave the hall. As he had supposed, the door led into the sacristy. He supposed, too, now that he saw it, that at some time before the house had been made into the hospital, this had maybe been part of a solar, the withdrawing place for the master and his family. It had been lessened by a wall added when the chapel was made by cutting through the hall's end, and what had been a generous window in the outer wall was now mostly blocked, to make what was left of the solar into a secure place for the keeping of the robes and stuff of the chapel.

He now had the choice of a shut door on the room's other side or stairs going up from the farther corner. Voices in talk from above turned him to the wooden-treaded stairs. The door at their head stood open and he made no secret of his coming, but the voices went on, neither Master Soule nor Master Hewstere, seated on opposite sides of a table near a wide window, pausing in their even-toned talk as he came in. Master Soule simply gave a beckon at Joliffe and pointed to show where he could set the tray on the table's clear corner while Master Hewstere tapped at a paper lying between them, saying, "Given he has no better thought of when he was born than in the spring in King Richard's reign, it's nigh to impossible to judge what will be best for him, not knowing under which planet or the time of the moon he was born."

As Joliffe crossed to the table, he saw enough to guess that when the room below had been a solar, this had been the best bedchamber. There was a small but stone-framed fireplace; the plastered walls were still painted with fading pictures of trees among which birds flew and small animal-shapes showed between tufted grasses. The floor was of well-smoothed boards, bare of even rush matting, and the furnishings were few and plain, the bed at the room's far end narrow, the curtains that hung around it of plain white cloth. It seemed Master Soule lived a surprisingly austere life. The only thing in excess here were books.

Supposing books could ever be said to be in excess, Joliffe thought.

On a thick shelf fixed strongly to the wall beside the window, perhaps a dozen were stacked or standing. Another was laid open on the slanted reading-board set on the table's end nearest the window. Joliffe tried to see what the book was as he set the tray on the table at Master Soule's elbow, but could not, only that—inevitably—it was in Latin. He stepped back from the table. Master Soule gave him a nod of dismissal. He bowed and withdrew, hearing as he went down the stairs Master Hewstere insisting, "More than that, we're still deep in the *caniculares*. Keeping all the men's humours in balance is all the more important and at the same time all the more difficult now."

As Joliffe went beyond hearing, Master Soule was replying, "Um. Yes. However—"

He realized as he returned to the kitchen that likely he would have to take Mistress Thorncoffyn's tray now, but found to his surprise that he did not, that he could join the sisters and Rose at the table for their own dinner that was not much different from the patients', while the boy Daveth sat on the floor under the table with his own meal in a bowl beside the child Heinrich still occupied with the spoon. The pottage was good, savory with its bits of mutton, and he asked, "Is this what I'll be taking to Mistress Thorncoffyn?" Because good though it was, he somehow doubted it would be sufficient to her apparent appetites.

The immediate answer to his question was Sister Letice's and Sister Petronilla's smothered laughter while Rose covered her full mouth with a hand, fighting a smile, and Sister Ursula said wryly, "No." Only Sister Margaret showed nothing, simply went on tearing a bite-sized portion of bread from the piece she held. Seeing he was missing something, Joliffe swept a questioning look around the table, to be answered by Sister Ursula, suspiciously straight-faced, saying, "Mistress Thorncoffyn doesn't care for our cooking of most things, you see." That brought more choked laughter from Sister Letice and Sister Petronilla. Sister Ursula went on, "She has her dinners and suppers fetched from a cookshop in the town. She has what she likes prepared there particularly for her and brought here."

Sister Margaret, very even-voiced and still intent on her bread, said, "The woman there cooks more to her taste, you see."

That, for some reason, brought a burst of outright laughter from Sister Letice and Sister Petronilla, but no one explained further. With the meal done and everyone rising from the table, Sister Ursula said, "If you're done eating, Joliffe, it's time you took Jack's dinner to him. Jack at the gatehouse," she added on the chance Joliffe had not yet learned his name.

Joliffe nodded and went to set a tray with a bowl of the meat pottage. Rose, putting a half loaf of the day's fresh bread beside the bowl, said, "He has ale. You needn't take him that. Call up the stairs to him, then go up. Don't have him come down."

With the man's humped and limping body in mind, it had not even crossed Joliffe's mind to have him come down. Besides, he was curious to see where and how the man lived, there above the gateway. Accordingly, when his call from the foot of the stairs was answered by Jack bidding him come up, he willingly did and was greeted at the head of stairs with, "You've taken Ivo's place, I hear, but Daveth didn't know your name."

"Daveth?" Joliffe said with surprise.

"He has lessons from me most mornings. Just set it there," Jack said, with a nod toward a broad shelf fastened table-height to the wall beside one of the windows.

"Joliffe," Joliffe said, crossing to set down the tray. "That's me. Daveth has lessons?"

"He's a little slow but not hopelessly so. Sister Petronilla hopes he'll be able to make his way as at least a simple clerk. Or maybe he can take over from me, fortunate fellow."

That last could have been bitter, but the man said it cheerily enough, and indeed Joliffe could see his life here might not be so bad, all in all, particularly given the man's no-chances in the world at large with his twisted body. The room was perhaps half the size of Master Soule's, with plain-plastered walls and bare floor, but the window beside the shelf looked out on the road and the church and churchyard and some of the houses along the road into town there, while a window in the opposite wall looked toward the hospital, meaning Jack had a high, wide view of things and sunlight in mornings and late afternoons. A small fireplace in one wall would give comfort in cold weather, and for furnishings there were a plain, uncurtained bed, a chair, a stool, a small chest to hold what belongings the man might have, a wallpole with a cloak hung over it, a candle in a holder on the shelf, and—

"Books," said Joliffe. "You have books." Three of them piled on the wide shelf that served for a table. Not restrained as he had had to be in Master Soule's and Master Hewstere's presence, he reached out to see what they were, belatedly recalled his manners, and looked at Jack for permission.

Jack, limping to join him, said, "The *Epistolae* is Master Soule's. He loans one and another of his books to me from time to time. Rolle, though, and the Macrobius are mine." A claim he made with open pride.

"Which of Rolle's purgative stages have you reached?"

Jack laughed. "As yet, I fear I only view them from afar. You?"

"I've read his *Incendium amoris* but, alas, have not yet been burned by it. I do carry a small book of Hoccleve with me, but he's another matter altogether."

"Hoccleve? I don't know him. What did he—does he?— write?"

"Poems on life. Life as it is, mixed with complaints of how it isn't what it should be."

"That can be tedious."

"So is life sometimes, after all, but he's mostly wry about it all. I've found him good company."

He saw Jack almost ask to see the book, then pull back. A book was not something to be handed around without thought. Still, if Master Soule trusted his books—books far more costly than Joliffe's little one—to Jack, then—

Joliffe pulled the thought up short. No, he would trust his book to Jack not because of Master Soule but because of Jack himself, and he said easily, "Tell you what. I'll bring it when I've had chance to dig it out of my bag. You can see for yourself what he's like." Jack gave a pleased nod of thanks while Joliffe went on, "But best I take myself back to the scullery now and leave you to your meal. We've let it grow cold. Do I come back for your dishes?"

"Daveth fetches them. Would you like if I asked Master Soule to lend you something of his books?"

Nearly Joliffe accepted eagerly, then thought better of it and shook his head. "Nay. By the look of things, I'll be kept busy enough there'll be not much reading for a while."

"Bed-pots," said Jack.

"Bed-pots and scullery work," Joliffe returned, pulling a face that left Jack chuckling behind him as he left.

Chapter 9

At the hall Joliffe put his head briefly around the corner in hope of a chance to trade a few words with Basset, but the curtains were drawn between the beds again, and he saw Basset was sleeping. So perhaps were the other men, and he drew back and went along the walk and to the kitchen where he found only Rose, on her knees scrubbing the broad stone in front of the hearth. She sat back on her heels to tell him, "The women take a rest at this hour, if all's well. When I've finished here and you've done the scullery, we can ease for a time, too, if things stay quiet."

"Where do they go?"

"Their dorter. It's above Mistress Thorncoffyn's rooms. If her dogs are in a yapping humour, there's not much rest, but at least they can lie down for a time."

"Where do you go?"

"There's the pallet in the pantry." She returned to her scrubbing. "Now go to your scullery, or there'll be no rest for either of us."

A short while later, scouring away on the wooden bowls

and cups and spoons for the second time that day, Joliffe began to suspect that the scullery was indeed going to seem, as Rose had said, "his."

He finished there as the sisters came back to the later afternoon's duties. For Joliffe, those proved to be much like the morning's, with bed-pots to empty and clean and various tasks and errands given him, including opening the curtains between the men's beds again. He did take chance when bringing Tom Lyttle's pot back to pause at Basset's side and ask quietly, with a tilt of his head toward the fevered John Oxyn and the priest seated beside him, one of the sick man's hands clasped in his own and his head bent in prayer, "Father Richard?"

"He comes every day," Basset returned as quietly. "Whenever he's not needed elsewhere, he's here, to pray over whoever needs him or asks. With Oxyn there, he's usually as quieting as any of the medicines the sisters give. That makes us always glad to see him."

There was not much to be told about him from his back and bowed head as he sat there, but Joliffe remembered, "He's the one who does the Offices and Mass sometimes, instead of Master Soule."

"That's him. But how goes it with you so far?"

Keeping his voice low because of the nearby praying, Joliffe gave a carefully crafted tale of over-work and woe in which bed-pots and firewood figured strongly. He soon had Bassett and Tom Lyttle in the next bed laughing and Dick Leek on Lyttle's far side asking, "What? What are you laughing at?"

Father Richard finished his praying, briefly laid a hand on the fevered man's forehead, said something, then stood up and turned away. He was far too thin for his height, as if maybe he took too much to heart the churchly admonitions on the value of poverty and fasting. Joliffe, having kept a corner of one eye on him, now looked full at him, half-expecting to be rebuked for story-telling while the man prayed. Instead, Father Richard gave him a friendly smile, a small nod, and a slight gesture of one hand that told him to go on with his tale. Then the priest looked past him to the door and his face lost all its friendliness.

Looking that way, too, Joliffe found Idany standing there, her mouth twisted as if she were disapproving of everything she saw and of the priest in particular as she said, "Father Richard"—making the "f" a hiss—"my lady has been waiting all day for you. You *know* she's ill."

"Others' needs are more immediate," the priest returned, coldly even-voiced.

"You're wrong if you think that," Idany huffed tartly. "You'll come now."

She swung around and left. Father Richard followed her, his hands clasped tightly together and against his waist. Possibly to keep from grabbing Idany's scrawny neck, was Joliffe's thought.

He looked at Bassett who, along with everyone else, had been watching, too. Bassett made a wry face and shrugged at him. Joliffe made an answering wry face, gave a shoulder-lifting sigh of over-played woe, and said glumly, "I'd best be about my work, too," and scuff-footed out the door with a hanging head, leaving Basset and Tom Lyttle laughing behind him, as he had meant them to be.

Despite all that, he was not truly in woe about the work. He knew himself well enough to suspect that in a somewhat short time he would be finding it all tedious, but at present everything and everyone were new enough to him to be diverting. But shortly, when Mistress Thorncoffyn—probably looking for some other diversion after she finished with Father Richard, sent Idany to bid Sister Ursula come to her—he amended his suspicion to a certainty that Mistress Thorncoffyn would become wearisome long before anything else did.

Sister Ursula went, not graciously, and returned, fuming,

to tell Joliffe, "What she wanted was to tell me you were to have the task of seeing her dogs out about their business twice a day or so. To spare Idany, she said. I told her no."

Before Joliffe could say his thanks, Sister Letice inquired, a little smiling, "No? You only said no?"

"I only said no. Although perhaps not so pleasantly as I might have."

"She's going to make complaint about you to the wardens," Sister Margaret warned.

"Again," Sister Ursula said, not as if worried. "None of them care for her meddling any more than we do. Letice, by way of parting, she said I should remind you she wants her medicine fresh-made every day, not something stale from yesterday."

"So long as there's sufficient sugar in it, she wouldn't care if it were last week's," Sister Letice returned.

"Let us be thankful she brought her own loaf of sugar with her," Sister Margaret said.

Joliffe ventured, "When I saw her, she didn't look all that ill. What troubles her?"

Sister Ursula made a brief, rude sound for answer, but Sister Margaret said more moderately, "She brought some on-going trouble in her stomach from home with her. Master Hewstere hasn't been able to make certain what it is, but a brew of herbs from Sister Letice eases it."

"My own guess is that someone at her manor finally set about slow-poisoning her," Sister Ursula said cheerfully. "The wonder is that someone hasn't tried the same on those dogs of hers, too."

"Oh, but they're sweet," Sister Letice protested.

"It may come," Sister Margaret said, not cheerfully at all. "There are too many of them, just as there's too much of her."

Fortunately the talk had turned other ways when Idany shortly came again, this time to complain that the two boys were too loud at their play on the greensward outside her lady's window, and Sister Petronilla was not curbing them. Sister Ursula left with her again, soon returning alone to say that of course it was Daveth who was too loud, that Heinrich was only sitting on the grass between Sister Petronilla's knees while she and Daveth rolled a ball back and forth between them, or else Sister Petronilla would roll it far aside for Daveth to run after.

"His laughter was upsetting her dogs, Mistress Thorncoffyn said. I told her to have Idany take them for a walk," Sister Ursula said disgustedly. "I barely held back from suggesting *she* take them for a walk and do herself some good."

When time for Vespers came, the sisters took advantage of Joliffe's being there to go together to the hall to hear the Office, leaving him to help Rose finish readying the men's suppers. This gave Rose chance to ask him, much as Basset had done, "How goes it with you this far?"

"None too badly. A pause in the bed-pots would be good. Nor would Mistress Thorncoffyn be much missed. Did you say she's likely to stay until Michaelmas?"

"If she holds to her usual way. It seems that once she reaches a place, she doesn't shift easily."

"I'm hard-put to see how she can shift at all, even from chair to bed and back again. Is it disease that's misshaped her, or just greed and gluttony?"

"Greed and gluttony," Rose said with immediate certainty. "She eats enough for three people at every meal and has a lust for sugar greater than even Piers does, and has the wealth for such indulgence which, thank goodness, he does not."

"So it's just as well," Joliffe said, "that she's chosen to get most of her meals from some cookshop. Otherwise the trouble of her here would be tripled, yes?"

Rose looked around the kitchen with over-large, pretended care, as if someone might somehow be lurking there, then leaned a little toward him and said, low-voiced and merrily, "She gets most of her meals from the cookshop because somehow almost any meal made for her here at the hospital is poorly cooked and badly seasoned."

"This morning's beef?"

"Oh, there's little can be done wrong to pan-cooked beef when we're forbidden to season it at all."

"But everything else?"

"Except her medicines. Yes."

"I take it not by chance?"

"Not even slightly by chance." The merriment went from Rose. "Not that Sister Margaret does it, but the others do, which is other than you'd think it would be, given that if I were Mistress Thorncoffyn, it would be Sister Margaret I'd not want anywhere near my food and drink."

Surprised at Rose's sudden seriousness, Joliffe asked, "Why?"

"Because Sister Margaret was married to her only son."

"She's Mistress Thorncoffyn's daughter-in-law?" Joliffe heard his voice scale up and pulled it down. "Then how is it she's a sister *here*?"

There was plainly wealth in the family. There should have been dower properties enough for the widow of the only son to live in comfort, not as a hireling sister in a hospital.

"She's here," Rose said, "because Mistress Thorncoffyn saw to it after her son's death that Sister Margaret got nearly nothing of her dower. Mistress Thorncoffyn and her grandson and a lawyer working together left her with almost nothing and hardly any choice but to become a sister here. Not that Sister Margaret ever says anything about it, but Emme seems to know all there is to know about everyone here, and she does like to talk."

"This grandson—not Sister Margaret's own son, surely?" But who else could he be?

"Sister Margaret's own son but entirely his grandmother's boy."

"And Mistress Thorncoffyn is brave enough to come here and stay," Joliffe marveled. "Or fool enough," he added.

"I think she enjoys seeing Sister Margaret brought down to this. Oh, there's Vespers ending. Let me show you how the trays are set for supper. Bring the bowls here."

The sisters returned from the hall, and there was no more time for talk except that Rose, as she readied to leave, made chance to say to Joliffe, with a smile as mischievous as any Piers might have, "Good sleeping to you."

He thanked her warily, and by the time he finally lay down on the bed in his small room that night, he understood the mischief in her wish well enough. After the men were given their supper—bread a little toasted, then broken into bits into the bowls, with warm milk poured over it—the sisters, the children, and Joliffe had their own in the kitchen. Then the men's trays were cleared back to the kitchen, and Joliffe took to the scullery again as Father Richard began Compline—the Office of prayers and psalms that closed a day—in the chapel for the men, while Sister Petronilla saw the children to bed in the dorter and in the kitchen the other sisters readied the men's evening sleeping draught.

Leaving the evening pot and the bowls to dry in the scullery and bringing the cleaned cups as he had been told to do, Joliffe went back into the kitchen. Sister Letice was gone now. Seeing him look around for her, Sister Ursula said, "With you here, she's able again to spend this last while of daylight seeing to the garden while we settle the men for the night. Set out the cups on the tray."

Joliffe did, and Sister Margaret filled them. At her bidding, he then took up the tray and followed the two women into the hall, where he kept to the aisle between the beds, and the sisters went from bed to bed, giving each man his cup and sharing small talk with each of them. At the far end of the hall, Sister Ursula had to help the fevered John Oxyn with his drink. While she did, Sister Margaret went along the hall again, back and forth from bed to bed, taking a last look at each man, making sure they were as comfortable as might be, and drawing the curtains between the beds to give them privacy for the night.

Joliffe watched and listened, waiting to see for what Sister Ursula might next want him and deeply interested by the concern and care she and Sister Margaret were showing for each man.

Sister Margaret finished and left the hall. Sister Ursula said something, kindly-voiced, to John Oxyn and helped him settle, then made beckon for Joliffe to follow her from the hall to the passage toward the foreporch. There, shutting the door to the hall, she stopped and said, "The door at the hall's upper end must be left open, and the door to your room, too, that you may hear anyone who needs you in the night."

"Yes, my lady."

"Sister. We've no time for being ladies here," she said, but with a smile. "You are on duty every night. We take night-duty turn and turnabout. Tonight it's Sister Letice who will sleep in the pantry off the kitchen. You're to call for her if there's anything beyond what you can do for the men. You do understand?"

"Yes." What he likewise understood was that a restless night for the men would be an unrested night for him.

"For now, see to lighting the hall's night-candle and then you had best go to bed, to better your chances of enough sleep, should there be need of you in the night."

Joliffe had already foreseen that, and after a day full of newness he not only welcomed the thought of bed as soon as might be, but thought sleep would readily come. At least he was hoping so as he bowed. Sister Ursula bent her head in return and went away toward the dorter, while he returned to the kitchen for a light for the night-candle.

Sister Letice was just coming in by the outer door, Father Richard with her. She had so far been the quietest of the sisters, saying little that Joliffe had heard, but she was talking eagerly enough now, saying, in the obvious middle of something, "Have you noted, too, how much Iankyn's breathing has eased since Sister Margaret added anise, of all things, to the electuary? It's eased his lungs far more than we dared hope."

"I've noted that, and that John's fever seems to have less hold on him." Father Richard smiled down at her. "That's as much your doing as anyone's. It was you who found the cuckoo sorrel that Sister Margaret wanted, and you who makes it into the decoction."

Sister Letice smiled up at him but by a little shift of her shoulders seemed trying to slide out from under his praise. "It was Sister Margaret who searched out that it might be useful."

"But it was you who found the plant itself," Father Richard said firmly. "There's no wrong in taking praise you deserve."

Sister Letice answered, tapping him on the front of his black priest's robe with a firm forefinger, "Mind that you remember that as well."

The lightness went from the priest as completely as from a snuffed lamp. "I remember what I must," he said, stepping back from her. He made the sign of the cross in blessing at, first, her and then toward Joliffe. "May everyone within this place sleep peacefully tonight."

"And you, also," Sister Letice returned gently, her momentary merriment gone.

"If God grants," Father Richard said and went away toward the roofed walk, presumably to leave the hospital by way of the foreporch.

Watching him go, Sister Letice said sadly, "He's wearing himself away with work and won't listen." She sighed, gave that small setting-aside shift of her shoulders again, and said, "But we can hope his prayer for a peaceful night will be granted us. Good sleeping to you, Joliffe."

"And to you, sister," he returned, but could not help wondering what was between her and Father Richard, that they were so easy together, familiar in a way with one another that none of the other sisters seemed to be with him as their priest.

Please, Joliffe thought—don't let there be secrets here that I don't want to know.

Chapter 10

So far as all went with the men in the hall, it was a peaceful night, but sometime in the dark hours Joliffe spasmed awake from a deep dream, his body knotted in fear, not knowing where he was for a long, black, heart-drubbing moment, until memory roused. Slowly, near to painfully, he shoved the dream away to the dark corner from where it came, and lay listening for anything beyond his dream that might have awakened him. There was nothing. Whatever the hour was, the darkness and stillness were of undisturbed night, and he forced his breathing to steady and his body to ease until he lay unknotted again. The mercy was that the dreams did not come every night. The last few nights he had been free of them altogether, but too many nights since he returned from France they were there, a nightmare twisting together of dream and memory that brought him awake taut with the fears of a fight long since lost. He had no thought of how to stop them. All he could do was deal with himself in their aftermath, and now, staring into the darkness, he began to run silently through his mind the words of the longest play he knew, filling his mind with words, giving weight to every one until at some unheeded point weariness drew his eyes closed and he slid back into sleep.

It was honest morning when he awoke again, to a day that proved, at first, to go much as yesterday had gone for him. There were the same chores—bed-pots to empty and clean, trays to carry and collect, sheets to change, firewood to fetch, scullery work to do—but at least no early demands from Mistress Thorncoffyn. Instead, today it was Master Hewstere who broke the day's even flow. Going his morning round of the men with Sister Margaret, he said aloud his surprise at Iankyn's claim to a quiet night. Joliffe, sweeping with a long-bristled broom at the hall's far end, heard Sister Margaret explain what she had done and saw Master Hewstere draw himself up like an affronted cockerel.

"You did wrong, sister. I've warned you before about your prideful attempts to share in what is beyond you. I warn you again. I grant that he did well in the night *this* night, but his stars were favorable to that without you ignorantly meddled. Trying something uncertain as you did, you might have countered the good there was for him in the stars."

Sister Margaret took what he said with bowed head and a murmured, "As you say, sir," and continued the round with him, while Joliffe swept to Basset's bed and asked, low-voiced, "What was he thinking—giving her that set-down in front of everyone?"

"Best place to give it," Basset answered. Like Joliffe, he had one eye on the doctor and Sister Margaret to be sure their backs stayed turned. "Keeps it in our minds that he's the master of medicines here, not her."

"But if . . ."

"Joliffe," Basset chided. "Joliffe, Joliffe, Joliffe." He took on the well-rounded tones of a grand preacher. "Master Hewstere draws on the wisdom of the heavens, is guided in all he does by the stars and sun and moon in their God-set courses. Sister Margaret knows no more than earthly ways."

"Earthly ways like the one that helped that fellow to a quiet night."

"All I know," said Basset, back to his own voice, "is that I'm not taking another clyster from him, no matter what he orders. Rubbing with whatever oils Sister Margaret has made have done me better good than any of that. Speaking of rubbing—" He held out a bare foot and waggled it at Joliffe.

Taking on a deep country peasant's thick voice, Joliffe backed off, saying, "Aw've no orders that way, mawster. 'Tis the broom Aw'm set to here," and busily swept his way out the near hall door, leaving Basset chuckling behind him.

Even aside from Basset's foot, Joliffe made quicker work of the sweeping than he might have, to be back in the kitchen when Sister Margaret returned. Master Hewstere was gone to what was apparently his daily attendance on Mistress Thorncoffyn, and as Joliffe had hoped, Sister Margaret gave way to what she felt, telling the others what Master Hewstere had said, then mocking furiously, "Uncertain, he said! Something that's been used time out of mind by herb-wives! I had it from Iankyn's aunt because I wasn't too proud—too *learned*—to ask what had been done for him in other years. The only difference this year is that, with his grandmother dead and the harvest and all, no one else had the time to brew it and tend to him as she would do."

"But what now?" Sister Letice asked. "If Master Hewstere is against it . . ."

"If Master Hewstere is against it, then Master Hewstere doesn't have to know about it," Sister Margaret snapped. "I doubt Iankyn will tell. Do you have sufficient supplies of the sorrel?"

"Oh, yes."

"There then," Sister Margaret said. Which seemed to settle it.

But later in the morning, sour-faced Idany stalked into the kitchen to demand she come to Mistress Thorncoffyn to explain why she had displeased Master Hewstere.

Joliffe was helping Rose lift a heavy kettle onto the hook above the fire. They traded looks, Rose lifting her eyebrows to him, but Sister Margaret said, while she went on decisively slicing carrots, "Tell your mistress—again—that I no longer come to her beck and call."

Idany's face drew in like a wrinkled date. "Mistress Thorncoffyn wants you to know she'll not have disrespect to a doctor in her hospital. She wants . . ."

On the far side of the worktable, without pausing at chopping an onion, Sister Ursula interrupted, "Mistress Thorncoffyn forgets—again—that this is not her hospital. The wardens, not her, have last say over us and what is done here. She is here as guest, not mistress. Now unless you want to make yourself useful by cutting some carrots, take yourself out of our way."

Idany gave an offended gasp. Everyone ignored her. She tried a wordless exclaim of anger to no better response. Altogether thwarted, she stalked out. When she was gone, Sister Ursula said calmly, "Sister Margaret, would you care to help Sister Letice in the garden for a while now?"

With matching calm, Sister Margaret said, "I think perhaps I would," laid aside her knife, and went out, wiping her hands on her apron as she went.

"Joliffe, finish the carrots," Sister Ursula directed.

So he was at the worktable when Mistress Thorncoffyn surged into the kitchen, her company of dogs scampering around her, and demanded furiously, "Where is Sister Margaret?"

Sister Ursula courteously laid down her knife before answering, "Gone out to help Sister Letice in the garden."

"She was here. I sent for her. I want to see her."

"She has her duties and should not be kept from them," Sister Ursula said evenly.

"She offended Master Hewstere!"

"And he has rebuked her. There is an end to the matter." Still evenly, and on the likely chance that Mistress Thorncoffyn needed it said more than once, Sister Ursula repeated, "An end."

Joliffe, watching as best he could while keeping his head down, saw Mistress Thorncoffyn's wide-fleshed face turn red. She looked to be working through several layers of anger, none of which she seemed to find sufficient words for, because finally she ordered at the dogs busily snuffling into every corner of the kitchen, "Fawn, Fox, Kydd, Swan, Falcon! Come!" and heaved herself around and away.

When her heavy tread, the thud of her staff, and the last click of doggie toenails were gone, Sister Ursula took up her knife, saying, "Joliffe, go and tell Sister Margaret it's safe to return. Or she's welcome to stay, if Sister Letice can use her help longer."

Joliffe had gathered by now, from talk around him, that most mornings after Mass Sister Letice worked with her herbs, either in the garden or the stillroom. Her skill with them was welcome, since they provided both medicine and changing savors to the daily pottages. Besides, the bee-humming garden in the warm morning sun, with its flowers and all the greens of the various herbs along its graveled paths, was a pleasant place to be, Joliffe thought. Presently, Sister Letice was gathering some yellow-flowered herb into a basket, while Sister Margaret sat on a bench tying some other herb into bunches before laying them carefully into another basket. She was much calmer-faced than when she had left the kitchen, making Joliffe suspect Sister Ursula had sent her here as much to be soothed as to avoid Mistress Thorncoffyn. Nor was she in any hurry to leave; to Joliffe's message, she said, "If there's no immediate need of me, I think I'll stay here a time, yes."

Sister Ursula received Joliffe's return message with a nod

of easy acceptance and no comment, and the day went on its way.

The next few days went their ways, too. Joliffe grew more used to his work. He did not dream again—at least not the kind of dreaming that threw him awake—but that might have been because that one night's solid sleep proved to be uncommon. More usually, twice or thrice each night one man and another seemed to have need of him, or need for him to summon whichever of the sisters was sleeping near that night. There never seemed any chance to see how much more friendly Amice might be, and Joliffe regretted that, but he did sit and talk with Basset a few times, and almost hour by hour his respect for the sisters grew—for their hard work and for their easy trust in one another and not least for their quietly deft handling of Master Soule and Master Hewstere who supposedly were over them in all things about the hospital and the men's care. Master Hewstere, because he came and went, could be listened to and his directions followed or altered after he had left. In truth, both the patients and the other sisters seemed to trust Sister Margaret's decisions more than his, if it came to a choice between. More than that, she tended to the men as if each one mattered in himself, while Master Hewstere rarely stooped from a physician's dignity to lay so much as hand on a forehead to feel for fever. So the women bowed their heads and said "Yes" to whatever he decreed, then went Sister Margaret's way when he was gone. There were even times, after all, when she agreed with what he ordered.

Master Soule might have been more trouble, being there in the hospital all the while, but he did not seem inclined to direct the women too closely. He did his daily duties in the chapel, and Sister Ursula went in late afternoons to tell him how the day had been and take counsel with him about any problems beyond the ordinary. Other than that he kept to himself. Or would have, if allowed. Among Mistress Thorncoffyn's continued small tyrannies and occasional large demands were summons to Master Soule to spend time with her, sometimes in an afternoon, often in an evening.

Joliffe kept his curiosity to himself until an evening when, as Sister Ursula and Sister Margaret were settling the men for the night, Master Soule came from the sacristy, started across the hall, paused to bow to the altar, and went out the other door, into the passageway that would take him either to the kitchen or else to the roofed walk. Since he had his private way from the hospital, from the sacristy through his own small garden and an alleyway to the road, and because Joliffe had never seen him anywhere near the kitchen, the guess had to be that the master was on his way to Mistress Thorncoffyn, which—to Joliffe's mind—accounted for his look of a man grimly determined on grace in the face of martyrdom.

Since he had never looked anything but grim the times Joliffe had seen him going to or coming from Mistress Thorncoffyn, Joliffe could not help but wonder why he suffered her company. Couldn't he refuse it?

Joliffe took the only way he knew to find out, saying to Sister Ursula as they left the hall, it being her turn at night-duty, "Master Soule and Mistress Thorncoffyn do well together, it seems."

"To her mind they do," Sister Ursula granted.

"Not to his?"

Sister Ursula gave him a sideways, upward look, then said, "She enjoys putting questions to him about God and the world and all, then arguing at him over his answers. Somehow I doubt Master Soule enjoys that as much as she must. As something of a patron to the hospital, she has to be endured. He'll be freed from her soon, though, when her grandson comes. She has small interest in anyone else when he's here. Saint Giles be thanked."

*   *   *

Sunday came with its half-day rest for the harvesters, giving families chance to visit their folk in the hospital. For Basset, that meant Ellis, Gil, and Piers came. Joliffe joined them briefly. It was good to jibe with Ellis again and be as rude to Piers as Piers was to him. Good, too, to see Gil include old Tom in the next bed, who had no one of his own come to see him because he had no one of his own left, Sister Petronilla had told Joliffe, adding, "He's going to be sorry to see your friend leave."

"Basset *is* going to altogether mend, then?" Joliffe had taken the chance to ask.

Sister Petronilla had looked surprised. "Oh, yes. Sister Margaret is sure of it. Until the next flare comes, of course."

"The next? It will happen again?"

She had looked concerned that he did not know that. "Not for years perhaps, but yes, almost surely. Sister Margaret has never known this manner of thing to burn itself out entirely."

If Basset knew that, he had not said. Nor had Rose. Nor was there any telling what Ellis, Gil, and Piers knew, jesting and laughing with Basset over his "life of ease and quiet," Gil reminding him of the saying that "ease can lead to vice" and Basset answering, "I can but hope so," as Joliffe left them to carry Jack's dinner to the gatehouse.

These past few days he had been carrying his own along with Jack's, for the two of them to sit in talk together while they ate. He had loaned his small book of Hoccleve's poems, as he had promised, and Jack was now copying them out for himself. So there was that as well as other books to talk of, and yesterday Jack had asked him about his life as a player. Until then, Joliffe had avoided talk that way, not knowing how much a man this much imprisoned by his twisted body would want to hear about a player's far roaming, but when he had answered Jack's questions only a little even then, Jack had guessed at his uncertainty and said, "I do truly like to hear about farther away than here. It's my mind that keeps me company most hours of the day. The more I have in it, the more company I have."

So Joliffe had answered more freely, and today meant to see if he could make Jack laugh at things Piers had got up to now and again, doubting there was much to bring Jack to laughter in his life, for all that he seemed a cheerful enough man on the whole. Assuredly, as Joliffe came into his room, he looked cheerful enough as he turned from the roadward window and said, "I have to wonder if Father Richard knows what goes on beyond the churchyard's charnel house."

Crossing the room to set the tray on the shelf that served for a table, Joliffe asked, "Goes on? I can't imagine much goes on at a charnel house." Where the bones of those long dead were kept when their grave-place in the yard was needed for someone newly gone.

"Not in it, to be sure," Jack agreed lightly. "But there's a sheltered place between it and the yew hedge, out of sight of everywhere. Anyone coming by way of the stile from the field path stands a good chance of reaching it unnoted, and once they're there, no one can see them."

"Except you?"

"Not even me. So I know no more what goes on there than Father Richard does, I suppose. But when I see first a man and then a woman go there, all careful there's no one in sight to see them, and they don't come out for a while and a while, I can't help what suspicions well up in my mind."

"Suspicions are a difficult thing to keep from welling," Joliffe granted. Having set the tray down, he took Jack's place at the window as Jack moved to see what was under the cloth today. Not but what it surely was going to be pottage as usual—all vegetables today—and bread and cheese. "Someone is there now?"

"They are. It's not even as if I'm looking in their windows, seeing this," Jack complained. "I'm looking out my own." But the complaint was lightly made, as was so much that Jack said, as if he found life a lighter thing than the burden his twisted body must make it. Now, as Joliffe joined him at the shelf, he asked, "How out of joint is Mistress Thorncoffyn's nose at all the visitors come to see other folk today?"

"She's summoned Sister Ursula to her three times about one thing and another, and sent complaint to Sister Petronilla about the boys' noise in the garth."

"But should anyone say aught about her yapping dogs—" Jack left the sentence hanging, no need to finish it. "How is her . . . it's her stomach this time, isn't it?"

They had begun to eat. Joliffe nodded around a mouthful of bread, swallowed, and answered more fully, "And her leg. She wants hot poultices for it. Master Hewstere wants cold. Sister Margaret thinks it would do best if she walked more and kept it raised while she sits, but neither Master Hewstere nor Mistress Thorncoffyn has asked Sister Margaret's thought on it."

"Nor will they," Jack said. He was soaking the end of his bread in the pottage, "She always has some ailment when she comes here. Something that needs Master Hewstere's heed and much waiting on by the sisters. Or as much as their tolerance will give her. It's been her leg before this, and her headaches several times, and now her digestion."

"Hai!" someone shouted from below the window. "Old halt and humble!" The bell jangled from someone jerking hard on its rope. "Get this gate open!"

Jack gave a sharp sigh. "Now here's the other 'ailment' she brings on us. Her unblessed grandson."

Chapter 11

Jack made to start toward the stairs, but Joliffe said, "I'll go. There's no need to stop your dinner since I'm here." Jack's thanks followed him as he went out. The bell was jangling again and went on jangling as he hurried down the stairs. Whoever had hold of the rope seemed not to care Jack could only come so fast and no faster, no matter what their impatience. As it was, Joliffe jerked the slightly open gate a little more open suddenly enough that the horseman beyond it was startled into a sharp answering jerk on his reins, making his horse throw up its head and back a few steps away. Forced to let go the bell rope, ending its jangle, he demanded angrily down at Joliffe, "Who are you?"

"Presently the one who's going to finish opening the gate for you," Joliffe returned. "So leave off the bell." He swung the gate wide aside, stepping backward with it, then—expecting what came next—stepping farther back, out of reach as the horseman, riding past, cut sideways at him with a stiff riding whip. Having spent much time in the past few months being lessoned to dodge blows, doing it now was no great matter.

The difficulty was in holding back from following through on the lessoning—in not grabbing the fellow's careless arm and jerking him from his saddle to the ground, momentarily helpless against whatever Joliffe could choose to do to him.

Joliffe did succeed in holding back, then half-wished he had given way as the man jerked his horse to a harsh halt and demanded, "Where's old Jack?"

As curtly, Joliffe said back, "Minding to other business. What's yours here?"

Not that he could not guess. The fellow was in the full glow of health and in need of no charity if his thigh-short green doublet, smooth-fitted yellow hosen, calf-high riding boots of dyed red leather, and the well-blooded horse were anything to go by. More than that, the darkly red hair showing below his in-fashion hat of padded headroll trailing a liripipe flung over one shoulder told the rest even before he said, no less sharply and ignoring Joliffe's question, "I suppose my grandmother is still here?" Making it sound as if it would be Joliffe's fault if she were not.

Not ready to take fault for that or anything else, Joliffe returned, "I could probably tell you that if I knew who your grandmother is."

So far he had given no heed to the second rider sitting his horse quietly behind the first because the man had made no move to add to the foolishness. Now, though, bringing his horse a little more forward, he said, courteously enough, "She's Mistress Cisily Thorncoffyn and surely she's here."

"Surely she is," Joliffe agreed, equally courteously to him. He looked back to the grandson, who was close enough to Jack in age to have no business calling him old. "And your name would be—?"

For answer he received "Take a kick in your cullions, you fool," as Thorncoffyn put his spurs to his horse's flank and rode sharply forward into the yard.

Feeling that his duty was somehow done by having irked

him, Joliffe gave a shadow-bow toward his back. Was ready
to give a better one to the second man as he, too, rode forward, but he surprised Joliffe by briefly drawing rein to say,
"On the likelihood you'll need his name later, he's Master
Geoffrey Thorncoffyn."

"And you, sir?" Not simply a servant. To judge by the
good cut of his clothing, sober-colored though it was, he was,
at the least, a clerk or household officer.

"Master Aylton. Her steward." And jestingly, "May I have
leave to pass?"

Joliffe gave a sweep of one arm and somewhat of a bow to
usher him into the yard and thought he heard the steward
softly laugh as he rode past toward where Geoffrey had already dismounted, flung his reins at a ringed post, and was
going into the hospital.

Thinking Master Aylton must be a patient man to put
up with Geoffrey Thorncoffyn for any length of time, Joliffe
went back up the stairs. He found Jack at the window over-
looking the yard, where he must have heard all of what passed
because he said, widely smiling, "You've upset the puppy."

"For which I shall feel everlasting shame. Sometime.
Maybe. Is this his usual way?"

"When he's in good humour, yes."

"And when he's in bad?"

"You'd best hope you never see it. He and his grandmother
are a matched pair. You know he's Sister Margaret's son?"

Joliffe nodded. "And how she comes to be here instead of
living a comfortable widow's life, thanks to them." He crossed
the room to collect the tray and cups. "Time I was back. If I
need to hide from them sometime, may I lie low here?"

"Surely, and be welcomed," Jack said but without the
laughter Joliffe had meant to have from him. As if Jack
thought the need indeed might come.

* * *

By the afternoon's end, Joliffe equally thought it might. Not, as he had expected, because of whatever unpleasantness Geoffrey chose to make, but because by then he had found that Geoffrey in high, fine humour could be as great a bother as Geoffrey arrogant and sharp. The mystery was why being in his grandmother's company was enough to put him in fine humour. Or perhaps there was no mystery about it at all, given they seemed so much of a matching kind.

Sent from the kitchen to Mistress Thorncoffyn with her tray set with slices of new bread and a bowl of clear honey ("We give what courtesy we can," Sister Ursula said. "That does not include cakes and fine wine."), Joliffe was met by the usual pattering surge of small dogs and wholly unusual merry laughter from Mistress Thorncoffyn, at a guess from something Geoffrey had just said, because Idany was widely smiling as she opened the door.

She must have been on her way out, since Mistress Thorncoffyn called to her, "Wait. Let him set down the tray. Then he can go with you and help to fetch."

She was on her chair, her face lightened with a smile and one of her meaty hands resting with affection on Geoffrey's head as he sat on a low stool beside her, an arm leaned companionably across her knees. He straightened and took his arm away as Joliffe approached, and at her gesture Joliffe set the tray there instead, then bowed and retreated, following Idany from the room and outside and along the yard to one of the doorways along the buildings there. The door was padlocked, but Idany had the key, and after a short wrestling between the lock and key, she swung the door wide to a small room being used as a storeroom for several large chests. Lined against its walls, they were all painted on their fronts with a pattern of flourished Cs and Ts, and on the one flat-topped one was a medium-sized cask, bunged and spigoted.

Joliffe's immediate thought was that if these were indeed

all Mistress Thorncoffyn's, in more ways than one she did not travel lightly.

He tried to be ashamed of that very poor jest at the woman's deformity, but he failed. He had never been given to mocking what another person could not help—would never have made jest at Jack's twisted body—but beyond Mistress Thorncoffyn's outward misshapenness she too often showed her inward deformity, and that let his mockery against her come too easily, perhaps by way of a shield against the fear that she seemed to prefer people have of her.

Fear?

Joliffe would have looked longer at that unexpected thought, but Idany had used another key to unlock one of the chests and was taking a gracefully long-necked pitcher of fine pewter from it that she thrust at Joliffe, saying, "Here. Fill it there." She tilted her head toward the cask. He took the pitcher, and as she turned to delve deeper into the chest, went to the cask, positioned the pitcher, and turned the spigot. Pale wine flowed out with a sweet smell that made him guess it was malmsey, and he could not help the thought of what a pity it was that all the sweetness in which Mistress Thorncoffyn indulged did not sweeten her nature.

Turning off the spigot, he caught the last drip on a fingertip that he quickly licked, enjoying the brief, rich taste, then turned back to Idany who had brought a tray and two goblets to match the pitcher out of the chest. Setting the goblets on the tray, she said, "Put the pitcher here. Then you can carry it to my lady. Now."

Joliffe obeyed, understanding that by "it" she meant the tray, goblets, and pitcher, and that "now" meant while she locked chest and door again. So it was by himself that Joliffe returned to Mistress Thorncoffyn and Geoffrey who was leaning back on the stool, holding a piece of honeyed bread above one of the dogs for it to dance on its hind legs, begging, while the other dogs clustered in hope of their turn, except for one on Mistress Thorncoffyn's lap, being fed bread in small bits. Wherever Master Aylton had been, he was here now, his hips leaned against the windowsill, his arms crossed as he answered an apparent question from Mistress Thorncoffyn with, "They're not getting as much as I think they could off the west field there. The reeve claims it needs marling. I think he's right."

"But they want us to pay for the marl," Geoffrey said and popped the bread into his own mouth, not the dog's.

"Of course they do," Mistress Thorncoffyn huffed. "Is there a way to claim the cost should be theirs, Constantine?"

"It's demesne land," Master Aylton answered. "So yours, not theirs."

"Fine them for something," Geoffrey said. "Pay for the marl out of that."

Turning from setting the tray on the table, Joliffe saw Master Aylton shake his head doubtfully as he said, "We've used that ruse too lately there. If we do it again so soon, they'll likely turn stubborn on us. If they start holding out on one thing and another, it could cost more than the marl would to begin with."

Geoffrey tossed a piece of bread across the room, sending the dogs into a scramble after it. "Idiot peasants," he muttered. He looked at Joliffe. "Pour the wine."

Joliffe turned back to the table to obey. They went on discussing matters at one manor or another while he poured and took the goblets to them one by one. Mistress Thorncoffyn first, Geoffrey next, Master Aylton last. Only Master Aylton gave him a nod of thanks. With better duties to do than wait on them and glad of the escape, Joliffe left as Idany returned after what must have been a long struggle with the lock.

Away from Mistress Thorncoffyn's rooms there seemed more air to breathe, and Joliffe wondered wryly if greed could be so strong it took the very air from others. But as he went along the covered walk to the kitchen, his mind went back to that momentary question about fear that had come to him in the storeroom. Was he indeed afraid of Mistress Thorncoffyn? Not merely irked by her, but fearful? A straight look at the thought said he was. Not of what she could do to him, because she had no power over him. He was the hospital's servant, not hers. But there seemed a wish in her to take stranglehold on any lives that came within her power. To throttle and crush them to whatever shape she wanted. It was a nastiness that, given free rein, would taint and misshape everyone around her. And all the while she would be declaring it was to their good to be as she said they should be.

He chilled inwardly at thought of what she would surely have done here in St. Giles if she had had the power, or the sisters not stood out so firmly against her.

To the bad, her grandson looked to be a piece with her— not careless in what he did to others but deliberate in his enjoyment of his power over "lesser" beings, whether a servant opening a gate for him or that dog teased with a piece of honeyed bread. How had Sister Margaret come to have a son like him?

As surprising as that to Joliffe, now that he looked at it, was his own carelessness toward the both of them despite the danger he saw of them. They were the kind of people he had learned to be most wary of in his years as a player. Coming into Lord Lovell's service had spared Basset's company some of the trouble their sort could cause, because a lord's men were not to be dealt with so lightly as lordless players, but the instinct of wariness had remained, engrained by too many years of deep necessity. Given that, where was that healthy wariness now? Had all he had learned and all that had happened in these few past months changed him that deeply?

And if that were so, then what else in him—besides what he guessed at—was changed?

Besides the obvious, he silently added, rubbing at his upper arm where the scar from last winter's wound, well-healed though it was, still sometimes pulled and panged, reminding him of what he would rather have forgotten—what it felt like to kill a man.

Leaving the covered walk for the passageway toward the kitchen, he found Master Hewstere and Sister Letice there before him, the physician saying to her in his curt way, "Will there be sufficient of it this year? There's likelihood of widespread illness to come when we're in the sign of Capricorn, and it's sovereign in that sign. We would do well to have sufficient of it."

"It's doing very well this summer, sir," Sister Letice murmured with far less than her usual confidence about her herbs, and Joliffe saw her head was a little downward so that she was looking up at the doctor almost shyly, not like someone being challenged or berated but like . . .

Oh.

Sister Letice was the youngest of the sisters. Still young enough to have hopes and longings perhaps. Joliffe had refused to give much weight to the perhaps-over-friendliness he had seen between her and Father Richard. After all, he had an easy friendliness with all the sisters; there was likely nothing particular between him and Sister Letice. But here she was again, and while whatever feeling she might have for Father Richard could supposedly go nowhere, he being a priest, did she have hope of something more from Master Hewstere? Or at least a *longing* to hope for more, without hope, because Joliffe had seen nothing in the physician's manner that showed any warmth toward her.

Not as there had been from Father Richard.

Master Hewstere swung around, away from her, seemed surprised to find Joliffe there, and went past him toward the covered walk (and probably Mistress Thorncoffyn) with a sweep of his wide gown that barely gave Joliffe time to make the deep bow due to someone so learned and far above him as a physician. By the time he straightened, Sister Letice was turned away and gone into the kitchen. He followed, since he was going there, too, and found Rose doing something at the hearth and Sister Petronilla mixing something in a bowl on the table under which Daveth was sitting cross-legged with Heinrich on his lap, the two of them gently rocking side to side. Or Daveth was gently rocking, carrying blank-faced Heinrich with him.

Sister Letice spoke quietly to Sister Petronilla, too low for Joliffe to hear, and went on across the kitchen and out the rear door. Because this was a time of day that usually found the boys in the garth, playing on the grass in sunlight for a while, Joliffe bent over to see them better, then straightened and questioned Sister Petronilla with a look.

"They don't like Geoffrey Thorncoffyn," she answered. "When he's here, they won't go where he might see them."

"I'm in sympathy with that," Joliffe said. "How long is he likely to stay?"

"A week perhaps, or until he and his grandmother quarrel. Whichever happens first."

"They quarrel?"

"They enjoy it. They shout and are loud and sometimes throw things. Then he goes away. That part of their quarreling we always welcome."

"Does he stay here in St. Giles with her?"

"For a blessing, he and Master Aylton put up at the town's nearest inn."

Her gaze went past Joliffe and her eyes widened. He spun around, not certain what could surprise her here, then joined her in surprise at sight of Master Soule just come into the kitchen from the passage. In his days here, Joliffe had never seen the master in the kitchen. The man's curious look around it now suggested it was never anywhere he came, at least not often. He answered with a nod to Joliffe's bow and Rose's and Sister Petronilla's curtsies, and with a small gesture stopped Daveth's spasmed move to shift Heinrich and uncurl from under the table. "No need," he said to the boy, and then to Sister Petronilla, "Have you been advised that Master Hewstere and I have been bid to dine with Mistress Thorncoffyn and so that I'll need no supper from here?"

"No, sir," Sister Petronilla said.

"I thought not."

"Thank you, sir."

He nodded silent acceptance of her thanks, and probably only Joliffe was near enough to hear him mutter as he left the kitchen, "And Saint Giles give me patience."

For her part, Sister Petronilla, looking down at what she had been mixing, said to the world at large, "Well, we shall have a goodly supper tonight then."

Chapter 12

Not that night but the next, another of the dark dreams twisted through Joliffe's sleep, this one so bad that he wrenched from it with a dream-shout, to lie rigid and gasping while he gathered wits enough to tell himself he was safely where he should be, lying in clean darkness on the now-familiar narrow bed in the now-familiar narrow room in the now-familiar St. Giles, and although the bed might be as narrow as a grave, it was not one, and the hard drubbing of his heart in the merciful quiet proved that he was not dead. He was awake and safe. He was trying to kill no one.

And no one was trying to kill him.

Assured of all that, he closed his eyes, knowing it would take time to will the terror out of his knotted sinews enough for him to sleep again.

But beyond his eyelids, the darkness changed. Someone had come with a light outside his partly shut door, and he snapped open his eyes and was already shoving clear of his tangled blanket and sitting up as Sister Margaret said, low-voiced, "Joliffe? Are you well? I heard you cry out."

So his dream-shout had not been entirely in his dream.

"A dream," he said, matching her low voice. For courtesy's sake, he rose and went to open the door a little wider. Sister Margaret stood with a lighted candle in her hand, her gray gown, white apron, wimple, and veil tidy upon her despite whatever night-hour it was. For some reason that added to Joliffe's apology, tousled as he was from his sleep and nightmare, with his shirt hanging loose around him, as he said, "That was all. A bad dream. I'm sorry I woke you."

As he said it, he realized she could not have been asleep, not been a-bed, even as she answered, "You didn't. I was already up, seeing to Iankyn. He was wheezing and needed quieting. He's asleep again now. But Tom Lyttle is dead."

She said it so evenly that for a moment Joliffe did not fully take in the words' meaning. Then it reached him, and he gasped, "What? Dead? When?"

"Just now. Or, rather, I only just found him as I looked in on everyone. But he's yet warm. So only a little while ago. Will you come with me?"

"Yes. Yes, surely." Joliffe fumbled his doublet down from the wall-pole. The night was warm enough that his bare legs would not matter, but there was chill enough he would want more than his shirt if he were to be up for any length of time. That practicality muddled with his other thoughts, his mind as clumsy as his movements, as he asked while shrugging into his doublet, "What happened?"

"He died in his sleep," Sister Margaret said calmly.

"But he . . . at Compline he was . . ." Joliffe tried to align his mind and tongue with one another. "He was well then."

"And he is now," Sister Margaret said. "Only in a different way."

"The Last Rites," Joliffe said. "He never . . ."

"Here the men confess every week. The older of them are in constant likelihood of death and know it. I doubt he passed in much sin. There'll be the Masses said for him, too," she added practically.

She moved away. Joliffe followed her, across the passage-way and into the hall where there was deep-night silence and curtained shadows around the beds, silvered by moonlight slanting in the high windows and barely touched by the small lamp burning over the altar in the chapel. It crossed Joliffe's mind that his outcry could not have been so very loud after all, and he was thankful for that. Sister Margaret must have heard him only because she was awake and prob-ably coming to wake him anyway, because the peace here was undisturbed, the only sounds the varied breathings be-tween curtains—Ned Knolles lightly snoring; Iankyn gently wheezing, a little labored but even; the others only a general, gentle susurration. There was no way to tell there was one less than a little while ago.

Even when he came to stand beside Tom Lyttle's bed while Sister Margaret set the candle on the bedside table, Joliffe could have thought the old man was only sleeping. Sister Margaret had already closed his eyes. Or perhaps, dying in his sleep, they had been closed. His jaw was sagged open, though, in that slack way only the dead achieve. That would have to be seen to before the body stiffened, Joliffe thought, using practicality to detach himself from other thoughts; but Sister Margaret was taking a long bandage from inside the front of her apron, and she bent to pass it under Lyttle's slack jaw and up around his face to the top of his head, lifting the jaw decently closed before she deftly knotted the cloth. Still keeping his thought to elsewhere, Joliffe noted she must have been bringing the bandage when she heard him. Better yet. For some reason, it mattered greatly that his outcry was as unknown as possible.

"There," Sister Margaret said softly as she straightened. "It's good to give what dignity we can."

Her calmness gave it all a dignity, too. She must have

seen a quantity of deaths here—enough to give her the calmness of familiarity, Joliffe supposed. Or even of indifference, perhaps. After all, Lyttle had been just an old man without family.

Then the candlelight glistened on a tear sliding down Sister Margaret's cheek, and Joliffe changed his thought. Indifferent she was not.

She wiped the tear away with the back of one hand, saw him watching her, and said, with an effort toward a smile, "How many of our tears are for the dead, I wonder, and how many are for ourselves, grieving to be left behind and at the same time newly fearing what will come to us in our turn."

For what comfort was in it, he offered, "I would guess that, moment to moment, that's all too mixed ever to sort out."

She gave him slightly more of a smile. "Very likely."

"Why don't you go back to bed while you may? I can keep vigil by him until the day starts."

As if his words freed her to be weary, tiredness was suddenly heavy in her shoulders and face. "I would be grateful for that," she admitted.

"Then go." Before someone else needs you, he did not add.

She went, a shadow of gray and white among the darker shadows. There was enough left of the candle that it might burn until dawn, but none of the shadows here were the foul and gibbering ones of Joliffe's dream, and he pinched the flame out between thumb and forefinger. He did not mind honest darkness, and candles were costly. He meant to stay awake, but did not know how much he would actually pray and was debating whether sitting on the stool beside the bed would be sufficient or whether he should kneel at the bedside, at least for a time for respect's sake.

"He's dead then," Basset said quietly from beyond the curtain.

"Gah," Joliffe said back, startled. "Don't do that in the dark like this."

"You're the one put out the candle. Put the curtain aside. I'll keep vigil with you."

Joliffe obeyed, trying to slide the rings as silently as might be along the pole and pausing to listen when he had finished, to hear if anyone had been disturbed. No one stirred, no breathing changed that he could hear, and finding he was glad of Basset's company, he sat down on the stool between the beds.

"So what was with that outcry of yours?" Basset asked.

Joliffe was abruptly less glad to have his company. He tried, "What outcry?" Basset answered that with a contempting snort, so he changed to, "An ill dream. That was all," and tried to take the talk away from himself with, "So why were you awake to hear me?" Then he wished he had said something else, because the answer to that was so obvious.

Basset gave it anyway. "Sister Margaret moving around here wakened me. But what was that with you shouting and thrashing? We're to wake *you* in the night, not other way round."

Joliffe wanted to make a lightly mocking answer back, but with the edges of the dream still raw in him, no light answer came in time, and Basset—as so often, too sharp for Joliffe's ease—asked with solid concern, "What is it, then?" And when still Joliffe could not find words, added, "Not something here. Not even the Thorncoffyns are worth that kind of nightmare. Is it something"—he lowered his voice even more—"from when you weren't with us?"

Joliffe swallowed down the tightness in his throat enough to force out, "Yes."

"Will it help to tell of it?" Basset asked, level-voiced and carefully not too gentle.

Joliffe had control enough now to say as evenly, "I don't know." But suddenly, whether it would help or not, he wanted to tell at least some of it, and he said, "I was in France. That's where I was sent after we parted ways."

"Not Northamptonshire, the way you said," Basset said, a little dryly.

"That was later. At the first I was in France. In Rouen. Then . . . in Paris."

In the dark Basset made a sharp, startled movement. "Paris," he hissed. "But Paris——" He broke off. A handful of months ago, Paris, that had been part of English-held France for these past fifteen years, had been brutally lost, along with much else England had won in France under the hero-king Henry V and since. Not everything had gone. Not Normandy. But Paris was, and it had not gone gently.

"I was there at the end," Joliffe said. "In the midst of it. I got out. Others . . . did not."

"Blessed Mary, Saint Genesius, and all the saints," Basset whispered, not hiding his horror.

"And now I have nightmares," Joliffe said flatly. And found there was nothing else he could bring himself to say.

Basset left him to his silence and each presumably to their prayers for Lyttle's soul and—on Joliffe's side, for other souls, too.

The night passed. Morning came. As understanding spread among the other men that one of them had gone, a silence different from the night's peace filled the hall, made partly of prayers, partly of the other old men's sense of their own waiting for their end. The sisters, for their part, saw to Lyttle's body while Joliffe went about his morning duties, finding that Rose in the kitchen shared the sisters' solemnity, and that even Emme and Amice were quieter than usual.

It had become a pleasant daily habit between him and Amice for him to suggest she was madly in lust for him and for her to laugh at him, and for Emme to say, mock-sternly, "You can do better than him that's just wandering through, girl," then threaten him with wet and soapy paddle, warning him to shift himself out of their way.

This morning there was none of that, and it made his return to the kitchen all the more jarring, to find Idany there, demanding at Sister Ursula, "She won't want *her* coming nigh her. Who else was there? Someone else had to be there."

Sister Ursula pointed at Joliffe. "He was."

"You," Idany said. "Come with me. My lady wants to hear all."

Joliffe cast Sister Ursula a questioning look, hoping for rescue. Rather than rescue, she merely nodded, and perforce he went with Idany away to Mistress Thorncoffyn's chamber where indeed she wanted to hear everything. Which old man was it had died? At what hour? Who was with him? No one? Who found him dead then?

"Sister Margaret," Joliffe said.

"Too late at her night round of the men, it would seem," Mistress Thorncoffyn sniffed. "Master Soule will have to speak to her. Nor was Father Richard there, I take it."

"No."

"Remiss in *his* duties, too." Mistress Thorncoffyn's eyes, small above her fat cheeks, were bright with looking forward to making trouble. "See that Master Soule knows I want to see him as soon as may be." She laid a hand over the highest swell of her belly. "Too, tell Sister Ursula I'm in need of more of that drink she makes with ginger and mint. My stomach was unquiet in the night."

Joliffe took that for dismissal, bowed, and made to withdraw. Idany followed him to the door, apparently to be sure it was rightly closed behind him but taking her chance to say at him, very low and with frowning fierceness, "You see to it that it's Sister Ursula who makes that drink. Not Sister Margaret. Nor that Sister Letice. Tell Sister Ursula I said so."

Joliffe did not see how she supposed it was his place to tell the sisters what to do or not do, and anyway no one but

Rose was in the kitchen when he returned. He told her, both about the drink and Idany's demand for Sister Ursula to make it, then asked, "What's the complaint against Sister Letice? I can understand distrusting Sister Margaret, but why Sister Letice? What's Mistress Thorncoffyn done to her?"

"To her brother more than to Sister Letice herself," Rose said. "Or to her brother and her parents, rather. But thereby to Sister Letice, I suppose. I doubt either she or he would be here if their parents hadn't died the way they did and if her brother didn't take it the way he does."

"Her brother is here?" Joliffe said in surprise. As he tried to think who he could be among the bedridden men, Rose said, "Father Richard."

Her brother. Then that small, easy exchange he had seen between them had been only sister to brother, no greater matter than that. Good. But he asked, "How did their parents die, to make such difference to them?"

"Unshriven," Rose said grimly. Meaning their souls' chance of Heaven was imperiled, if not altogether broken. "Six winters ago they fell ill together of a rheum in the lungs. You know how that can sometimes go. It starts out seeming none so bad, turns worse, seems to better, then suddenly goes very bad and kills quickly. That's what happened with them. Letice was tending them, understood what was happening, sent for her brother to come quickly. He was here, this being his parish even then. So was Mistress Thorncoffyn, making one of her visits and somewhat unwell with a slight, aching fever. She's the sort who knows that whatever she has, it's worse than whatever someone else has. If someone else is dying, she's dying sooner. She wanted her own Last Rites before Father Richard left her. No one thought she was dying, so he refused it. She clamped down on his arm and wouldn't let him go. Those ham-hands of hers look like no more than much meat, but there's strength in them. Sister Ursula was here then. She says that Father Richard argued and argued with her, and that when he finally gave up trying to persuade her and fought to break her hold on him, they left bruises on each other. Mistress Thorncoffyn was that determined to have what she wanted. His sister had been right—their parents were dying very quickly. He came just in time to hear his father's death-rattle. His mother was already dead. He was too late for both of them. He's made his life a penance for it ever since, Sister Ursula says."

Joliffe held silent a moment, taking in the full, cruel weight of the burden Father Richard must carry. Then he asked, "And Sister Letice?"

"When her brother sold off everything their parents owned, he should have provided her with a dowry out of that, but he begged her to put her share along with his into Masses for their parents' souls, to try to save them in death since he had failed them in life. He was in such a pitch of misery, so determined on a wrenching penance for his failure, she could not say no. So the money went to pay for Masses at Ely, to add to Father Richard's own prayers for them. Since all that Letice had left in her life by then was her brother, she took service here. That's been to the hospital's good, what with her skill with herbs, but it means she and her brother have to deal with Mistress Thorncoffyn time and again."

And if Mistress Thorncoffyn did not worry about that, Idany did, Joliffe thought. He shook his head over the pity of it all and went to tell Master Soule that Mistress Thorncoffyn wished to see him as soon as might be.

Master Soule received the message with down-drawn mouth and, "To complain of something, no doubt. Do you know of what?"

A sensible servant would have denied any knowledge or at the least answered circumspectly. Joliffe, who had never had inclination to be a sensible servant, said, "That Sister Margaret and Father Richard didn't foresee Tom Lyttle was going to die and weren't there when he did."

"Even over that she has to make trouble. As if to go to God in sleep isn't one of the more merciful ways to pass." Master Soule shook his head and gestured for Joliffe to go.

Joliffe went back to the kitchen. All the women except Sister Petronilla were there, with Sister Letice just finishing pouring something from a pot through a sieve into a pottery cup. He heard the pad of soft-soled feet behind him but was not in time to turn before Idany shoved at his arm to have him out of her way, demanding as she came into the kitchen, "Where is my lady's drink? Didn't you tell Sister Ursula it's wanted?"

In the moment of warning there had been, Sister Letice had moved away from the table, was several yards away, her back to it as Sister Ursula took up the cup and held it out to Idany, saying, "It's just finished steeping. You'll add the honey if she wants it?"

"Of course." Idany took the cup with her usual brisk ill grace, no bother of thanks, and ordering over her shoulder as she left that, "She'll want more in a while. Her stomach is badly uneased."

Too low for Idany to overhear, Sister Margaret murmured, "It might better if she chewed her food instead of gobbled it."

The day went its solemn way. Late in the morning, Father Richard and Joliffe carried Lyttle's shroud-wrapped body across the road to the church where it would lie until its burial tomorrow. Since there was no family to keep vigil over him, the sisters were to take turns at it through the day, with Father Richard to keep the watch in the night. Meanwhile, in the hospital itself the curtains were left drawn around what had been his bed, but the bedding, blanket and all, went to the laundry, and at Sister Ursula's order, Joliffe carried out the straw-filled mattress and pillow and hung them to air over the garth's fence in the sunlight.

The quiet familiarity with which it was all done showed

these were all-too-usual duties. Only little Heinrich showed himself unsettled, not keeping to his usual silent place under the table despite Sister Petronilla putting him there several times. Instead he wandered the kitchen vaguely, sometimes straight into the table or, worse, into a wall where he would stand gently knocking his head against it until someone turned him away to his wandering again.

"He's like this whenever there's a death," said Sister Petronilla. "He somehow senses it and is unsettled. Daveth will be back from lessons soon and take him."

"What about a quieting draught of something?" Joliffe suggested.

"Whatever we've tried, he never seems to take it same way twice. Sometimes what ought to quiet him only makes him worse."

"Can't he be tied to a table leg or something?" Rose asked a little desperately, leaving off stirring the mid-day pottage in time to turn him aside as he wandered blankly toward the fire.

"He wails and rubs himself raw on the rope," Sister Petronilla said, catching him as he turned around and headed toward the hearth again. Even her usual serenity sounded strained.

"Joliffe," Sister Ursula ordered impatiently, "take him and do something with him for this while until Daveth comes back."

Dismayed, Joliffe caught the child by one shoulder as Sister Petronilla let him go. Then he mercifully had a thought and said, "Come, Heinrich," and steered him from the kitchen with the same light touch and gentleness Sister Petronilla and Daveth used.

Did Heinrich even know the difference between one person and another, or was everyone and everything much the same to him in the small and shadowed place that was his mind? There was no way to know. At least he was biddable: he went the short way to Joliffe's own room without trouble and sank straight down cross-legged onto the floor when Joliffe, with a slight downward press on his shoulder, told him to sit. There he began his usual rocking front to back, which was safe enough, and Joliffe left him to it while getting out his lute from his hanging sack, then sitting himself down cross-legged in front of the boy and setting to fussing the strings into tune. After the lessons he had been put through—done in the evenings after the brutal weapons work of most of the days—his skill with the lute was still nothing that would excite the truly skilled but assuredly better than it had been. Not that he would have to stretch himself to divert Heinrich, he thought. If Heinrich heeded music at all, of course.

Heinrich did.

As Joliffe stroked one simple song and then another from the lute, the child's gaze never once strayed up from the floor in front of him, but his rocking slowed, almost stopped, then changed to a sway from side to side, not quite in time to Joliffe's playing but nearly. Joliffe wondered if that might be the best approval his lute-playing was ever likely to have.

"He likes it," said Daveth from the doorway.

"Has anyone ever played for him before now?" Joliffe asked without stopping.

"Not here. I don't know about before here."

Those were more words together at once than Joliffe had ever heard from Daveth without Sister Petronilla prompting him. The boy's eyes were on Joliffe's fingers, watching intently. Joliffe stopped playing. Heinrich went completely still for a moment, then began to rock forward and back again. Joliffe lifted the lute toward Daveth. "Do you want to try?"

Daveth hesitated, then limped forward. With his bent leg, sitting on the floor would be awkward. Joliffe stood up, nodded him toward the bed, sat there himself, and when Daveth joined him, handed him the lute. The boy took it, still uncertain. Joliffe showed him how to hold it against his body and then a simple placing of his fingers on the neck.

"Now stroke across the strings with your other hand. Gently. You want to learn the feel of the lute, not break its strings," Joliffe warned, all too aware of most boys' urge to strum vigorously.

Daveth, though, had a gentle touch. Leaving Heinrich to his rocking—at least he was not wandering again—Joliffe enjoyed, for a brief time, being teacher—the more especially after having spent the past months as mostly pupil himself. He thought Daveth was enjoying it, too, until from the doorway Geoffrey Thorncoffyn said, "So you're a string-strummer, too, fellow?" and Heinrich, from near-stillness, flung himself sideways and made to crawl under the bed. Daveth pushed the lute into Joliffe's hands and plunged forward in time to wrap his arms around him and hold him back. Joliffe, taken off guard in both directions, was momentarily uncertain whether it was Geoffrey or the boys he should deal with, then left Heinrich to Daveth and said, standing up from the bed, "Among other things, yes."

"A player, for one, I hear," Geoffrey said down the length of his nose, taking the unnecessary trouble to show how far below himself that was.

"The thing is," Master Aylton said behind him, "until just now, when Master Soule did, no one had bothered to tell Mistress Thorncoffyn that your whole company is hereabouts."

"So she wants you all to put on a play for her. Today, if possible," Geoffrey said.

"It is not possible, sir," Joliffe answered. "They're at work in the fields."

"Tomorrow then," Geoffrey said, turned sharply enough that Master Aylton had to move smartly out of his way, and left. Master Aylton made a wry face and a shrug at Joliffe and followed him. Joliffe, his own face wry, set the lute aside and knelt down to do what he could to disentangle Daveth and Heinrich.

Chapter 13

Ellis glowered at Joliffe. "This is your doing, isn't it? This gets you off your right work there, but us—after we've worked ourselves bow-legged, bent-backed, and shuffling in the fields all day—we're supposed put on a play, all merry and capering. Is that the way of it?"

"We could do *Tisbe and Pyramus*," Joliffe suggested, straight-faced. "There's no merriment or capering in that."

"Oh, I do laugh at your sharp wit. Hear me laughing," Ellis said, not laughing.

"Or *Dux Moraud*," Joliffe said thoughtfully. "No capering in that one, either."

"I hate that play," Ellis snarled. "So do you!"

Joliffe did, for more reasons than one, but that would not have kept him from a goading reply except Rose cut in with, "This isn't Joliffe's doing." She paused as if in momentary thought, then added, "For once."

"Hai!" Joliffe protested.

Rose went on, ignoring him, "It's all because that Thorncoffyn woman is bored and wants diverting. Her and her grandson."

Ellis grunted a grudging half-acceptance of that and pushed another stick into the fire under the pot of pottage heating for their supper. Rose was slicing bread, and Piers was cutting the day's portion of cheese into large pieces. Gil from where he lay with his hands clasped behind his head on a pillow, taking his turn at having no evening task, said toward the tree branches above him, "Just not *The Baker's Cake* or *Fox and Grapes*. Please."

Joliffe, standing, his shoulder leaned against a tree trunk, understood the plea. Both of those plays called for far too much of the undesired capering and merriment.

"Nor *Abraham and Isaac*," Ellis said. "We want something simple to set up and do. I'm not unpacking half the cart for this."

"*Saint Nicholas and the Thief*," said Piers. "It's simple." And one of the oldest plays in their set of plays. They could all do it in their sleep.

But Ellis asked in protest, "Without Basset?"

Indeed, it was difficult to think of the play without Basset being massively dignified as the statue of Saint Nicholas that comes alive to deal with a thief. Time was that Joliffe had played the woman who leaves her chest of treasure in the saint's safe-keeping and has it stolen by Ellis as a thief. Later, while Gil learned his craft as a player, he and Joliffe had traded turns as the woman, but Gil had had the part all to himself in the months that Joliffe had been gone. That made it all the easier for Joliffe to say now, "I'll play the statue."

"You?" Ellis protested. "You're not old enough to be the saint."

"First, who says Saint Nicholas has to be old? Second, aren't you fortunate that Basset isn't here to hear you call him old?" Joliffe said.

"I never said he—" Ellis broke off, glowering at having

been diverted, and returned to the main point. "You don't look the way people expect Saint Nicholas to look."

Joliffe rolled his eyes in a way that Piers had perfected and said, "I'd put on Abraham's white beard and powder my hair with flour. Just as Basset does."

Ellis glowered suspiciously at so reasonable an answer, but Rose said firmly, "With that and bishop's mitre and robe and crozier, yes, Joliffe, you'd do quite sufficiently as Saint Nicholas."

"So we do the *Saint Nicholas*," Gil said before Ellis could make more trouble over it.

Ellis immediately said, "So where are we going to do it?"

By the time they had thrashed out both that *and* the matter of when they would play, twilight was well along toward darkness and Joliffe was late to his evening duties. He had warned Sister Petronilla that he might be. She had said not to mind, she could always have Daveth's help if need be. "He's reaching a size to be of some use that way," she had said with her usual air of taking calmly whatever came. "Besides, we'll put something in the men's evening drink to help them settle better for the night. We always do after a death. Otherwise, the first night is almost always hard for everyone."

So Joliffe might have hurried less than otherwise but in truth he hurried not at all, instead strolled at ease through the orchard, across the little stream, and into the garden. There, in the deepening blue twilight, where the herbs' subtle mingled scents still hung in the lingering warmth of the ended day, he paused, put his head back to look at the first stars pricking into being overhead, and simply let the world be around him, not demanding anything from it.

Or, in that moment, anything from himself.

For that moment everything was simply there; everything simply was; and simply so was he. He closed his eyes and let the feeling deepen in him, grateful for the peace of it, then after a time opened his eyes, drew a deep breath, let go of his thoughts, and went on his way, quieter in himself than he had been for a long while.

The quietness was still there when he awoke in the morning after an unbroken sleep, letting him look at what he would not yesterday. Two mornings ago old Tom Lyttle had been alive. Today he was not, and some day, soon or late, Joliffe would not be either. He had no desire for his own end—he had seen too many ends of late—but in the quietness of himself just now he did not protest the inevitable. It was simply as things were. The pattern of things. Just as this year there had been spring and then summer, now harvest and all too soon winter, some day he would die.

But not today, probably, and here and now there was work to be done, and he got himself out of bed and set about the day's necessities, grateful to the sleeping draught that had kept the men at peace all night.

Basset insisted on hobbling to the funeral that morning, using a staff, Joliffe's arm, and soft shoes padded with folded cloth as thickly as might be. Only Ned Knolles among the other old men chose to go, too, shuffling along with Sister Petronilla's arm and Daveth's shoulder for his support. At the church there were only Father Richard, the boy Will, and the sexton. Candles were few, too, and there was no incense, but Father Richard was in full funeral vestments and said the Mass with all care, neither scanting nor hurrying.

At the end, the sexton and Joliffe carried the shrouded body from the trestled boards where it had rested before the altar out of the church to the readied grave on a far side of the churchyard. That was too much more walking for Basset and old Ned. They waited on the church porch with Daveth while Sister Petronilla followed Joliffe and the sexton and Father Richard for the priest's final prayers over the body when it had been lowered into the ground. After that, there was nothing but the slow return to the hospital, leaving the sexton to fill the grave and Father Richard to whatever his own next duties were.

Later Joliffe took the chance, when he carried the mid-day meal up to Master Soule and Master Hewstere, to ask Master Soule about where and when the play might be done, only to find that Mistress Thorncoffyn had been before him in the matter.

"She summoned me to her this morning," said Master Soule. The way he said it told something of how he felt about being "summoned" in his own hospital. "She wants it played in the garth, where she can watch from her window. What, by the by, is it you mean to play?"

He was so openly ready to disapprove that Joliffe was pleased to be able to say it would be *Saint Nicholas and the Thief.* He told the story, and Master Soule granted, "That sounds well enough."

Encouraged, Joliffe said, carefully the humble servant, "If we play, it should be for the men in the hall as well as for Mistress Thorncoffyn, and if for them, then it will surely be easier for her to shift into the hall than for them to shift out of it, such of them as could; and some couldn't, after all. If we played it at the chapel end, we'd have to set up nothing but a box, just use the doors that are there for our coming and going, and making as little disturbance of matters here as might be. There, the men could see all without leaving their beds."

Master Hewstere, only listening until now, said, "Won't my lady balk at sharing this play she sees as being done for her?"

Master Soule slightly stiffened, probably at thought of how unpleasant Mistress Thorncoffyn would try to make his life and everyone else's if she were displeased; but Joliffe said smoothly, "By your leave, sirs, we aren't doing the play for Mistress Thorncoffyn. We're doing it as a gift to the hospital."

"She won't pay you for that," Master Hewstere said in flat warning.

Mentally shrugging aside Ellis' undoubted irk at that, Joliffe said, still to Master Soule, "We can do the play as soon as this afternoon's end if you like, sir," and saw his own thought of "not leaving her much time to complain" pass across the master's face. "But my fellows will need time to unpack and ready our playing gear. Nor they can't come straight from the fields to do this. At best, to ready themselves and everything they need to be let off the harvest by mid-afternoon."

Hindering the harvest was never lightly done. It was likely the thought of that gave Master Soule almost as deep a pause as thought of Mistress Thorncoffyn's displeasure had before he said with decision, "Let it be so. When you go to fetch them from the fields, say I gave the word for it. Tell Sister Ursula it's to go forward and all."

Joliffe bowed, ready to leave, but Master Hewstere said, "Will you be in this play?"

"I will, sir."

"So you need time off your duties, too."

"Some."

"No wonder you're so eager for it all."

Several sharp answers to that wanted loose from Joliffe's tongue. Holding back from them all, he answered with face and voice both empty, "Sir," which was no answer at all, and with another bow got himself out of the room, fighting his anger to quietness as he went down the stairs. After all, this was hardly the first time he had encountered that manner of thought about his work. All too usually, doing a play was thought to be merely light sport by people who did not know how a player could spend more of his body and mind in the while of playing than, say, a clerk might in a whole day at his desk. It depended on the play, of course, and on the player, but at the best it was not simply a matter of moving yourself around the playing space and saying the right words when you were supposed to. Poorly skilled players were satisfied with being no more than themselves in a play, enjoying simply showing off to the onlookers, but a truly skilled player worked to put himself aside and become the part he was playing, all the while never forgetting he was only playing at being someone else. That meant that to all outward show he was someone other than himself but at the same time, inwardly, he was remembering not only all the words he had to say and where to be when he said them, but having to pay heed to where the other players were and what they were doing, *and* judging how the lookers-on were taking what was being done. To do all that all at the same time took skill and strength of both mind and body, and if either mind or body—or one of the other players—faltered, so might the play. That meant that failure or success depended not only on one player having it right but on all of them, all at that same time.

So, no, doing a play was not the light-hearted sport and excuse to avoid "true work" that people like Master Hewstere seemed to think it was, and, yes, Joliffe and Ellis and Gil and Piers needed time to ready for even something as outwardly simple as *Saint Nicholas and the Thief.*

Sister Ursula at least made no trouble over him leaving when the time came. She even asked Rose if she needed to go, too. Somewhat too readily, to Joliffe's mind, Rose answered, "No, I'll not be needed," as if she were more than willing to have no part in the business at all, and he left the kitchen wondering just how tired she had become of the players' life, to want not even this small part of it here and now.

On his part, he was finding how much he missed his right work as a player. Close to nine months away from it was far too long—long enough that he was even looking forward to doing tired old *Saint Nicholas and the Thief.* More than that, he missed being day by day on the road, always on the way to somewhere else. There had been change and travel and different places in plenty these past months, but much of it had been . . .

He shook his mind away from where the nightmares came.

He was leaving the hospital's rear-yard, setting out along the cart track for where he was told the harvesters were at work today, when another thought slapped into his mind, bringing him to a stop. Did it matter, after all, if people wondered how the players came by a second horse? If anyone thought to question it, why not say a bounty from Lord Lovell had made it possible? That was not altogether a lie: Lord Lovell had set them on the way that had brought Joliffe to Bishop Beaufort's sight. The point was that with another horse to the cart, Basset would be able to ride instead of walk and they could be away from here, could be about their right business, with Basset bettering while they traveled, now that he was so much better already.

Joliffe started walking again, poking at the thought as he went, disconcerted, now he looked at it, to find how wide apart in his mind he had been keeping his life of these past months from his player's life. Was he was trying to make himself into two people, the halves of himself walled away from each other? His nightmares, let alone his common sense, should have shown him how impossible that was going to be, but he had been trying it, even blocking one part of his life from the other when there was help to be had between them. He felt a fool.

Or did he mean a coward? What had he thought to gain by keeping his life in separate pieces? Yes, surely when he first became a player there had been a separating in his life, old part from new. There had been no way not to separate from all his earlier life; no one in his earlier life would have understood his choice or even—probably—forgiven him for taking that choice, had he given them the chance. Some would likely have gone so far as try to stop him. So he had left all that part of his life—and them—behind.

But that had been a matter of going onward, with never

a denying to himself who he had been or from where he had grown, never this trying to hide one part of himself from another as he had been doing lately.

But now that he had seen what he was doing, he was going to . . . do what?

Think about it, he supposed.

But not now. It would keep until later. Whatever tangles he had made—was making—would make—in his life, here and now there was a play to do, and in a player's life, all else went to the side when there was a play to do.

On Master Soule's word there was no trouble having Ellis, Gil, and Piers away from the harvest, although Tisbe had to stay behind, given over to another boy to lead, and all their readying went smoothly, the necessary garb and gear readily unpacked from the cart and carried to the hospital. From visiting Basset, Ellis, Gil, and Piers had some knowledge of what would be their playing space in the hall. Now, coming in through the kitchen, Joliffe showed them how the pantry led between the kitchen and the sacristy on the chapel's far side. They would change into their garb in the sacristy, and Gil as the Merchant Woman enter from there, first with Piers staggering behind her, carrying her "heavy" money chest to put in Saint Nicholas' keeping, and again when she returned to find the chest had been stolen, while Ellis would go back through the pantry into the kitchen and into the small passageway beside Joliffe's room, to enter from the hall's other side as the Thief.

Ellis and Gil went back and forth several times, muttering each other's lines from the play as they went (they all had done this play so often that everyone knew everyone else's lines) to be sure they would be in time for whenever they had to enter. Joliffe used the time and Piers to shift joint stools to where the sisters and Rose could sit between beds to have good view without blocking any of the men's or Mistress Thorncoffyn's. He presumed she would be sitting where she did when she came to Mass since there was enough of her to block several men's views if she sat closer. He knew that was an unkind thought, knew that in charity he should curb it, but unkind or not, it was also the truth and would be the truth whether or not he thought it. So he shrugged away any guilt for the unkindness and let Piers persuade him back to the kitchen where Piers undoubtedly had hope of wheedling something to eat from someone.

That happened to prove no challenge. Ellis and Gil were already at the table, being given bread and ale by Sister Ursula. Piers happily joined them for a share while Joliffe went on to the laundry, to tell Emme and Amice they should soon come to the hall.

"Unless you can't bear to leave your laundering for a while," he suggested lightly.

"The laundering will wait for us," Emme said cheerily back. "Sheets and all can soak while we're away."

Amice, already untying her apron, asked, "Is someone gone to tell Jack?"

"Daveth will," said Joliffe, glad to be reminded, and when he was back in the kitchen he asked if Daveth would.

Sister Petronilla promptly sent the boy, then asked in her turn, "Will it be all right for Heinrich to be at your play?"

Knowing that if Heinrich did not come, then either she or Daveth could not, Joliffe said, "Surely. You can hold him on your lap, say?"

She said, smiling, "That would be no trouble."

Ellis, Gil, and Piers were already gone to the sacristy to change into the play's garb. Joliffe's change into the bishop's beard and robes would be easier to do once the complications of Gil being gowned for the Woman Merchant were done, so rather than joining them straight away, he went back to the hall, going along the cloister walk to enter by the far door, closest to Basset's bed. Basset was sitting up. So were as many other of the men as could, the others were propped on their pillows as much as might be. Even John Oxyn was in one of the respites that came in his fever and taking an interest. As Basset had said, they were all ready for something that would put their fellow's death further off from them, and with a hard look Basset asked him, "What are you doing here instead of readying?"

"Giving Gil a chance to be ready before I take my turn. The sacristy is narrow."

Basset gave a nod, accepting that, then said what was probably truly on his mind. "Do you know, I've never seen my players play."

Joliffe gave a short laugh of surprise, but saw that was true. Basset oversaw them in their practicing, but when they actually performed for lookers-on, he was always *in* the play, not seeing it. With equal surprise, Joliffe said, "Come to that, I haven't either." Not since he had talked his way into the company those years ago. "Nor have I seen this play from Saint Nicholas' side of it," he added. How different a shape would it have for him, played from that way?

Idany came in, ending their talk. Behind her, Master Aylton was carrying Mistress Thorncoffyn's stool that served her at Mass. "There," said Idany, pointing toward the chapel. "Put it right there, between the first two beds."

Joliffe did not need the protesting lift of Basset's hand. He was already stepping forward into Master Aylton's way, saying, "No."

Brought to a stop, both Master Aylton and Idany stared at him, before Idany said tartly, "Yes. That's where my lady means to sit. Close. She's said so."

"She'll block some of the men from seeing all the play if she sits there," Joliffe returned. "She can sit here and see as well as anybody." He pointed to where he was standing at the foot of Basset's bed.

"That's not where she means to sit," Idany repeated.

"She's not going to sit where she blocks what everyone else sees."

"Fellow," Master Aylton put in. "This play is being done at her behest and for her."

"We're being allowed to do it here by Master Soule's leave, for the sake of the men," Joliffe returned. "She'll see it all very well from here without trouble to her or anyone else."

"You are a servant here," Idany said. "It's not for you to say what's done and not done."

Joliffe felt the subtle shift in his body from simply being there to a straightening into command and heard the same change in his voice as he said, "I'm speaking for the players now, not as anyone's servant. If I answer to anyone, it's to Master Soule as our patron for this time." He shifted his look to Master Aylton and pointed. "The stool goes there."

Something suspiciously near to a smile twitched in the steward's face as he set the stool down, but he sounded solemn enough as he said to Idany, "He knows what will work best for his own play. Come away now."

"Neither Mistress nor Master Thorncoffyn will be pleased," Idany threatened.

"They will be when they see the play, I'm certain," Master Aylton assured her. As she unwillingly started to leave, he added to Joliffe, "Nor will I move the stool when you're not looking, or let anyone else."

Joliffe gave a slight, silent bow of thanks for that and, behind his back and Idany's, exchanged a lift of eyebrows with Basset. He did not know what Basset's thought might be, but his own was a true wonder at how Mistress Thorncoffyn could turn even a play for a hospital of ill men into argument and trouble.

Chapter 14

The play went perfectly despite the gap of time and place since Joliffe last worked with the others. That was partly because they all knew the play so well, partly because they knew each other so well. Whatever unease or quarrels there might sometimes be among them outside their work, within their work each fully trusted the other. All else in the world dropped away. There was only the play.

Piers began it. Wearing the bright red and yellow tabard of Lord Lovell's livery, he marched from the sacristy into the hall, tootling on a recorder held in one hand, with the other beating on the small drum slung from a strap over his shoulder. Directly in front of the chapel, centered on the aisle between the beds, he stopped, faced everyone there, and declared the players and he were come to do a play and now, by everyone's kind leave, they would. This served, as it usually did, to draw the lookers-on out of their talk among themselves and their eyes toward the playing place, and Piers, his duty done, gave a deep bow and continued his march, tootling and beating again, out the opposite door, into the passageway. As he went out of sight—to dash around to the sacristy and rid himself of drum, recorder, and tabard and come back in a few moments as the Merchant Woman's Servant—Joliffe came out of the sacristy in bishop's robes and mitre, white of beard and hair, carrying a tall crozier and deeply dignified. As Saint Nicholas—or rather as a statue of Saint Nicholas—he paced solemnly to his place in front of the chapel, stepped up onto a low box waiting there for him, and struck a proper statue-pose, his right hand raised in blessing, his empty gaze into empty air above everyone else's heads, no movement in him anywhere. He and Gil had paced the distance earlier and determined on a slow count of ten for him to be in place. Now, as he finished his deliberate count of ten, the Merchant Woman entered from the sacristy with a proud sweep of skirts.

How to move as a woman had been one of Gil's first lessons after he joined the company, just as it had been Joliffe's. Besides becoming at ease with all the treacheries long skirts could work around legs, they had had to learn to use their bodies differently and to seem not simply "a woman" but a young woman, an old woman, a comic woman, a proud woman—all the sorts of women there were. As Basset had had to say more than once, "If you can't stop being you, you've no business trying to be a player. You have to be whoever the play needs, not just yourself spouting words, and that means every kind of woman as well as every kind of man."

Watching Basset as an elderly widow in gown and wimple and veil in *The Steward and the Devil* was a revelation of just how far one could go from being oneself.

So now, to all appearances, it was a proud and wealthy Merchant Woman who swept into the hall from the sacristy, cloaked, gloved, and carrying a riding whip to show she was about to travel. Her Servant Boy followed her, staggering with the supposed weight of the chest he carried. At her gesture, he set the chest down in front of the statue. She explained how she must go on a long journey and was commending her treasure to the saint's keeping. Then she swept out, all wealth and confidence, her servant behind her, and Ellis as the black-cowled Thief came in from the passageway.

Skulking was the word that best applied as he looked all around, saw no one, spotted the chest in front of the statue, opened it, gloated aloud over what he saw inside, mockingly thanked the saint for his bounty, closed the chest, took it up, and skulked out the way he had come. Few people skulked as well as Ellis did, and his turn around at the last moment before leaving, to raise a finger to his lips to warn all the lookers-on to silence about his crime, raised laughter, just as it always did.

The Merchant Woman returned. Finding her treasure gone, she railed at the saint for failing her and beat on the statue with her riding whip.

Gil's business was to look as if he were hitting hard while hardly hitting at all. Joliffe's business, as a statue, was to stand completely still until, weeping, the Merchant Woman threw down her whip and left. With her gone, the Thief furtively returned, carrying the chest. As if he were in some other place than where he had stolen the chest, he set it down and began to gloat over it, not seeing, behind him, the statue of Saint Nicholas come to life, step down from its "high place," and pick up the whip. Here the lookers-on began to laugh, easily able to guess what was coming. With solemn dignity, St. Nicholas paced to the thief who heard him and swiveled around to be appalled at the sight. Saint Nicholas proceeded to belabor him with the whip, explaining this was in return for the beating from the Merchant Woman, then uttered dire warning against greed and theft and sins in general and paced back to become a statue again. The terrified Thief scurried to put the chest back at the statue's feet and fled. The Merchant Woman returned, still weeping, only to be overcome with joy when she saw her treasure was restored.

She thanked and praised Saint Nicholas, bade her Servant Boy take up the chest, and swept out, all wealthy pride and happiness again. Piers, comically playing the chest's heaviness for all he was worth, staggered after her, earning a last burst of laughter. On that laughter and the clapping that came with it, Saint Nicholas stepped down from his place, made solemn sign of the cross toward everyone, and followed the others out of the hall.

The clapping had not yet ended when Master Aylton put his head into the sacristy, his face still full of laughter, and said, "Mistress Thorncoffyn wants to see all of you. To give her thanks."

He was gone too quickly to hear Ellis' muttered, "And some coins with it, I trust."

He had already stripped off the Thief's black cowl but he shrugged back into it while Gil straightened his veil, Joliffe set aside the crozier, and Piers threw on the bright Lovell tabard again.

Going back into the hall, they were met with more clapping. Gil swept everyone a deep curtsy. Joliffe, Ellis, and Piers made sweeping bows, Joliffe remembering only just in time to catch his bishop's mitre from falling off his head. They then made their way down the hall to where Mistress Thorncoffyn sat wide-hipped on her stool, waiting for them. Master Soule and Geoffrey Thorncoffyn stood on either side of her, with Master Hewstere a little behind Master Soule, Master Aylton a little behind Geoffrey. Idany on her feet directly behind her mistress was making short, sharp beckons for the players to hurry and present themselves.

Ellis, as senior among them, strode forward first. Gil and Joliffe followed side by side. Piers, who never took to modest last if he could, skipped around them to join Ellis. That could have warranted a good cuff to the back of his head in another time and place but not here, Joliffe regretted before he forgot to be irked at Piers, first with pleasure to see how widely Basset was smiling at them from his bed, Rose sitting beside him looking equally glad, then with surprise at Jack and Amice standing together just inside the door there, their arms around each other's waist and heads bent close together, she saying something in his ear and both of them smiling smiles that looked to be more for each other than for the play they had just seen.

Oh.

Jack had never so much as hinted . . .

Joliffe let go the last of his already well-faded hopes of sharing more than talk with Amice and was glad for Jack who looked to have more reasons to be content with his life than Joliffe had guessed at.

He and the other players made their courtesies to Mistress Thorncoffyn, to Master Soule and Master Hewstere and Geoffrey. She briefly enthused to them about the play. Ellis, bowing again, said in his best manner that their pleasure in pleasing her was even greater than the pleasure she had taken in their playing. She snapped fingers over her shoulder at Geoffrey who had coins ready and put them into her raised hand. Piers, confident of his childish charm and golden curls, went quickly down on one knee, smiling up at her most winsomely. As usually happened with women when Piers did his "sweet small boy" trick, Mistress Thorncoffyn cooed at him and held out the coins for him to take. As he did, she put a hammy hand on his head and tousled his curls, telling him what a dear child he was. If anyone among the players had tousled his hair that way, they would have needed to dodge a hard kick at their shins, but for Mistress Thorncoffyn, Piers beamed and looked as if he were about to wiggle with happiness like one of her dogs.

A small box was nestled between her thighs. She took something from it and held it out to Piers, saying, "Have this candied ginger, child. A reward for your struggle with that heavy chest."

Joliffe at least among the other players had to hold in a derisive snort. The "treasure chest" weighed less than the bucket of water that Piers was supposed to carry to camp. Piers, though, took the ginger, beaming at her, and piped, "Thank you, my lady," making Joliffe pray with greater devotion than he gave to most of his prayers that Piers' voice would change soon. He would find his life a little more difficult without that childish treble, indeed he would.

Master Soule cleared his throat, perhaps readying to assert his own thanks as the hospital's master; but beyond him Jack and Amice were moving aside from the doorway and turning around as two men came into the hall. They were no one Joliffe knew. By their rough-woven tunics and hoods and loose hosen, they were country men, villagers from somewhere. By their general dustiness and well-used shoes, they had been traveling. Faced suddenly with an assembly of people turning to stare at them, they stopped short, staring back. Neither looked ill. They looked hale and hearty in fact, and Joliffe's first thought was that they had left an ill companion outside and were looking for permission to bring him in; but as they hastily pulled off their soft-brimmed caps, Geoffrey exclaimed in surprised, "Cawdry. Wyke. What brings you here?" And added to his grandmother, who was heaving her bulk around to see what everyone else was looking at, "It's Dick Cawdry. He's reeve at Tybchurch for you. And Simond Wyke. He's reeve at Crofte."

"Those are both twenty and more miles from here. What are you doing here?" Mistress Thorncoffyn demanded. "It's harvest time. You're needed where you live. You've no business vagabonding around the countryside." She seized her staff from Idany and began her cumbrous rising. Geoffrey and Idany quickly had hands under her elbows, helping her as she ordered, "Come here. Don't try to hide yourselves now. It's too late."

Neither man had shown any sign of trying to hide himself. Indeed, the older one was already coming forward. His fellow was only a half-pace behind, and by the time Mistress Thorncoffyn was on her feet, they were side by side again, both bowing to her. Whatever it was that had them here, Joliffe did not think either looked guilty, only very grimly determined as the older man said, "My lady, it's about the harvest we've come and it's not a thing that could wait." He pointed a finger at Master Aylton behind her. "Your steward there, he's told me I'm to lie in my Michaelmas accounting, so that you don't get your full count of oats and barley. He has a man out of Peterborough will buy them, he says, with him to have the money and a little to me to sweeten my thieving."

Master Aylton took an angry step forward. "You're a lying cur, Cawdry! Shut your mouth!"

"He said if I didn't do it," Cawdry stubbornly went on, "he'd see to it my rent on my holding went up, or that I lost it altogether, and assuredly I'd never be reeve again."

Master Aylton started, "My lady, this man . . ."

"Deserves a hearing," Mistress Thorncoffyn said, staring at Cawdry angrily. "If only to learn why he's lying about you."

"I don't lie, my lady," Cawdry protested. "Wyke here will tell the same. Master Aylton threatened him the same as me, only at Crofte, if he didn't write his accounts false."

Wyke nodded strongly in agreement. "He did, my lady. Nor I wouldn't have dared come if I hadn't happened to meet Dick Cawdry on last market day in St. Neots, and we fell into talk. Over the ale, like, we found out each other's trouble. There being two of us to say it, and minded we'd heard you were here and not likely to be nearer, we decided to come and lay our charge against Master Aylton."

"Liars and surely thieves!" Master Aylton said angrily. "Trying to cover your thievery by throwing it on me!"

Her look still fixed on Cawdry and ignoring Aylton, Mistress Thorncoffyn said, "Geoffrey, you were with Aylton the while he was at those manors. What do you know of this?"

Geoffrey paused so long at answering that his grand-mother finally took her gaze from Cawdry, turning her glare on him instead. Joliffe could not tell if the red flooding Geoffrey's face was embarrassment or guilt as Geoffrey gave way and muttered, "I, uh, I was not with him those days. Not just then."

His grandmother's gimlet stare demanded to know why not. Fumbling more, he ventured, "There was a place—a woman—some women—there's a place . . ."

"A brothel. You were brotheling instead of seeing to my business."

Geoffrey hung his head and admitted with deep guilt, "Yes, grandmother."

It was a quite passable copy of what Piers did when pre-tending to be sorrowful for something he had been caught at. Joliffe, Basset, Ellis, and Gil never believed he was sorrowful over anything except being caught; Rose believed him only in her most forgiving moments. Mistress Thorncoffyn must have been having one of those or else was completely besot-ted where her grandson was concerned, because she turned her wrathful look from him to Master Aylton. He, able to see which way things were going, said, angry and maybe some-what desperate, "My lady, you won't take these men's word against mine, surely. I probably spoke sharply to one and the other about something I don't even remember now. They're here for nothing more than revenge on me for it."

"A long way to walk for a petty revenge," Master Soule murmured.

Master Aylton darted an angry glance at him but went on strongly to Mistress Thorncoffyn, "What have they got to show against me? Nothing except words. I've done well for you all these three years I've been your steward, and they've been hard years as you well know, my lady."

"Aye, m'lady," Cawdry cut in. "That's what he said. That we've had these several famine years, so now there's a good one, and some of the profit skimmed away into his pouch instead of yours wouldn't show like it might have in other times."

"Words," Master Aylton said. "All they have against me are words."

Wyke had been loosening the drawstring of his belt pouch and now pulled out a folded piece of parchment. "There's this, m'lady. From Henry Multon. He's bailiff at . . ."

"I know Harry Multon," Mistress Thorncoffyn snapped. "Have known him for years." She shoved her staff at Geoffrey, who took it while she snatched the parchment from Wyke.

As she unfolded it and started to read, Wyke went on with a kind of trudging certainty that had probably done as much as anything to get his village through the past few hard years, "We stopped there on our way here to ask him if Master Aylton had done the same with him. He would have come with us, but his wife was in the midst of childing. So he had the priest write this out and witness he'd swore it's true."

"He was going to go to you himself, even without we'd come," Cawdry said. "But there's the harvest and his wife about to bear and all. That's what kept him back."

Master Aylton said, furious, "You suborned him to this. Or else *he's* behind it all and suborned *you*!"

Suborn might be more than either man knew but they understood the accusation and Cawdry answered resentfully, "We've done what needed doing, that's all. We're no liars, none of us."

"Aylton," Geoffrey said, sounding as if he were following a thought just now forming in his mind. "It was you said there'd be no reason I shouldn't linger in St. Neots. You encouraged me to it."

"As if you needed encouraging," the steward snapped.

"You did," Geoffrey said, becoming more certain. "And the day and night we were at Multon's, you pointed me toward that wench, and you stayed up with Multon after I went—"

He became aware his grandmother had switched her glare from Aylton to him again. "Um," he said and stopped.

Mistress Thorncoffyn returned her glare to Aylton as Master Soule ventured, "This might be better talked over in a more private place. I would . . ."

Mistress Thorncoffyn waved the parchment at Aylton. "This says what they say it says. I've known Harry Multon, boy and man. Longer than I've known you, that's sure. I take his word over yours. Take these men's, too, if he vouches for them. You've been looking to cheat me, Aylton!" She shoved the parchment at his face. He put up both hands to protect himself. She pushed the parchment into them and grabbed her staff away from Geoffrey.

Aylton, fumbling with the parchment, did not see the first blow coming. Mistress Thorncoffyn's staff cracked along the side of his head and he staggered sideways. Dropping the parchment, he put up his hands to protect his head from her next blow, but she swung in below his raised arms, thudding the staff hard against his ribs, staggering him again as cries of alarm broke out all around them, Idany drawing back, exclaiming, "No! No!" while Geoffrey tried to catch his grandmother's arm and Cawdry did the same and Wyke stepped back well out of reach of any chance blow.

Master Soule was ordering, "No! Not here! My lady!" but retreating, too. It was Master Hewstere who moved to catch the staggering Aylton and barely missed being hit by Mistress Thorncoffyn's next blow as it came down onto Aylton's right shoulder, driving the steward to his knees and opening his head for a blow that would have probably knocked him insensible or maybe plain killed him except Geoffrey got tight hold on her arm and pulled her around and away from Aylton as Cawdry twisted the staff from her hand. Scarlet-faced and panting as after a hard run, Mistress Thorncoffyn gave up the assault and sagged against Geoffrey. He straddled his legs, bracing to take her weight.

Aylton stayed on his knees, moaning and holding himself around the ribs. He moaned worse as Master Hewstere made to raise him to his feet but did stand, albeit bent over and still moaning. The physician looked around and said at Ellis as the largest man there not part of the trouble, "Come. Help."

While Ellis went to help hold up the bent and moaning Aylton, the other players started backing away, Gil drawing gawking Piers with him, crowding aside from Sister Ursula as she came past them purposefully, saying, "Best lay him here, Master Hewstere," pointing to the bed that had been Lyttle's. "Master Thorncoffyn, also best is that you and Idany take your grandmother back to her chamber."

The other sisters had begun to move among the beds at the hall's other end, telling what had happened to those who had not clearly seen and heard, making light of it and soothing. Master Soule was shepherding Cawdry and Wyke toward Jack at the door, making sounds about seeing them out and recommending they stay at the inn just along the street while things were sorted out here.

The players left them all to it, making good their escape into the sacristy, where Ellis shortly joined them, not needed once Aylton was to bed. With all their well-honed instincts to get away from trouble—little though any was likely to come their way out of this one—they quickly and with no talk changed into their own clothing and packed their garb into the hamper for carrying back to the cart. They had given up expectation of ale and maybe something to eat as extra reward for performing. After all, they had got coins when the likelihood had seemed they would not, meaning they were still ahead. But they had failed to take account of Sister Ursula's firm hand on matters. As they went into the kitchen on their way to the back door, Gil and Ellis carrying the hamper between them, Rose was setting out wooden cups and a pottery pitcher at one end of the long table and beckoned to them, saying, "You're not forgotten. Sister Ursula said you were to have your due."

Sister Letice was at the table's other end, mixing herbs with a broad wooden spoon into a thick paste in a bowl. Beside her, a length of linen cloth lay ready to wrap it into probably several poultices. Catching Joliffe's look at them, Rose said, "Whether anything is broken or not, there'll be bruises."

"And a headache," Joliffe said.

Sister Petronilla came in. "She wants something for her heart and something to steady her breathing. She's heaving for air like a man who's run a mile when he shouldn't have."

Sister Letice handed the broad spoon to her and nodded at the linen cloths. "I'll fetch what she needs. You make the poultices."

She disappeared into the stillroom. Sister Petronilla, doing as she was bid, said to the players in her serene, firm way, "We all enjoyed your play. Thank you for it very much."

"Heinrich, too?" Joliffe asked.

"He sat quietly through it. I've put them in your room for now. Out of the way until things settle. I hope it's no matter Daveth meant to take your lute in hand? He says it helps Heinrich to hear it."

"He has gentle hands. It's no trouble if it helps," Joliffe assured her.

Sister Margaret came in. To everyone's asking looks she answered, "Master Hewstere says Aylton has a rib or so probably cracked, but not his skull, and his shoulder is only deeply bruised, not broken."

"That's all to the good then," said Sister Petronilla.

"I'm none so sure about his skull, though. The bone is not broken inward, but I'd not swear it's uncracked, and there could be an inward bruising of the brain. I don't think we can know that for a while yet, if there is. Joliffe, when you tend him, keep watch that his pupils stay even. If the blacks of his eyes go uneven, that tells there's something wrong beyond what poultices can outward do."

Joliffe nodded that he understood and offered, for what ease there was in it, "It would likely have been worse if Mistress Thorncoffyn hadn't been so close she never had a full swing at him."

Sister Petronilla, now spreading the herb-mess onto one of the linen cloths, said, "He'll be looking at worse in a different way before she's done with him if he's been looking to cheat her the way those men say."

"He will that," Sister Margaret agreed. "Or maybe to save the cost of lawyers and courts, she'll be satisfied by having Geoffrey simply finish her beating of him."

She did not sound, to Joliffe's ear, as if she were altogether jesting.

Chapter 15

The evening busyness of Vespers and supper went not much differently from usual despite everyone's sharp awareness of Aylton sometimes softly moaning behind the curtains drawn to hide his bed. Joliffe, bringing his supper, found him lying on his side with legs drawn up and head tucked down, curled in on his undoubted pain in side and head and shoulder. He had been undressed down to his shirt. The poultices and the bandages holding them to his ribs and shoulder were lumps under the shirt's fine linen, while another bandage wrapped his head, holding a third poultice there. Joliffe had no chance to see his eyes as Sister Margaret had bid. Aylton opened them only so far as needed to see who was there and why, then shut them again and slightly moved one hand in a gesture that refused the food.

Joliffe set the bowl and bread on the little table beside the bed, carefully quiet, as if even the clunk of wooden bowl on wooden table might jar the man to more pain, and said, "One of the sisters or I will come later to see about feeding it to you."

Aylton made a sound that meant nothing and did not stir. The easy-mannered, pleasant-worded steward was vanished, utterly gone from this undressed, bandaged, disheveled man in pain. Pain at its worst tended to cancel all else in a man, and Aylton was assuredly in pain that was mostly of the body at present, but Joliffe suspected there had to be a strong current of fear-pain in his mind, too, over what Mistress Thorncoffyn would purpose against him next. However well Aylton healed or did not heal, Joliffe doubted she would be satisfied with a beating as sufficient punishment for attempting to cheat her. More than likely, she would set the law on him.

Had she thought yet that he could set the law on her, too, because of the beating? Not that it would matter much to her. At the most, that would probably come to her having to pay a fine that she could readily afford, while Aylton almost surely could not afford whatever more her wrath might bring down on him. On the whole, he had more reasons than his aching body to lie there and groan.

Handing Basset his supper, Joliffe slid a look to the curtain hiding Aylton, questioning. Basset answered with a silent nod, agreeing they would not trouble the man with their voices, but no one among the other men in the hall had any care to spare Aylton their talk. Any of them who had not directly suffered himself from a corrupt steward in their time knew stories enough of others who had and were gladly telling them to each other. Joliffe, returning to the kitchen, was thankful the players had not played *The Steward and the Devil* today, because in it he would have been the Devil who took the Steward to Hell at the end, and the jesting at him now about when he would take Aylton away would have surely become tedious both for him and Aylton.

Joliffe was clearing the supper dishes to the scullery, Master Soule could be heard saying Compline in the chapel, and the sisters were finishing their own supper when there was a hurried padding of feet in the passageway, bringing Idany at a rush into the kitchen demanding as she came, "My lady is in pain. You." At Joliffe. "Go for Master Hewstere. Tell him her stomach is cramping worse than ever, the pain worse than it has been." And at Sister Letice, qualms against her apparently forgotten, "She needs something to help her. Be quick at it!"

Sister Letice looked to Sister Ursula, who nodded. As Sister Letice started for the stillroom, Joliffe heard her saying mostly under her breath, "Mallow. No, not at this season. Mint? Horehound, yes," while he asked at Sister Ursula, "Where's Master Hewstere likely to be now?"

"Home. He lives three houses beyond the church."

"Hurry!" Idany ordered, and because for once she sounded truly urgent rather than merely sharp, Joliffe hurried. In the foreporch passage, he took a quick look through the doorways to Mistress Thorncoffyn's rooms as he passed, left open by Idany in her haste, and saw the woman sitting bent forward in her broad chair to as nearly double as she could go. Her arms were wrapped across the bulge of her belly, and Geoffrey was bent over her, his arms around her shoulders, either to comfort or brace her as she gave a groaning cry long and loud enough it followed Joliffe into the yard. The pain in that cry was real and deep, and Joliffe broke into a run.

Master Hewstere answered his own door at Joliffe's heavy knocking. At Joliffe's quick telling of Idany's message, he bid Joliffe return to say he was coming, only he needed to gather some things. Joliffe bowed and returned to the hospital at a run, to find Idany hovering with wringing hands in the inner doorway of Mistress Thorncoffyn's rooms.

Sister Ursula and Sister Letice were already there, with Sister Ursula and Geoffrey on either side of Mistress Thorncoffyn, trying to steady and maybe comfort her while Sister Letice hovered close, holding a cup.

At Joliffe's word that Master Hewstere was coming, Idany gave an impatient exclamation, shoved him from her way, and hurried out. Joliffe wondered if maybe she was intent on dragging the physician faster if he would not hurry on his own. It was his own chance to escape, but he did not take it, held by sight of Mistress Thorncoffyn suddenly straightening and straining backward in her chair, head thrown back as if she were trying to pull away from the pain in her guts clutched under her hands. Sister Letice leaned over her, trying to hold the cup to her lips, but Mistress Thorncoffyn, eyes and mouth tightly shut, twisted her head from side to side, refusing.

Joliffe heard Idany returning and shifted out of her way. Idany, ignoring him, hurried past, exclaiming, "He's here! Master Hewstere is come!"

Not far behind her, Master Hewstere strode in, ignoring Joliffe as thoroughly as Idany had, and instantly demanded at Sister Letice, "What are you giving her?"

Sister Letice startled back, her face reddening, but Sister Ursula said firmly at him, "Horehound and honey in warmed wine. What you've always said is safe for a troubled belly."

Master Hewstere granted ungraciously, "That's well enough." And then to Mistress Thorncoffyn, suddenly smooth with persuasion, "You'd do well to drink it, my lady. Here." He took the cup from Sister Letice. "Gently now." Obedient to him, Mistress Thorncoffyn drank.

Joliffe suddenly wondered where her dogs were, why they weren't underfoot and yapping, then saw them in a huddled heap against the pillows at the head of the bed, all curled and tucked around each other, with here and there a bright and watching eye fixed on their mistress. No fools they, getting themselves safely out of the way but still able to see everything that went on with their mistress, he thought.

"A vomitive first," Master Hewstere was saying with firm authority. "Then perhaps a purgative, to completely cleanse."

Joliffe decided the dogs had the right of it: safely out of

the way was what he wanted to be, too, and he quickly withdrew, hoping as he went that he would not later be called
back to help with the outcomes of what Master Hewstere
purposed. Cowardly desire or not, he was not in the least
ashamed of it.

In the kitchen, he found Sister Margaret readying to make
the men's evening drink. "On the chance Sister Letice isn't
freed in time," she said. "It's to be stronger again tonight, to
help after today's upsets. Has Master Hewstere come?"

"He's there now."

"Then likely Sister Letice and Sister Ursula won't be
wanted much longer. Sister Petronilla is in the scullery, seeing to the bowls and cups."

Joliffe went to take her place and found that with Daveth's
help and despite Heinrich sitting on the floor between her
feet, she was well along toward being done. He thanked her,
she welcomed him with her ready smile, dried her hands on
her apron, scooped up Heinrich, took Daveth by the hand,
and left, to see about putting them both to bed. Setting to
scrubbing, Joliffe briefly wondered how it would be when
Heinrich was too big to scoop up and carry.

He finished what little was left to do and returned to the
kitchen where Sister Ursula was standing with two of the
pottery jars from the stillroom in her hand, asking Sister
Margaret, "But both a vomitive and a purgative? Is that wise,
do you think?"

"That's not for me to say," Sister Margaret said with sus-
picious sweetness. She took up the pitcher and began to
pour the men's herbed ale into cups already set out on the
tray on the table there. "I'm sure Master Hewstere will do
what's for the best for her."

"What's 'for the best for her' will likely mean a hellish
night for Sister Letice and me," Sister Ursula pointed out.
"And for Geoffrey," she added, noticeably more cheerfully.

"His loving grandmother is keeping him right there beside her, grabbing hold on him when the pains are worse. He'll have bruises by morning."

Sister Letice hurried in. "Couldn't you find—" She broke off, seeing the jars Sister Ursula held, exclaimed, "Those are the ones, yes," seized them, and hurried out again.

"These are ready," Sister Margaret said, setting down the pitcher, the cups filled, and for a little time the evening went its usual way, with Joliffe carrying the tray for Sister Ursula and Sister Margaret to give the men their drinks, helping the men to settle for the night, making sure they were all as comfortable as might be and in need of nothing. Only Aylton resisted the sleeping draught, refusing to uncurl or even open his eyes. "Later. Leave it," he muttered.

"It will ease the pain and help you to sleep," Sister Ursula urged gently, bending over him. "Drink now, while I'm here to help you." She leaned closer, as if waiting for an answer. None came, or if it did, it was muttered too low for Joliffe to hear, and was refusal, because Sister Ursula straightened, set the cup on the small table beside the bed, said, "It's here if you want it," and came away.

The day should have been done then, but there was still Mistress Thorncoffyn. As Joliffe and the sisters left the hall, Sister Letice came from the kitchen carrying a large basin of steaming water. To Sister Margaret's question of how Mistress Thorncoffyn did, she said, "The vomitive has worked. Master Hewstere is going to bleed her next. Then will come a purgative, he says. Thank you," she added to Joliffe as he took the basin from her, finding it as heavy as it looked. Then to Sister Ursula she said, "He wants you there now, but I'm dismissed, I'm afraid. I questioned the dose of purgative Master Hewstere means to give her. He said I was overly bold and foolish into the bargain to question anything he did."

Sister Ursula sighed. "It's assuredly not you who is the fool. Since I doubt Sister Margaret would be welcomed more than you, best you go and tell Sister Petronilla of her misfortune. Sister Margaret, go to bed."

Sister Margaret went away toward the bed in the pantry, her place for tonight. Joliffe had a belated fear that by carrying the basin he had opened himself to having to help clean Mistress Thorncoffyn and was relieved when that martyrdom was not asked of him, when at the outer door of Mistress Thorncoffyn's rooms, as Sister Letice went on to the stairs up to the dorter, Sister Ursula took the basin from him, thanked him, and told him he had best take this chance to have what sleep he could, should the men prove restless despite all that had been done to give them a quiet night. He thanked her in return and willingly went to do as she bid.

Either the stronger nighttime drinks served their purpose, or else the day's excitements had tired the men enough to ensure they all slept deeply. No one needed Joliffe until just at dawn, when Deke Credy needed help with his bed-pot. That tended to, and with stirrings in other beds along the hall, and the certainty that Sister Margaret would be up from the pallet in the pantry soon and the other sisters down from their dorter—supposing Sister Ursula and Sister Petronilla had eventually got to their beds—Joliffe put aside thought of returning to his own bed. Instead, he went to see how Aylton did.

The bed was empty.

Joliffe stood staring at it, momentarily bemused to see only the pillow, rumpled sheets, and a blanket where there should have been a man. Then he bent and looked *under* the bed because the man had to be *somewhere*.

There was only the bed-pot and a crumpled heap of cloth that were the bandages of Aylton's poultices.

Out of sight beyond the curtain to the right, Basset whispered, "How does he?"

Joliffe stepped sideways and to Basset's side before answering softly, "He's not there."

The hall was still in gray shadow, morning light not yet falling through the high windows; Joliffe could not see Basset's face clearly but the pause then was as blank-minded as his own had been, until Basset said, "He's gone?"

"He's not there, only his bandages. I'd call that gone. So are his clothes." That had been laid on the stool beside the bed. "You didn't hear him leave?"

"I slept soundly all the night, heard nothing. How could he leave?"

"Very slowly?" A pain-huddled shuffle was the most Joliffe could see Aylton able to do after yesterday's beating.

"You're sure he's gone?"

"Well, he's gone from bed. How *far* he's gone is another matter."

"As far as he can get from Mistress Thorncoffyn would be my guess."

Joliffe shrugged in silent agreement with that and went to see if Aylton had maybe collapsed somewhere between the hall and the outer gateway. He had not, and since the bar was still across the gate, no one had gone out that way unless they had asked Jack's help, which Jack was unlikely to have given to an injured man in need of care. To be thorough, though, Joliffe unbarred and opened the gate enough to put his head out to look both ways along the road. Out here there was daylight enough—and more by the moment as sunrise neared—that if someone had been lying on the road, he could have seen them, but he saw no one. That Aylton might have fallen into the ditch along the sides called for more of a search than he was ready to make, and he pulled his head back in, barred the gate again, and went to tell the sisters they had lost one of their patients.

He found all of them in the kitchen, setting about breaking their fast. Sister Margaret looked the better for what

must have been a full night's sleep like Joliffe's, but Sister Ursula's and Sister Petronilla's gray-shadowed eyes and slumped
shoulders told their night had been very otherwise.

"It went on for hours," Sister Ursula was saying. "Whatever
it was, it was terrible. First there was the vomiting. It started
even before Master Hewstere dosed her. Then he set her to
purging. That wracked her so violently that Master Hewstere
couldn't bleed her until well toward morning, when she was
finally able to lie quietly for a while."

"It never came to sending for Father Richard, though,"
Sister Petronilla said with an escaping yawn she only barely
covered in time.

"Thanks be to the Virgin and Saint Giles for that," Sister
Ursula said wearily.

"And Master Hewstere," Sister Petronilla said around the
end of her yawn.

"And him," Sister Ursula agreed. "Whatever it was he
fetched from his house made the difference at the end, I
think."

"What was it?" Sister Margaret asked, with more interest
in that than she had shown for whether or not her erstwhile
mother-in-law survived.

Both women shook their heads that they did not know.
"I'll ask later," Sister Ursula promised. "Sister Letice, I think
I took the last of the mint from the stillroom last night.
Master Hewstere needed it to mix with honey to settle her
stomach."

"Um." Nodding, Sister Letice swallowed a mouthful of
bread and started to draw back from the table as if more than
willing to go to the garden on the instant. "I'll get more now,
to have it ready at need."

"There's something else," Joliffe put in. "Aylton is gone."

Four sets of startled eyes widened toward him. "Have you
looked for him?" Sister Margaret demanded. "He's hardly fit
to go far."

"I only just found his bed empty. I've only looked to the foreyard yet."

"Poor man," Sister Letice said. "To be that afraid to stay that's he's dragged himself away."

But she was already done with her surprise and went on out the door while Sister Ursula was saying to the others, "He has reason enough to be afraid. Mistress Thorncoffyn means to have the sheriff on him. That will be gaol at the very least."

Sister Margaret, having paused with one hand on the loaf the sisters were sharing, her other hand poised with the breadknife over it, went back to slicing as she said, "I don't see why we should trouble ourselves to look for him, though. We've all duties enough."

A moment of considering silence met that suggestion before Sister Ursula said, "Yes. Master Aylton is no concern of ours now he's out of our care. He's a matter for the Thorncoffyns to pursue or not, as they choose. Too, with him gone, it means we can send word to Agnes Kemp that she can bring her grandfather today after all."

From earlier talk, Joliffe knew this Agnes was someone who had been wearing out herself in care of her increasingly decayed grandfather while trying to help her husband in the fields and tend to three children. She had been promised her grandfather would have the next bed that came empty; the only reason he had not been in it yesterday was he had refused "another man's bed before the fellow is fully cold in his grave," as one of her sons had come to tell Sister Ursula. He might have had to wait longer because of Aylton, so Aylton's flight was to the good there, whatever stir the Thorncoffyns might make because of it.

Idany came into the kitchen, for once without her usual thrusting haste. She looked even wearier than the sisters, with her headkerchief limp and her apron stained in ways Joliffe took care not to see too closely. Her tongue was uncurbed, though. With almost her usual sharpness, she demanded, "My lady wants a warm posset."

"Has Master Hewstere advised she eat yet?" Sister Ursula asked wearily.

"He hasn't come yet this morning. It doesn't matter. She wants it. It's *you* who must make it, mind." Her baleful sideways look at Sister Margaret, making clear who was not to touch it, was interrupted by Sister Letice and Rose coming in, in such a rush together that everyone turned toward them, beginning to be alarmed even before Sister Letice exclaimed, "It's Master Aylton!" and Rose cried out, "He's dead!"

Chapter 16

Everyone stared at them, startled beyond words or moving until Sister Ursula demanded, "He's dead? You're sure of that?"

Both women, short of breath, jerked their heads in assurance. Rose sank down on the bench beside the table, but Sister Letice gathered breath and said, "He was in the stream. He was lying there, his head in the water. I pulled him out and turned him over and he's dead, yes."

With open satisfaction, Idany declared, "He must have tried to slip away in the night, only he hadn't the strength for it and collapsed into the stream instead and drowned. As served him right, the thieving coward," she ended viciously.

Sister Margaret, as harshly and with something of the same satisfaction, said back at her, "That makes Mistress Thorncoffyn guilty of manslaughter, doesn't it?"

The satisfaction disappeared from Idany's face. She gaped at Sister Margaret, then whirled away and hurried from the kitchen. Behind her, the sisters were already steadying out of their first sharp surprise. Death was too familiar a matter here, was something to be dealt with, not exclaimed at, and Sister Ursula said, "She'll see to telling Mistress Thorncoffyn and Geoffrey. Joliffe, you must find the bailiff. He's John Borton. His house is on the right just the other side of the marketplace as you go into town. By now he may be gone to the fields, but someone will know where he is. He'll send someone for the constable and crowner."

Joliffe would have liked a word with Rose but could only lay a hand briefly on her shoulder as he passed, catching her glance and strained smile up at him in return. Behind him, as he went out, Sister Ursula was saying, "Sister Letice, go back and keep watch by the body, to be sure no one moves it more. It should stay untouched until the crowner sees it," at the same time that Sister Margaret was saying, "I'll fetch a sheet to put over him."

Jack was unbarring the gate for the day as Joliffe came from the hospital. Told what had happened, he shook his head over it and hoped Joliffe would find Borton still at home. Borton was, and at Joliffe's report, asked, "This Master Aylton. He's the fellow got himself beaten yesterday?" At Joliffe's surprised look, he added, "There was talk at the tavern last night."

Joliffe's surprise went away. "That's him."

Borton sent one of his servants to find the constable, someone named Credy, telling Joliffe, "Happens he has an uncle in your place," before adding, "He'll know who best to send for the crowner," because a crowner might take some finding. Only a few and largest of towns had their own. Mostly, two crowners served for a whole shire and so could be anywhere besides home when needed, since one or the other of them had to be summoned to look into all unexpected deaths, to rule whether there had been simply an accident or else a crime that turned it into a matter for the sheriff and royal fines and punishment.

"After you've given him the word, though," Borton told

his man, "you go straight on to the field. I'll be along as soon as might be." And to Joliffe, "Let's go, then," not troubling to hide his impatience at having to delay his day's right work. Harvest, being life or death for everyone, was more important than one unfamiliar man's death.

As they came to the hospital, they encountered Father Richard leaving the church. His look of surprise at seeing Borton changed to distress when he was told why. "I should come, too," he said. "Prayers for his soul are needed, surely."

"Surely," Borton agreed.

As the three of them were crossing the foreyard, Jack called from his window above them, asking why they had not gone by way of the orchard gate. "It would have been shorter."

Father Richard made an impatient sound at himself and said, "Of course it would be. I wasn't thinking."

"Nor was I," Borton said easily. "I raided apples enough there when I was young. Never mind. Come on then."

Joliffe was fairly certain he should give over following them and turn to his own right work, but only Rose was in the kitchen as they passed through, and she did no more than catch his eye and raise her eyebrows at him. He raised his in return and kept going, leaving her shaking her head. Outside again and trailing the two men along the path through the garden, Joliffe saw Sister Letice, standing beside the stream in her appointed guard over the sheet-covered form on the grass. Emme and Amice were hovering not far off, no more seeing to their work than Joliffe was to his. That no one else was there meant word of the death had not spread beyond the hospital yet, to bring the curious. And that Sister Ursula, Sister Margaret, and Sister Petronilla were either more devoted to their duties, Joliffe thought wryly, or better restrained in their curiosity than he was.

Sister Letice moved away, joining Emme and Amice, as the men approached. Borton gave them a nod but his heed was on the body, and while Father Richard knelt, signed a cross toward it, and bent his head to pray, Borton said with heavy resignation, "Best have a look, I suppose." And to Joliffe, "You, help me lay the sheet back."

With the strangely large respect so often given to a dead body surely past caring, Joliffe and Borton each took an upper corner of the sheet and lifted it back into careful folds at the corpse's feet.

As Sister Letice had said, it was Aylton and he was beyond doubting dead. After pulling him from the water and turning him over, she must not have touched him again. His legs were twisted one over the other from when she turned him over, his arms were flopped out loosely at his sides, and his head was canted crookedly, the hair flattened wetly to it, his mouth gaping, his eyes a little open. He was fully clothed. Either before or after getting himself out of the hospital, he had managed to dress, and that must have cost him some pain, given that by then he must have been stiffened with his bruises and all. To suffer through that, he had been very determined on escaping.

Well, he *had* escaped, although more thoroughly than he intended, Joliffe thought. He had made it this far, then collapsed, unfortunately into the stream, either senseless or too weak to push himself out. That yesterday's violence to him had played a part in that was probable, but how much his death would be ruled his own accidental doing versus how much Mistress Thorncoffyn might be held responsible for it would likely turn into a matter giving several lawyers a good income before it was settled.

That was all for later. Here and now, what caught most deeply at Joliffe was, as always, the utter emptiness of a dead body. Where there had been someone alive a while ago, now there was only a dead and useless corpse, all its point and purpose gone. That was likely why the immediate urge was always there to straighten and tidy a dead body, to give it what little dignity it could have in the while left to it. This particular body, though, no one moved to straighten. Given the death was unwitnessed and therefore uncertain, the body was supposed to be left as it was for the crowner to see. With the warm weather and all, if the crowner was likely to be too long delayed in coming, the constable might decide to have it moved after all and the town pay the fine for doing so. For now, though, waiting for the constable, Father Richard prayed and Borton stood staring away into the apple trees, rocking a little back and forth on his heels. With nothing more to see or do, Sister Letice drifted away into the garden, and Emme and Amice, too, were starting to draw away when Jack came limping through the garden. Leaving Emme, Amice went to him, took his hand. He gave her a gentle kiss on the cheek, then looked past her to the little gathering beside the stream and said, "He's truly dead then. Mistress Thorncoffyn won't be best pleased." He took another step forward for a clearer look. "Daveth will be, though."

"Daveth?" Joliffe echoed in surprise. He could imagine Mistress Thorncoffyn displeased at being forestalled from whatever miseries of the law she had planned for Aylton, but, "Where does Daveth come into it?"

"Daveth was afraid of him," Jack said. "Aylton liked to slap or hit him if he chanced on him alone. Daveth told me he once kicked Heinrich, too. Heinrich doesn't seem to notice much, but he's sense enough to be afraid of Aylton afterward. It was Daveth asked me to come be sure Aylton was really dead. Now I can tell him that he is. Ah, well, back to the gate with me."

"To the laundry with us," Emme said. "Come on, girl."

The three of them went away together. For them, Aylton's death was no more than a briefly interesting interruption of their usual days, while for Daveth it would be welcome; for Mistress Thorncoffyn and possibly Geoffrey, a disappointment; for those like Borton whose duty required them to deal with it, an annoyance. Was there anyone to whom Aylton's death would mean more? It was a sad thought that perhaps, no, there was not.

Despite knowing it was time he went back to his own right duties, Joliffe went forward, to the other side of Aylton's body from Father Richard, bent, and lifted the corpse's nearer hand. Besides clay-pale, the flesh was cold and slack, as if already beginning its slump off the bones, but the arm moved only unwillingly. Borton made a half-inquiring, half-disapproving sound. Joliffe laid the hand carefully down where it had been and said, "He's stiffened. He's been dead a fair while."

"Since well before dawn, I'd guess," Borton agreed. "He wasn't trying to make his escape by first light anyway."

The year was not so many weeks past the short nights of mid-summer that a night's hours were all that long yet. They were long enough, though, that if Aylton had got himself from the hall soon after Sister Margaret made her last round for the night and got his horse out of the inn's stable and away, he could have been a good many miles from here by now, with no one likely to know which way he had gone.

But if Aylton had headed back to the inn to get his horse and maybe whatever else he had left there, he must have been counting on Geoffrey being still here with his grandmother. Had he known she was ill? Probably not, and would not have dared risk going to the inn while there were folk up and about and the chance of meeting Geoffrey. So had he stayed in his bed until he thought it was late enough to chance going, or had he left the hospital, meaning to lurk somewhere near the inn until the hour was late enough he could hope to slip in unnoticed?

Then again, did it matter when he left? Whenever he did, he had only come this far and no farther.

Or was it just too . . . simple that Aylton should have struggled this far only to collapse in the one place and one way sure to kill him?

Simple sometimes happened. In fact, simple was usually the way of things. Simple stupidity. Simple greed. Simple carelessness.

But sometimes simple was . . . too simple.

Joliffe's eyes had been traveling while his thoughts did, and he heard himself saying aloud, "No sign of struggle here."

Borton said in surprise, "Why would there be?"

Joliffe shrugged. "I only say it."

Father Richard signed himself with the cross, sighed, stood up, and said sadly, "He passed from aware to unaware and fell and died without time for even a prayer for God's mercy. A great many prayers are going to be needed for his soul."

"Not that Mistress Thorncoffyn is likely to pay for them," Borton said. "She's more likely to stomp on his grave once he's in it. Here comes Credy."

Joliffe looked up and around from his thoughts woven among the long water weeds waving in the swirling clear flow of the stream just beyond Aylton's head to see a tall man coming through the garden. He looked no happier at having to be there than Borton did. He greeted Father Richard, traded a wordless nod with Borton, apparently summed up Joliffe as a servant, and gave his heed to the corpse, brooding down at it for a long moment before saying, "Aye, he's dead. He's the fellow someone here beat on yesterday?"

"He's the one," Borton agreed.

"Think that's what killed him?"

"Hard to say yet. Could have drowned."

"Not of purpose," Credy said, flatly enough that Joliffe was uncertain whether he meant it seriously or was making a jest of someone trying for self-murder in so shallow a stream.

"Accident then," Borton suggested.

"Likely."

Credy changed his heed to Joliffe. "You found the body?"

"No, I . . . ." Was there for no better reason than naked

curiosity, but he was saved from having to say so by Master Hewstere, saying harshly from behind them, "Why wasn't I summoned immediately? Why did I have to hear of this only after I came to the hospital to make my morning round?"

All the men turned to stare at him. A little beyond and aside from him, Sister Letice was standing, her hands twisted into her apron. If he had troubled to greet her at all, it must have been by no more than a silent gesture, set on his indignation as he was. "I should have been called immediately when he was found!"

Borton shrugged, openly not so impressed as Master Hewstere intended him to be. "No point in having you here. There was no doubting he was dead."

With every show of outrage at someone presuming to usurp his prerogative as a physician to recognize death and life, Master Hewstere demanded, "On whose word was that determined?" As if death, several hours on as this one had been, was not simple enough for anyone to determine, physician or not.

Softly, Sister Letice said, "I told them."

Master Hewstere turned on her. "You?" He sounded both incredulous and offended. "You presumed to determine he was dead?"

"His head was in the water. He wasn't moving. I—pulled him out," she said as if suddenly uncertain she should have.

"You *moved* the body?" Master Hewstere exclaimed. "You're supposed to leave bodies where they're found!"

"Ah, but he might not have been a body yet, see," said Joliffe, to draw Hewstere off Sister Letice and deliberately sounding as thick as the plank across the stream, "Might have still been alive, see. Couldn't tell, with his head in the water like that."

Master Hewstere turned on him with a glare. "You. Why are you here?"

Joliffe was spared answering that by Amice calling from

the far side of the garden, "Joliffe! Emme says we'll be needing water and wood soon. When are you coming?"

"Now," he called back, made a single hurried bow to priest, constable, bailiff, and—vaguely—physician all at once, and escaped. Behind him Credy was saying as he went, "What we need from you, sir, is to know whether there are any hurts on him new from yesterday when you saw him. Anything that might have put him in the water. Head bashed or something."

That was to the good. Even while openly wishing he did not have the bother, it seemed the constable meant to know all he could about Aylton's death.

Joliffe was stacking his last armload of firewood in the laundry when Emme said to Amice and him both, "Come see," and they joined her at the doorway to watch Sister Ursula leading a small procession into the yard, Borton and Credy following her with Aylton's body carried between them, followed by Father Richard, Master Hewstere, and trailing them all, another man Joliffe did not know, carrying a wooden box of no great size. Sister Ursula stopped outside one of the open-sided, empty sheds on the rear-yard's other side, said something to the men with a gesture that seemed to invite them to use of the shed, and left them. She might have gone straight back to the hospital, except Emme called to her and she turned aside to the laundry, answering before anyone could ask, "I know it's over-soon to be moving the body, not even giving the crowner time to be here. But our Master Hewstere claimed he couldn't look for new hurts on Aylton if he wasn't laid out somewhere and properly stripped." She glanced over her shoulder to where Borton and Credy had set down the body and were dragging forward trestles and boards to the shed's middle. She lowered her voice. "I think he was hoping to put it off altogether."

"Umph," said Emme. "That's like enough. Would rather deal with men decently dead on a bed, where they ought to be, than gone astray and some place he might get his hands dirty."

"His luck missed him this time. John Credy wasn't having it. So—" She beckoned her head toward the shed. She fixed a look on Joliffe. "Are you done here?"

"Nearly." There was still the water to raise from the well.

She nodded and went away. At the shed, the constable and bailiff were lifting the body onto the trestle table they had made. Father Richard had stationed himself to one side, still praying. Master Hewstere was as yet keeping his distance. The man whom Joliffe did not know had slid down onto his heels with his back against the wall of the neighboring shed, his box set on the cobbles beside him. Emme waved to him; he waved back. Joliffe asked, "Who's he?"

"Dick Denton. He's barber-surgeon hereabout. John Credy must want to go a bit deeper with things," Emme said. She chuckled at her own jest as she turned around to her work. Amice, making a small sound of disgust, followed her. Joliffe with a small, agreeing groan turned toward the well. "Deeper" meant slicing Aylton's body open to see what could be learned there, and since no physician with any respect for himself cared to dirty his hands on a body—most especially dead ones—barbers, with the sharp-bladed razors and the basin of their trade, were called on to do cutting and sewing when nobler medicines were not enough. There were even guilds of barber-surgeons, to make plain their double calling. In some places abroad there were schools, Joliffe knew, where surgery was taught as a learned skill, but men with that learning were mostly only to be found in such places as London and York and Paris. For most folk it was their plain barber-surgeon who was to hand to do the ugly work to which physicians would never stoop.

Finished with filling the large laundry kettles and woefully behind on his other morning duties, Joliffe knew it was time he returned to them but somehow found himself strolling across the yard and sitting down on his own heels beside the barber. They traded friendly nods, and Joliffe asked quietly, tipping his head toward the shed where Master Hewstere had now joined Credy and Borton at the body, "What do you hear from there?"

The man was at ease about it, happy to talk. "They haven't found anything more than the bruises he got yesterday, seems. When it's my turn, I'll be looking to see if the skull is cracked more than Master Clean-Hands thinks it is. Something like that will kill a man slow but sure and not show much. Then Credy wants me to see if there's water in his lungs or not. Doesn't think the fellow looks for sure like he drowned. Be interesting to see." He grinned with broad mischief. "You want to watch?"

Joliffe had not a moment's hesitation at grinning back and answering, "No. Best I get back to my right work, come to that." He stood up. "When you're done, they'll likely let you wash there." He nodded at the laundry.

"Oh, aye. Emme is cousin to me. She'll see me clean."

They traded final, friendly nods, and Joliffe—all too aware of how far ahead the morning had gone—finally returned to the kitchen. The sisters were gathered around the table, chopping vegetables; Heinrich was with his wooden spoon under the table; Rose was stirring a pot over the fire. He immediately apologized to Sister Ursula for being so late back. Continuing to reduce an onion to small pieces, she answered, undisturbed, "Rose said you would likely be a while."

Joliffe shot a look at Rose. She stayed very occupied with her stirring.

"So I thought I would leave you to it," Sister Ursula continued. "That way you can tell us what is toward. No one else is likely to. So. What have they found so far?"

"There's no sign yet he died by other than plain ill-luck."

Sister Ursula let the onion rest; Sister Petronilla stopped cutting carrots; Sister Letice paused at chopping herbs. Sister

Margaret, her knife poised above the cabbage she was slicing, joined their look at him and asked, pointedly and for all of them, "Yet?"

Quite aware of how sharp these women were, he said, "From what's said so far, there are only yesterday's hurts on his body. The constable wants the barber—Denton?" The women's heads all nodded. "Wants him to see if maybe the blow to Master Aylton's head was worse than Master Hewstere thinks it was, and to make sure there's water in his lungs to show he drowned. If there's water in his lungs or the blow to his head was worse than it seemed, then likely that will be the end of it. Maybe the constable or crowner will want to know when he left the hospital. Maybe he'll even ask why all the other men slept soundly after their night-drinks but Aylton did not."

"Because he never drank it," Sister Ursula said. "I left it for him, remember, but this morning . . ."

". . . we found he'd poured it into his bed-pot when we came to empty them," Sister Petronilla said.

Instantly guilty, Joliffe said, "I'm sorry about the bed-pots. I . . ."

"We've had to do the bed-pots before this," Sister Petronilla said serenely. "Did us no harm at all. Daveth and I scrubbed the breakfast bowls and mugs, too."

"It's no matter," Sister Ursula assured him. The wicked merriment she sometimes betrayed glinted briefly. "Not if you can go on telling us what we might not otherwise hear about all this, to recompense whatever work you slack."

"So long as you don't slack too much," Sister Margaret put in.

"I'll not," Joliffe rashly promised. After all, his duties in the hall would let him draw talk about last night from the other men, on the chance they might not all have slept as thoroughly as the women thought they had. Someone among them might help him with his worry over how Aylton had left the hospital. That was the way his curiosity was turned now. The shortest way from the hall to the garden and the stream there would have taken Aylton past his own door, and since France and after these past months of training he did not sleep either as easily or as deeply as he used to. He would have awakened at the slightest sound of someone moving anywhere near his door. The stealth of a footfall meant to go unheard past his door would have jerked him awake.

Nor did he doubt that if Aylton had left the hall by the door into the sacristy and tried to cut through the pantry to the kitchen, Sister Margaret would have awakened. So Aylton must have gone through the sacristy and out by way of Master Soule's small, private garden. Someone would have to ask Master Soule if the door to the garden had been locked or barred or on the latch last night and whether it had still been that way this morning.

Idany's all-too-familiar tread along the passageway warned she was coming. Sister Ursula gave a deep and resigned sigh, laid down her knife, and began to wipe her hands on her apron. Idany, coming into the kitchen, had something of the same resigned air and only said heavily, instead of with her usual sharp demand, "Do you know where Master Hewstere is? My lady wants him to come. One of the dogs is sick."

Chapter 17

Sent to fetch the physician, Joliffe was glad to see him coming out of the shed and Denton readying to go in. When told why he was wanted, Master Hewstere said disgustedly, "One of her *dogs*. It's not enough she eats whatever she chooses, pleasuring the gross matter of the body against all common sense, no matter what I say of how the body's humours must be balanced. And she feeds those dogs the same way. You, come with me on the chance I have to send for something." He stalked, still muttering, toward the hospital. His tiredness after his long night had likely betrayed him into saying all that for someone as nothing as Joliffe to hear and surely among the following mutters Joliffe was not meant to hear, "The *exceedingly* gross matter of her body."

Joliffe did not care what Master Hewstere muttered. His own thoughts were gone back to the problem of Aylton. The steward must have left the hall by way of the sacristy and through Master Soule's small garden, but if so, then why had he come around to go through the kitchen garden? It made little sense. From Master Soule's garden and from there to the road into town, to the inn and his horse that were his most likely goals, the simplest way was along the alley that ran along the master's garden and that side of the hospital. At one of its ends, the alley opened onto the road itself. At the other, it met the cart lane that ran between the rear-yard and the fields beyond. Maybe Aylton had been wary of taking the road, though he could have probably gone unseen that way in the deep dark if he held off until late enough in the night.

The other way, the one he must have chosen, was by the cart track behind the hospital. By it, he would have come to one of the side ways into town, closer to the inn with less time to be seen on the road. Well enough. But if that was what he intended, why had he left the cart track for the hospital's rear-yard and gone almost its full length, almost back to the hospital—the one place he had most reason to be away from—to reach the alley into the kitchen garden? Did he know the players were camped in the orchard near the cart track and feared to go past them? But why would he think there was less risk in circling back close to the hospital than going past the players, unlikely to trouble about someone going along the cart track if that someone did not trouble them?

The one sure thing was that he must have meant to go through the orchard. That was the only reason Joliffe could see for him having gone the way he did. But that would have simply brought him back to the road no more than a little closer to town than if he had gone straight there along the alley outside Master Soule's garden. Had he feared Jack seeing him from the gatehouse? In the middle of the night? In the deep dark? The hospital did not keep a lantern burning by the gate all night. Even if Jack saw a man-shape passing by, Jack would not have known who it was.

His choice must have made sense to Aylton, but it did not to Joliffe. Not sufficient sense. Not sense sufficient for him to stop wondering about it. Because if Aylton dying where he did did not make sense, could there be something else wrong about his death? Something more than plain mischance?

Joliffe's thoughts were taken away from Aylton by sight of Mistress Thorncoffyn as he followed Master Hewstere into her chamber. She was sitting in her wide chair, wrapped in a violently yellow bedrobe, her hair bound up under a coiled cloth, and the past night's misery showing in the great slump of her body and her face's paleness, under-shadowed at the eyes by gray. One of her dogs was cuddled under each of her over-fleshed arms. Two others were crouched against her skirts at her feet. The ill one lay twitching and whimpering in a cushioned basket on the chest at the bedfoot, with Idany hovering beside it and Geoffrey standing a few feet away with a look on his face that could have been either pained sympathy or else an attempt to hide disgust.

"It's Kydd," Mistress Thorncoffyn said at Master Hewstere, her voice weak but her fierceness still there. "He's in pain. Make him well."

"If I can, my lady." Master Hewstere made a bow that included both her and Geoffrey and went to the dog. Joliffe, not needing to be told to keep out of the way, stopped just inside the door, watching from there as Master Hewstere briefly handled and slightly prodded at the dog before stepping back and saying with no shading of doubt, "He's dying. There's nothing I can do."

Geoffrey went quickly to his grandmother, putting a comforting hand on her shoulder as she flung back, "I won't have it. There's something you can do. Do it."

"My lady, I can't stop death."

"You had better!" She made to rise but had strength only to lurch a little forward in her chair before sinking back, gasping.

Geoffrey, hand still on her shoulder, said, "Grandmother, some things aren't possible."

"But he was well as any of them yesterday!" she wailed.

"Why is he dying?" Tears rose in her eyes, and the broad bulges of her bosom heaved with coming sobs. "*Why?*"

With a practiced sympathy meant to slide oil-smooth and soothing over someone else's grief, Master Hewstere said, "Death comes in its own way, in its own time, my lady. It's all as God wills."

Idany, not soothing at all, declared from beside the bed, "It's the candied ginger. That's what's done it."

"But ginger is *good* for the stomach," Mistress Thorncoffyn protested at the same time Master Hewstere exclaimed, "You fed *ginger* to the dog?"

"Not of purpose," Geoffrey said in hurried defense. "She dropped a piece. Kydd gobbled it before anyone could stop him. They're all used to her dropping treats and bits to them. He thought it was for him."

And had gulped it down too fast to taste it, Joliffe supposed, because he could not imagine any dog chewing through a sharp-tanged piece of even sugar-soaked candied ginger on purpose.

"A dog's gut is not made to take ginger," Master Hewstere pronounced. "It's undoubtedly lodged in his bowels. There's surely nothing to be done."

Kydd writhed and moaned as if to make his point the plainer. Mistress Thorncoffyn moaned, too, and cried out, "A purgative would do it! Give him a purgative."

"Since his bowel is obstructed by the undigested matter, a dose of anything strong enough to shift it would kill him in even worse pain."

Kydd writhed and yelped. Mistress Thorncoffyn clutched the two other dogs to her more tightly. "At least ease his pain," she moaned.

"That I can do," Master Hewstere said. "You," he ordered at Joliffe. "Move the basket to that table," pointing to the one midway between the bed and door.

As Joliffe moved to obey, Idany went quickly to clear a

place among the table's clutter of things, then retreated to her lady's other side from Geoffrey. Joliffe carried and set down the basket as carefully as he could, to jar the dog as little as might be, then withdrew to the door again. Master Hewstere, coming toward the table, reached inside his long physician's robe as if to find something in an inner pocket or pouch, but brought his hand out empty as he put himself with his back to Mistress Thorncoffyn and the others—Idany offering a handkerchief for the tears rolling over Mistress Thorncoffyn's cheeks; Geoffrey still making useless soothing sounds. Only Joliffe could see how Master Hewstere put his hands to the whimpering Kydd's small head, lifted it slightly, and gave a sharp twist.

If there was any snap to the neck breaking, Joliffe did not hear it. What was heard was the sudden quiet where Kydd's pain had been, and as Master Hewstere took his hands back from the lifeless body, Mistress Thorncoffyn cried out with hope. Solemn-faced, the physician turned, held out his hands in a gesture of helplessness, and said, "It was all too late, my lady. He died as I touched him."

Well, that was true enough, Joliffe granted. More than that, the killing was a kindness in its way, the death a mercy to both poor Kydd and Mistress Thorncoffyn. What was unsettling was how Hewstere had done it with as little care as a housewife snapping a chicken's neck. Almost as unsettling was how he had not minded that Joliffe saw him do it, expecting a servant would know it was not his place either to exclaim or say what Hewstere had done.

Hewstere was right in that, of course: it was *not* Joliffe's place to say anything. But Hewstere had brought him along to help with the dog. With the dog dead, Joliffe chose to decide he would not be needed, and as Hewstere went to Mistress Thorncoffyn, adding his sympathy to Geoffrey's and Idany's, Joliffe slipped out of the room and away.

When he had passed through the kitchen with Hewstere,

he had hardly given the women a look, too busy with his thoughts about Aylton. Going now the other way, he caught their curious looks but only said as he passed them, "I'll be back directly," and went out.

Credy and Borton were standing outside the shed, looking very thoroughly away from where Denton was still at his work. Joliffe was equally careful not to see accidentally past as he asked, "Was Aylton's neck broken?"

"What?" said Credy.

Borton, catching the question more quickly, said, "No. Why?"

"I just watched Master Hewstere snap a dog's neck."

The two men's startled looks made him add, "It was dying and in pain. He helped it die more quickly, that's all. But it was deftly done." And hardly something taught in any medical school, Joliffe supposed.

"No neck snapped here," Borton assured him. "Why wonder?"

"Nor any skull broken," Denton called cheerfully from inside the shed. "Bruises and a lump are all there were on his head."

Answering Borton, Joliffe shrugged and said, "A man is dead unexpectedly. Just thinking of possibilities."

"That he fell and broke his neck on that little slope?" Borton asked.

"Only bruises otherwise," Credy said, holding to the apparent point. "No ribs or other bones broken. That much we could tell. Along with not the neck."

Behind him, Denton said, "Right then. I've the lungs open. You'll want to see for yourselves, to tell the crowner when he comes."

Credy and Borton looked at one another, each seeming to wish only the other need go in. The yearly autumn butchering of hogs and cattle, or gutting a snared rabbit for the

spit, were one thing. Seeing a man laid open in something
of the same way was something else, and they liked it no
more than Joliffe did, it seemed. They had already moved the
body, though, and so had both best be able to give clear tes-
timony when the inquest came, and they went into the shed
together. Joliffe had seen too much in Paris, knew more than
he wanted about the inside of men's bodies, and stayed where
he was, willing to be told what the others saw.

Credy came out. He seemed to have his mouth shut tightly
over more than words—holding his gorge down maybe. Behind him, Denton was asking, "I'll sew him closed now?"

Joliffe, on a new-come thought, said, "Best check his
stomach if you haven't."

"His stomach? Why?" Denton asked.

Borton joined Credy in the doorway. With both their
questioning looks on him, Joliffe followed along the stray
end of his half-thought and answered, "To see what's there.
Or isn't."

"I'll look," Denton returned cheerfully.

It was good when a man could that much enjoy his work,
Joliffe thought with far less cheer, and offered to Credy's and
Borton's still questioning looks, "It just crossed my mind he
might have eaten something he shouldn't have. What did you
see in there?"

Letting go by that feeble reasoning, Credy said, "There
was water in his lungs. He drowned, just as it looked."

"That makes it all simple," Borton said, openly pleased
and eased. "He was trying to take himself away before Mistress Thorncoffyn could bring the law in on him, but he mis-
judged his strength after her beating of him, collapsed into
the stream, and didn't have the strength to pull himself out
again."

Credy was not so eased, pointing out glumly, "That means
there's no getting around that the Thorncoffyn woman as-

saulted him yesterday. Beat him soundly. Maybe this Aylton wouldn't have brought charge against her for it, but if he died because of what she did to him, that's manslaughter."

"She's not going to like to hear that," Borton said, matching Credy's glumness.

"Stomach is out and open," Denton said. "Who's going to look?"

Borton said at Joliffe, "This was your thought. Best you come look with us."

Seeing no way out of it, Joliffe went into the shed with them. Inevitably, it had a slaughterhouse smell but Denton was good at his work: there was no widespread mess and Joliffe took care to see only the dark mass that was the stomach laid out and open beside the body. Denton was prodding inside it with various implements, lifting bits out with a small pair of pincers and taking closer look at them than Joliffe ever intended to.

"Bread," the barber-surgeon said. "Not much digested, so eaten not long before the body stopped its work. He'd had something to drink, too. Not wine, surely? You treat your folk that well in this place?"

"New ale is the best we give," Joliffe said.

"Must not be wine then. Didn't much chew the bread. Gulped it more like. See?"

He held up something at the pincers' end. Everyone seemed willing to take his word for it, and Denton grumbled, "You might as well have stayed outside if you're not going to look."

"Right you are," Borton agreed and went out.

Credy and Joliffe followed him, Credy saying as they came into the sunlight, "Here's Father Richard come to pray over him some more."

"Hold him back a time, will you?" said Denton. "Doesn't like to see a body all to pieces, he doesn't."

"Who does?" muttered Borton.

Rather than prayers, Father Richard had come to say Sister Ursula wondered if Joliffe would come help with the men's dinners. Taking his new thoughts with him and ready to apologize to everyone in the kitchen for leaving off his duties the whole morning, Joliffe went immediately, only to find that none of the women wanted apology from him, only to hear everything he knew of what was being said and done. He answered readily that Aylton had indeed drowned.

"Master Hewstere and Denton, too, say there were yesterday's bruises and bumps and no sign of trouble on him else."

"Mistress Thorncoffyn will have to answer for his death then," Sister Margaret said.

"Seems likely," Joliffe agreed, keeping to himself that the sign of trouble had not been *on* Aylton but *in* him. That bread. Busy setting the men's dinners on the trays and keeping any great interest out of his voice, he asked, "Aylton ate no supper at all last night, did he?"

"Nothing," Sister Margaret said. "I tried to have him eat even a little, but he would not."

"And nothing was missing from the kitchen," Joliffe said, rather than asked, but Sister Ursula answered, "Nothing." Then added rather too quickly, "Why?"

Picking up the first trays, Joliffe shrugged. "It's just that if he had taken something, even a bit of bread, to eat on his way, he might not have fainted and fallen as he did."

He left the kitchen to a general nodding of heads agreeing that pain and hunger were assuredly bad companions when setting out on an escape.

When the men had been fed, he put his dinner and Jack's on a tray and made for the gatehouse. Passing Mistress Thorncoffyn's open doors, he heard Mistress Thorncoffyn declaring feebly but stubbornly, "Not if there's chance she was anywhere near it, no! She hates me. They all hate me! Don't you know that?" Then there was the dry retching of someone being ill on an empty stomach.

Crossing toward the gatehouse, Joliffe had the sorry thought that if Mistress Thorncoffyn was now adding heavy self-pity to her arrogance, the mix was going to be dismal for anyone caught in it. Not least for Mistress Thorncoffyn herself, he added and was surprised by an odd twinge of pity as he wondered if she found it *easy* to be as utterly centered on herself as she was. Surely it must take a wearying amount of will to be so constantly demanding this, that, and everything for herself from everyone around her. *Let the world be her way or let the world be damned* was how she seemed to see life. Or feared it.

That last thought brought him to a stop at the foot of the gatehouse stairs.

Could it indeed be fear that had her throwing constant demands and commands at the world? Assuredly there was enough and plenty in the world to be afraid of, and although with her wealth and all, she had less to fear than many folk, some people were more cowards than others. Was that it? Were her demands and her great bulwark of flesh attempts to wrap herself against the world's buffeting?

Or was she just what she seemed—a shallow woman given over to self-indulgence, cruel because, at least for her, cruel was easier to be than kind?

Did that mean the hospital's sisters were kind because, for them, kindness came more easily than cruelty?

Joliffe doubted it was that simple. Knowing himself, knowing choices he had made, he could more readily believe that kindness and cruelty were equally possible in any person. He equally knew that to be kind often took more courage than to be cruel. So . . . did that mean cruelty was a form of cowardice?

He welcomed going up Jack's stairs to put an end to that turn of his thoughts. Jack of course wanted to talk about Aylton's death and hear whatever more Joliffe could tell him.

While they ate, Joliffe obliged him, even to the matter of the bread there should not have been in Aylton's stomach.

At the end Jack said, "No wounds on him except the bruises from yesterday, and nothing of those would kill him?"

"That's what Denton and Hewstere both say."

"Tom Denton knows his work. Pulls a tooth with a sure hand. Gives good shaves and haircuts. Even took himself off to Cambridge for a time, to learn what he could pay a surgeon there to teach him. Knows his business inside out, as it were." Joliffe groaned as that "jest" deserved while Jack went on, "So if he says there's no sign but that Aylton drowned, I'll believe him. It's the bread in his belly that's the trouble, isn't it? If you can't find that he ate anything here, that means he was somewhere else." Jack paused, then went on slowly, seeing the same trouble with that as Joliffe did. "Then he came back and was going away again and fell into the stream and drowned."

"This place is far too easily come and gone from," Joliffe complained. "The gate and wall here makes good show but the wall doesn't even go all the way around the place."

"It used to," Jack said, sounding amused by Joliffe's indignation. "Back when it was built, this was a properly defended manor and all. When Mistress Thorncoffyn's father was founding the hospital, he decided to gift the parish with a stone bridge over the river a mile or so on for good measure."

"And used the stone from the wall here for it," Joliffe guessed.

"You have it. The story runs that he pointed out this was to be a hospital, with no one to defend the place but sick old men and cripples, and why bother to pretend they could, wall or no? Besides, here is too far from the coast for the French or Bretons to come raiding, and nobody has stirred armed trouble hereabouts since who-remembers-when. So away went the stone. We're just in fortune that Mistress Thorncoffyn hasn't decided *she* wants something built or I might have nowhere to live."

"So Aylton was easily able to go away, get something to eat, come back, and start to leave again. Can you make that make sense?"

"What if we leave the stream out of it for a time and just follow the question of where he went?"

"To the inn for his horse and maybe his belongings. There would be food there, too. Your constable will have to ask if he was seen there."

"Neither belongings nor horse were with his body," Jack pointed out.

"Umph," Joliffe granted. "Unless they were there and were stolen by—" He saw his own hole and finished, "—whoever did not strike him down and leave him in the stream. Damn. I wish he had some extra hurt to his head or somewhere."

"Of course he may not have gone to the inn straight off. He had to have been in pain. Maybe he went to Master Hewstere. His house is close."

"Who did what? Gave Aylton something that sent him senseless, then hauled him to the stream and put his head into it?"

"It's possible," Jack said, less as if he would insist on the thought and more as if he was simply playing with the possibility. "Master Hewstere would have next to no chance of being seen carrying him into the orchard by the gate from the road in the dark, dark time of night."

"There's the small problem of Hewstere being busy all the night here with Mistress Thorncoffyn."

"Ah," said Jack. "There is that." Then he asked with disconcerting sharpness, "Why do you sound so regretful?"

"I just don't much like Hewstere," Joliffe admitted. "The way he lords it over the sisters and keeps his distance as best he can from the men in the hall. Then there's the way he broke Kydd's neck just now."

"He did? What for? Not but what I've wanted to do as much to one or another of the little beasts when the pack has come yapping around my ankles."

Driven to be fair, Joliffe said, "The dog was sick, in pain and dying. Mistress Thorncoffyn wanted Hewstere to at least stop the pain."

"So he broke its neck."

"It was a mercy. It was just—" It was just that Hewstere had neither stroked the dog in pitying kindness nor looked the least sorry at the need, had simply done it. "It seemed to no more matter to him than snapping a stick would."

Jack nodded with grim understanding. "I've seen him look at Heinrich that way when the boy is in one of his fits."

"Heinrich has fits?"

"Rarely now. I think Sister Margaret and Sister Letice found some brew of theirs that helps. Anyway, both Sister Petronilla and Daveth take care to keep him out of Master Hewstere's way. Not that he would actually harm the boy, surely. Besides, Aylton's neck wasn't broken. Besides that, why would he want Aylton dead?"

"Because he likes killing?" Joliffe ventured. "Or as a favor to Mistress Thorncoffyn? Or because Aylton was a danger to him in some way?"

"What way?"

Joliffe fixed a mock-irked look on him. "You play devil's advocate far too well, Jack. It's no use my coming up with satisfying thoughts if you keep pulling them down."

"Not pulling down. Just asking to see the foundations. How was Aylton a danger to Master Hewstere?"

"He knew something Hewstere didn't want him to know? Or at least something Hewstere could not chance him telling?"

"About what? Except for here, they never crossed each other's way."

"Something to do with the hospital or Mistress Thorncof-fyn?" Joliffe tried. At Jack's deeply doubting look, he gave way with a rueful grin. "Right enough. I grant we have no reason for Hewstere to want Aylton dead or chance to do it. Come to it, we lack reason for anyone at all to want Aylton dead. For all we know of why he was killed, you could be his murderer, Jack."

"*If* he was murdered," Jack pointed out.

Joliffe heaved a deep, deep sigh. "Right again. It's just that for him to go somewhere he could get bread, then come back to the hospital, and then be going away again makes no sense."

"Come to," said Jack with a small snort of not-quite-laughter and following his own thoughts, "I'm more likely to be murdered than most. Sitting up here. Seeing all I do. Guessing what I do from what I see. Someone may get murdered for being ignorant, but I'm willing to wager more people are murdered for what they know."

"If that's the way of it, what did Aylton know? Any guesses that way?"

"Something against Mistress Thorncoffyn? Not that she waddled out and dealt with Aylton herself, but her loving grandson on her behalf? Of course there's our fine Geoffrey Thorncoffyn himself. Maybe he had more part in Aylton's treachery than anyone but Aylton knew and with Aylton dead he's safe from anyone ever knowing?"

"There's Idany, too," Joliffe offered. "She has Mistress Thorncoffyn's confidence and keys. She could be abusing her mistress' trust, and Aylton knew it."

Jack, openly enjoying this, said, "Or she and Geoffrey could be together in deceiving Mistress Thorncoffyn! That's an alliance that would be profitable for them both, and if Aylton was part of it, then both Idany and Geoffrey had good reason to be rid of him."

Joliffe heaved a regretful sigh. "Imagining reasons they

might have to want Aylton dead is easy enough. The trouble lies in how either one of them would have had the *chance* to do anything against him last night, either one or the other, let alone together."

"True," Jack granted with equal regret. "There would have to be a conspiracy between them and with Master Hewstere, too, for any of them to have been gone long enough to deal with Aylton—to feed him and all. Come to it, you'd think that if they were bent on murdering someone, it would be Mistress Cisily Thorncoffyn herself, the thorn in everyone's sides. If she was the one who was dead, there'd be people in plenty to suspect of wanting to kill her and no lack of 'why'."

That would have been a jest yesterday. Now it was no jest at all, and feeling stupid at having come so belatedly to the thought, Joliffe said, "She was ill last night. Sick to her ample stomach. And today her dog went ill after stealing food from her it was not meant to have."

Jack looked as startled by the thought as Joliffe was. He made to answer but was cut off by the sound of hoofs of several horses coming at a canter along the hard-packed road. He limped to the window, leaned out, pulled back in, and said, "Looks to be the crowner and his men coming. That was soon. I'd best get down to open the gate for them."

"Want I should do it for you?"

"It should be me does it this time. You'll be better employed hurrying to let Sister Ursula know he's here."

Chapter 18

In the kitchen, Sister Ursula took the news with her usual calm, only saying, "So soon? That's well," before adding to Sister Petronilla who had been rolling out a pie's crust at the worktable, "Heinrich?"

"Best, yes," Sister Petronilla agreed, laid aside the rolling pin, wiped her hands on her apron, bent, scooped up Heinrich from where he had been sitting against her skirts between her feet, and settled him on her hip as if he were a much smaller child. "You come with me, poppet. Maybe it's time for a little sleep now you've had your dinner."

Rose went to take up the rolling pin as Sister Ursula asked, "Daveth?"

"Already in the dorter, last I knew," Sister Petronilla said and was gone.

Looking down at her apron, probably to make certain it was clean enough for receiving an officer of the crown, Sister Ursula said, "Joliffe, pray, warn Credy and the others that Master Osburne is here. They're still in the rear-yard, I think. If not, you'll have to find them."

"They're there," said Rose. "When I took them out the ale, the constable's man had come back with word the crowner was on his way, so they decided not to bother heading out to the harvest, just to have to come back."

She sounded oddly taut, and Joliffe, starting for the rear door, took his first full look at her since she and Sister Letice had come into the kitchen with news of finding Aylton. Was she still unsettled by that? Or was she worried because, as a first-finder of the body, she would be questioned by the crowner? None of that would account for the betraying shadows under her eyes of a sleep-short night, though. She looked almost as drawn with tiredness as Sister Ursula and Sister Petronilla. He wanted to ask her what was the matter, but Sister Ursula was going on, "That's good then. And Sister Letice is in the stillroom and can stay there until called, surely. Sister Margaret is in the hall. She can go out with me to greet Master Osburne. Joliffe, once he's here, stay with him if you can, to hear how things go. Rose, when you've finished rolling out the crust, take cups and a pitcher of ale to his men in the foreyard. He probably has two with him besides his clerk."

Joliffe found the constable, bailiff, and Denton comfortable on the bench outside the laundry door with a pitcher of the hospital's ale in their midst and Denton sharing his cup with his cousin Emme who must have just stepped out of the laundry's heat and was pushing her straying hair back under her cap with one hand as she took the cup with her other. Done with their work on Aylton, the three men were cheerful enough, Borton calling that if Joliffe had brought his own cup, he could join them. Then he took in Joliffe's look and said with a sigh before Joliffe could give his message, "Here already, is he?" He slapped Denton's knee. "Up and at 'em, lad. Master Osburne is not a man to waste time and he'll want all you have to tell."

Borton had that right. Too soon to have spent time on

greetings or going to see Master Soule before all else, as well
he might have and maybe should, Master Osburne came
into the rear-yard, a clerk following him. The crowner was
a narrow-faced man with the somewhat yellowed skin of the
slightly jaundiced, and he walked as if he might have a fistula, but he looked and sounded wide awake enough as he
greeted the three village men by name. He then looked at
Joliffe in a way that had Credy saying who he was without
being asked. Master Osburne accepted that with a brisk nod,
answered Borton's comment about him being here sooner
than hoped by saying, "I was only five miles off, as it happened. An old woman fell into a pond while washing out a
grandchild's clouts and wasn't found until too late. Nothing
but an accident but I had to say so. Your man overtook me as
I was leaving there. Where's your body?"

Joliffe stayed outside the shed, not wanting to see Aylton's
mutilated body again. The clerk who had followed Master
Osburne into the yard seemed to be of the same mind; like
Joliffe he stayed outside, able to hear without seeing while he
scratched with a pen at a piece of parchment stretched over
a wooden tablet. Unfortunately, Joliffe heard nothing new
before the four men came into the sunlight again with Master
Osburne saying, "If you say that's all there is to be learned
from him, there's no reason not to move him to the church.
Borton, Denton, if you'll see to that. Then you can get back
to your right work. Credy, I want you to keep with me while
I see to the other questions I have to ask. Who was first-finder
of the body?"

"One of the sisters and a servant here found him together,"
Credy said.

He looked toward Joliffe, who answered in turn as Master
Osburne looked at him, "Sister Letice went out to her morning work in the garden. Rose Basset, the servant, was just
coming from the other way, on her way to her work. Sister
Letice saw him first, I think, lying facedown in the water,

and together they pulled him out, rolled him over, and saw he was dead."

"All that will be for them to say." Master Osburne shifted as if his fistula were troubling him. "Where will I find them?"

Joliffe led the crowner, Credy, and the clerk to the kitchen, where Sister Ursula and Sister Margaret were waiting for him. Sister Ursula said, "Master Soule wishes to see you, Master Osburne."

Like someone who had expected that, he said back, "In good time. I've questions to ask first. Unless he knows aught about this man and his death?"

"I think not. I think he merely wants you to understand this is his hospital and he has authority here."

There might have been the smallest touch of laughter behind her words' outward respect. There was maybe even some in Master Osburne's as he answered, "I'll not tread on toes that shouldn't be trod on. Now where are the women who found the body?"

"Rose is here. Joliffe, if you'll tell Sister Letice she's wanted now?"

"I'll talk to them apart," Master Osburne said; and to Rose, "If you'll come into the yard with me?"

Rose nodded and went with him. Sister Margaret followed, unasked, with the clerk. Joliffe, relieved the sisters were keeping watch on their own and his worry for Rose useless just now, went to tell Sister Letice she was wanted, too.

The stillroom was a peaceful and well-ordered place. It smelled richly of all the varied herbs hung to dry from the rafters and wall-poles, and the varied bowls, the mortar with its pestle, the pottery jars, wooden boxes, and all else were orderly in their places, ready to hand for use. Sister Letice was using nothing, though. Instead she was leaning forward with her hands braced on the long shelf against one wall that served for table and workbench together, her head hanging as if she were enduring either bodily pain or heavy thoughts.

Joliffe wondered, startled, if she was as upset as Rose had seemed to be about being questioned. He said her name and she straightened and turned to him with the care of someone ill and working not to show it. Quietly, with effort, she asked, "The crowner is come?"

"And wishes to speak with you. Sister Ursula said I should bring you."

She gave a small nod and came. He followed her back to the kitchen, where Sister Ursula told him, "It might be well if you see if anyone needs aught in the hall, since all of us are taken up with this for now."

Joliffe bowed and went willingly, taking the covered walk along the garth, to go in by the door at the hall's far end. Tom Lyttle's dying had made the men quiet, turned them inward to their own thoughts, but Aylton's death was another matter altogether. He had not been one of them nor died properly in his bed. Once they heard of it, the men had spent the morning in eager talk and had used their dinnertime to throw questions at Joliffe and the sisters. Now, with the curtains drawn between the beds for what should be their afternoon rest, Joliffe was able to come to Basset's bedside unseen, avoiding the questions and talk that would otherwise have been hurled at him from one end of the hall to the other.

There was the chance, of course, that Basset was sleeping as—judging by the quiet—the other men were, but instead he was sitting on the edge of his bed rubbing ointment from a pottery bowl into one bare foot and more than ready to hear whatever Joliffe could tell. That being partly why Joliffe had come, he sat down beside him and, low-voiced, told him everything about the morning, ending with his talk with Jack and their sudden suspicion about Mistress Thorncoffyn's illness.

Basset, who had finished with one foot while Joliffe talked and was now working on the other, nodded understanding and kept on rubbing. "Yes," he agreed slowly. "If she's being poisoned in truth, rather than in her imagining, it would nearly pass belief for that to be separate from Aylton's death. As for Aylton, it's the bread that's the trouble, isn't it?"

"How he came by it, since it wasn't here, and why he came back, having escaped once."

"If he ever left at all. Maybe it was Jack's bread and cheese he had, and he never went any farther at all."

Joliffe had not thought to consider Jack in the matter at all and found himself uncomfortable with the thought that maybe he should have, but asked, "Why would Jack lie?"

"Why wouldn't he lie, if he'd killed Aylton?"

"How would he have moved the body all the way around to the stream?"

"A humped back and a heavy limp don't mean he's a weakling."

"His crippled arm would make it nigh to impossible."

"But still possible," Basset insisted.

"But what reason would he have to kill Aylton?"

"That's the root trouble, isn't it?" Basset said. "We don't know any good reason for anyone to want Aylton dead. Those men from the manors might have, if they couldn't have turned Mistress Thorncoffyn against him, but as it was, they had to be satisfied Aylton was no more threat to them."

"It's not only a matter of wanting Aylton dead," Joliffe brooded. "It's a matter of chance. Who had chance at him last night?"

"If he left the hospital, anyone he might have happened on," said Basset unhelpfully.

"Someone who fed him, killed him, then thoughtfully returned the body here."

"Except of course that he wasn't dead when his head went into the stream. But he wasn't in his right senses then either, I gather."

"No. There was no sign of struggle. I looked. There was no dirt or tearing to the fingernails like there might have been if he had scrabbled to push himself free while someone held him under. No bruises either, of someone forcing him down."

"Just the old bruises from the afternoon."

"Yes." A new thought came, belatedly perhaps. "Maybe you're right at thinking he never left here. Maybe he only went so far as to Mistress Thorncoffyn, thinking to plead for mercy or pardon."

"From Mistress Thorncoffyn?" Basset said dryly.

"I'm not saying he was in his right mind," Joliffe returned as dryly. "But suppose he went to her. Or maybe he sought out Geoffrey. Geoffrey was here all the night and maybe knows more of Aylton's doings than he or Aylton admitted to yesterday. Aylton could well have not accused him then in just the hope of his help later."

"So he somehow got Geoffrey away from his grandmother in the night, and Geoffrey fed him and got him senseless and hauled him to the stream," Basset suggested, not very encouragingly.

"I didn't say it was a likely thought. I'm only saying Geoffrey might well have better reason than anyone else to want Aylton dead."

"Anyone else we *know* of."

"Don't go adding to the problem," Joliffe said, aggrieved, then added to it himself by saying, "There's Master Soule, of course. It would have been easiest of all for Aylton to have gone to him in the night."

"I want to overhear you questioning Master Soule," Basset said as if the thought diverted him.

"I'll let you know when it's likely to happen," Joliffe returned. He knew his place here, and it did not include asking questions of the master. Why that suddenly irked him he did not know. As a traveling player, he was almost always among the lowest of the low, and it had never much troubled him before now. Possibly the "traveling" made the difference.

If you were always on the move, no one lorded it over you for long. This staying in one place was maybe beginning to wear on him. Restful in its way though it was after the rigors of the past months, it was not his own life back again, and yesterday's playing had shown him how much, under his weariness, he wanted his own life back. "How much better are your feet?" he asked.

Basset stretched his legs out and flexed his toes, then his feet at the ankles. "Far better. Couldn't do that three weeks ago without yelping with the pain, let be that two months ago I was in pain most everywhere else in me, too. Sister Letice and Sister Margaret know what they're about with their herbs and all."

"And Master Hewstere?" Joliffe asked despite himself.

In a tone that matched the physician in high dignity and assured authority, Basset answered down the length of his nose, "He says that Saturn has shifted sufficiently away from Mars for conflict to ease within those bodies of men whose humours are so regrettably unbalanced as to be balefully affected by their influence." He dropped Hewstere's masterful tone, returned to his own. "Which may well be, but I'm glad I had the sisters' herbs and ointments in the meanwhile."

From the hall's upper end a rattle of curtain rings being pushed aside told something was happening, even before they both heard Sister Ursula quietly saying for everyone to hear that the crowner was come and had something to say to them all. As Basset set aside the bowl and swung himself around into his bed, Joliffe stood up, pushed back the curtain there, and went on to put back the next one along and the one after that, meeting Sister Ursula coming from the other way. Sister Margaret was doing the same on the other side of the hall, and when all the curtains were open, both sisters stood together between the last pair of beds, with Joliffe a servant's few paces behind them, all facing the length of the hall toward Master Osburne now taking up a stance on the chapel step. From there the crowner swept a slow look over everyone until sure that everyone was looking back at him before he said, "Good men, you all know by now that one of you came to a bad end in the night. Master Aylton was here when you all settled for the night. Sometime after that he left. Did any of you hear him go?"

That brought a general looking at one another and then back to him, followed by a general shaking of heads. Because he had surely already been told of the sleeping draught by now, Master Osburne did not look surprised or press further that way; instead tried, "Do any of you know anything about why he left?"

"To escape Mistress Thorncoffyn coming after him with lawyers instead of her staff!" Deke Credy readily answered.

Laughter skittered among the men. Master Osburne permitted himself an agreeing smile before asking, still to everyone, "Did he say anything to any of you while he was here?" The general shaking of heads came again. Master Osburne fixed his look on Basset. "To you?"

"Nothing, sir." Basset was all humble respect. "He took to his bed and the sisters drew the curtains around him, and except for a groan now and again when he moved, that was all I saw or heard of him."

Master Osburne shifted his gaze to Dick Leek on the other side of the empty bed that had briefly been Aylton's. "You?"

Leek beckoned his head toward Basset. "As he said. No more than that."

Master Osburne spent a moment giving a long look around at everyone again before nodding as if satisfied. He stepped down and, followed by his clerk, came down the hall toward the sisters. "My thanks," he said to Sister Ursula as he reached her, and added past her to Joliffe, "I'd speak with you now."

Without waiting for answer, he went out the near door. Joliffe, carefully not trading even a glance with Basset and aware of the clerk at his back, followed him into the passage and out to the foreporch that was maybe too near Mistress Thorncoffyn's door, because Master Osburne went from it to well out into the yard before he turned around and said bluntly, "The most likely way for this Aylton to have left was past your room. You didn't hear him go?"

"No."

"You didn't hear him, follow him, kill him?"

Hiding how much the crowner's boldness diverted him, Joliffe said with the startled surprise and protest of a simple man, "No! Why would I do that?"

"That's for you to tell me."

Joliffe thought better of telling him anything at all, just stared at him as if utterly bewildered to be asked at all.

Master Osburne paused, accepted his silence, and accused, "Come to it, you might not have followed him by chance. You could have lured him out on purpose to kill him."

Truly taken aback, Joliffe exclaimed, "What?"

"You were maybe hired to it by Master Thorncoffyn. To save his grandmother trouble. Or to save *him* trouble if he was deeper with Aylton's mischief than anyone yet knew."

The crowner was very sharp. From what he had probably been told while coming here and from the questions he had already asked since arriving, he was shifting possible pieces of who and why and how around with fine speed. But Joliffe would just as soon he shifted them some other way than toward him and said, "That's more than I know about Master Thorncoffyn's business. Nor he didn't ask anything of me. I don't know the last time he spoke to me, but it's not since early yesterday or longer. Long before there was any trouble over Master Aylton. Besides, Master Aylton didn't drink the evening drink. The sisters surely told you they found it in his bed-pot."

"They did."

"So he must have been meaning, all on his own, to leave from the very first."

"On his own? Or at someone's instigation?"

"That I couldn't say," Joliffe said with the firmness of a simple and innocent man. "It wasn't me. That's what I know. I know, too, he didn't go past my door in the night. I sleep light and I'd have heard him."

It was the only solid help he could give the crowner, for what it might be worth, and Master Osburne did not seem to think it was worth much, his gaze still fixed on Joliffe's face with no sign of belief in it; but giving no sign of what he believed was maybe a deliberate trick, like now letting the silence draw out between them, waiting for some guilty filling of it. That being a trick Joliffe knew, he said nothing but shifted from foot to foot and blinked with the uneasy, bewildered, almost-resentment of an innocent man who did not understand why he was being questioned and doubted. It was a manner he had perfected over the years as a player, because among the troubles of not belonging where you were was that when the untoward happened, folk looked first at you, hoping that if someone were guilty, it was someone no one much knew. The problem had eased when the company gained Lord Lovell for a patron, and now, beyond Lord Lovell, at the last push he could claim protection from Bishop Beaufort.

That being something to be called on only at the very furthest need, he presently put his hope in his own innocence and the crowner's willingness to accept it and go on seeking the true answer, encouraged in his hope because, very unlike some encounters with other such officers, he did not have the sense that Master Osburne was intent on choosing him guilty to keep matters simple. The man was prodding and questioning to see what he could learn, not because he had made up his mind to what he would find, and for now it seemed he thought he had found out all he could from Joliffe, because after a long, fixed look at him, he gave a nod that seemed both of decision to himself and dismissal to Joliffe and said, "That will do for now. You can go about your business."

The crowner went first, though, quick-strided toward the hospital again, his clerk behind him, while Joliffe was still bowing. Left to follow, Joliffe did. With presently no thought of how he might get answers to his own questions and satisfied that Master Osburne was being fair-handed at the business, he was thinking he might go back to his right duties for a time after all his neglect of them today, but was forestalled by Master Osburne and his clerk stopping in the passage outside Mistress Thorncoffyn's open outer door. Joliffe expected them to go in, out of his way, but they did not, and as he stopped behind them he heard Mistress Thorncoffyn declaring loudly, hoarsely, "I'm not asking in holy ground, no! Don't be a fool. All I want is a prayer or two over him. That much I'll have!"

Joliffe stayed where he was, shamelessly willing to listen unless told to go on his way. Could Mistress Thorncoffyn be arguing against Aylton being buried in consecrated ground?

Master Osburne took a step backward, making his clerk shift quickly aside from his way. The crowner looked around to him and gave a short nod. The clerk nodded in return and went past him, rapped sharply at the door frame, and went in without waiting for leave. He must have spoken very quietly, because next heard was Mistress Thorncoffyn snapping, "Finally come to me, has he? I'm where he should have started. You go tell him he'll have to wait now," and returned to her harangue at whoever else was there with, "I'll have it and no mistake. Either you or Father Richard, one or the other of you will say prayers over my poor Kydd at his burial or you'll both be the sorrier for it."

Master Soule's voice was sharp with reproof as he said back at her, "You weep more over that dead dog of yours than you have for your man who died without the Church's prayers."

"I don't weep for Aylton at all. Supposing anyone troubles to say enough prayers for him, *his* soul stands at least a chance of Heaven, no matter he meant to rob me. But my poor Kydd? He's more worth my tears than Aylton ever was, but you priests say there's no heaven for dogs."

"They're soulless animals," Master Soule returned sternly. "They die and they're done."

"Then all the more reason to shed tears over their loss!" Mistress Thorncoffyn stormed. "Nor do I believe you! I've seen more of a soul in my dogs than ever I do in most people!"

"That," Master Soule snapped back with sudden wrath, "would be because you look with more love at your dogs than ever you do at people! For which fault may God have mercy on *your* soul!"

Master Osburne's clerk, either dismissed with a wave of a hand or giving up on being properly dismissed, came into the foreporch then. He raised eyebrows at the crowner who nodded back and straightened his shoulders as if bracing himself to go in, asked or no, only to be forestalled by Rose coming into the far end of the covered walk and along it at a flurried run, calling as she came, "Master Osburne! You're wanted! Hurry!"

Chapter 19

aster Osburne, his clerk, and Joliffe all started toward her. Breathless with both alarm and haste, Rose cried, "It's Sister Letice! In the kitchen!" The crowner broke forward into a run, his clerk an instant after him, Joliffe still behind them both. Rose stood aside to let them pass and would have followed at their heels but Joliffe slowed, caught her arm, and held her back to a swift walk as he demanded, "What is it? What's happened?"

"Mistress Thorncoffyn's vile candied ginger! She's poisoned herself."

"Sister Letice? With the ginger? How did *she* come by any of it?"

"Given the way Mistress Thorncoffyn was ill, she had the thought that it was poisoned. She had Sister Ursula ask Idany for a piece and ate it!"

"But why—" he started. Assuredly neither he nor Jack had said anything to Sister Letice about their guess at a link between Mistress Thorncoffyn and Kydd being sick. There had been no time to say anything about it to anyone.

But Rose was already saying, "It was because Piers was so sick in the night, just like Mistress Thorncoffyn was. That gave Sister Letice the thought."

"Piers was sick?" Joliffe echoed, alarmed. That, then, would be why Rose had been late coming to the hospital this morning and had looked—still looked—so drawn with tiredness. "How sick? How is he now?"

"Terribly sick. He was better enough by dawn that I could leave him to Ellis for the day, but for a time in the middle of the night he was very sick. Sister Letice remembered the piece of ginger Mistress Thorncoffyn gave him. It was the only thing alike between them."

"Why try it herself if she thought it was poisoned?" Joliffe demanded as they came to the kitchen door.

"She didn't know how else to find out for certain otherwise!"

He followed Rose into the kitchen. Sister Letice was on one of the benches, resting forward on the table on her crossed arms. Her headkerchief was gone. From the edges of her close-fitted coif at the nape of her neck and on her cheeks, black tendrils of her hair were curling free, all the darker against her unhealthy, sweating pallor. Master Osburne was leaning close over her, and she had raised her head to him. Both his clerk and Sister Ursula were standing discreet distances aside, but Sister Margaret was on the bench beside her, gaze watchful on her, one hand resting near a wide basin on the table as if she expected it would be needed soon.

"Yes," Sister Letice was saying, faint-voiced. "The signs are all the same. It has to be the candied ginger. There's nothing else we've had to eat in common."

"You're certain it's poison then?" Master Osburne asked.

"As certain as can be."

"Couldn't you have found another way to prove it?"

She gasped, "No," and wrenched around, away from him and toward Sister Margaret who was already snatching the basin toward her. Sister Ursula came, too, to brace her with a hand on her forehead and a hand on her back as an almost-dry vomiting took her. Master Osburne stepped well out of the women's way, probably knowing himself as helpless with this as Joliffe was, but Rose went quickly aside and was back and ready with a cup of the hospital's thin ale when Sister Letice finished with a weary gasp and sagged backward against Sister Ursula. Putting the basin aside, Sister Margaret took up a damp cloth and began to wipe her face.

Joliffe, at last seeing something he could do, went for the basin and was carrying it away to the scullery as Master Osburne asked, very gently, "Sister, do you know what manner of poison it is?"

A little trembling with weariness, Sister Letice answered, "No."

Firmly, Sister Ursula said, "That has to be all for now. She's told what she can." And to Sister Letice, "You've done what you needed to do. Now you will lie down and rest. If there's more you have to say, it will have to be for later."

Master Osburne must have accepted that. Joliffe returned from the scullery to find he was gone aside to say something to his clerk, while Sister Ursula and Sister Margaret were helping Sister Letice from the kitchen, toward the pantry where she would be able to lie down. Sister Margaret held out her hand for the basin. Joliffe gave it.

At the last moment before they were gone, Master Osburne said after them, "Do any of you know how Mistress Thorncoffyn came by the ginger?"

Without looking around, Sister Ursula answered, "It was a gift from Master Thorncoffyn. The carrier from St. Neots brought it, yesterday, I think. She said something about it last night, that it was good he'd thought of it; it would help her stomach. But Master Hewstere said no and took it from her."

Master Osburne said thanks after her, but the three women

were gone and he returned to saying something to his clerk as they both went out to ask more questions of Geoffrey, Joliffe guessed, as well as tell Mistress Thorncoffyn she had been poisoned. Joliffe was glad not to be there for that and that none of the sisters would have to do it.

Left alone in the kitchen, Rose and Joliffe looked at one another for a silent moment before she said, "The ginger would be a good choice for poisoning, I suppose. The sharpness of the ginger would serve to conceal any taste the poison had."

"Even supposing Mistress Thorncoffyn didn't gobble every piece down too fast to note any off taste," Joliffe said. "Then, when the poison made her gut ache, she would eat more of the ginger to settle it."

"Ginger being good to settle the stomach," Rose agreed. "Although an honest infusion of ginger in boiling water and drunk straight down would surely settle it better."

"Something Mistress Thorncoffyn should have considered, given how much stomach she has to be unsettled," said Joliffe. "Come and sit. You look done to the bone with weariness."

To show her how, he sat on the bench beside the table and patted it encouragingly.

"I should do something toward the men's suppers," she said, but came and sat anyway, leaned a companionable shoulder against his before she said, "Piers didn't gobble his piece. He savored every sharp and sugary bit of it and must have noted nothing."

"That would be Piers, and fortunately he had only the one piece. It was enough to make him sick, being boy-sized, while one like piece was enough to kill the dog, it being so much smaller."

"The dog? One of Mistress Thorncoffyn's dogs? Oh, the one that was sick. I'd forgotten that among all the rest. He died?"

"Not of the poison, but that's what he was sick with and

would have died, Master Hewstere said. The little beast was in pain enough that Master Hewstere broke its neck."

Rose flinched.

"Not so she saw him do it," Joliffe added. "Not so she knew he'd done it. Likely *he'd* not have survived that if she'd known."

That won a small sound that might have been a corner of a laugh from Rose, but Joliffe's thoughts were going forward— or circling back—and he said, "If the candied ginger was a gift from Geoffrey and it only came yesterday by the carrier, how did it get poisoned?"

Rose sighed, knowing the question was to himself, not her.

"Who could come to it to poison it?" he persisted. "Geoffrey in the while after he had it from the carrier. Aylton in that same while, I suppose. Idany after it was here . . ."

"*Idany?*"

"Why not? Who suffers more from the Thorncoffyn tyranny than she does?" He warmed to the thought. "She could poison Mistress Thorncoffyn's food and drink more easily than anyone else. Could have got the ginger and poison and done it all with no one's help. Safer that way. But I could see her and Geoffrey in it together."

Rose sat up, away from him. "Joliffe, little though I like either one of them, I do *not* think either is murderous."

Joliffe agreed with a regretful nod. "Somehow I don't either." Something about Geoffrey's and Idany's devotion to Mistress Thorncoffyn was as addled as the woman herself. The unwholesome twining together of pride, greed, gluttony, and ire among the three of them was like twisting vines dependant on each other for support even while they strangled one another. Whatever it was among them, it might well go too corruptedly deep for one of them to murder another.

"What I can't see," he said, "is why Mistress Thorncof-

fyn keeps coming here where she has to know at least three
people have deep reasons to hate her."

"Three people?" Rose echoed with surprise. "Who?"

"Sister Letice and Father Richard, from what you've told
me, and Sister Margaret, surely."

Rose actually laughed. "Oh, Sister Margaret can't be troubled to hate either Mistress Thorncoffyn or Geoffrey."

"You told me they cheated her out of everything that
should have been hers. How can she not at least deeply loathe
the both of them?"

Rose was smiling with open delight. "That's where the jest
lies! Without either her son or Mistress Thorncoffyn knowing it. She hated being married to John Thorncoffyn. He was
as much his mother's creature as Geoffrey is. Instead of setting up his own household after he married, he stayed in his
mother's, and Mistress Thorncoffyn expected her daughter-
in-law to be the same as he was. But Sister Margaret—
Mistress Thorncoffyn herself, as she was then; just think of
it—refused to be—to be—" Rose paused, searching for what
she wanted to say.

"Refused to be devoured?" Joliffe offered.

"Devoured," Rose agreed. "When she was widowed, she
hoped she might escape, could go to live on her dower land
and be free. But Mistress Thorncoffyn would have none of
that, and Geoffrey took his grandmother's side. What neither of them knew was that Sister Margaret—only she wasn't
then, of course—saw from the very start how they meant to
cheat her *and she let them*. It was her escape, you see. You've
seen how skilled a *medica* she is. If she wasn't here, all that
skill would be wasted. So she let herself be robbed of everything they supposed she wanted and came away to here."

"Where she's glad to be," said Joliffe, "while her son and
erstwhile mother-in-law enjoy the thought that she's humili-
ated and miserable. Because they do think that, don't they?
And enjoy it."

"Yes."

"And yet Mistress Thorncoffyn is mad enough to put herself in Sister Margaret's reach at the same time that Sister Letice and Father Richard have to endure serving her, too, despite what she did to their lives. I can see why Idany is wary over who sees to Mistress Thorncoffyn's medicine, but given the misery Mistress Thorncoffyn spreads around here, I have to wonder why Idany thinks *anyone* here is safe to make food, drink, *or* medicine for her."

Rose laughed. "I suppose because neither of them truly believes anyone would dare do anything against her." She sobered. "Or didn't believe it until now, when they'll have to. Sister Ursula says the problem is that Mistress Thorncoffyn always knows that everything she does or wants is right and sees anyone who doesn't agree with her as a fool."

To be that sure that one is forever right and righteous, and that everyone else is wrong, must be a constant comfort, Joliffe thought acidly.

"Oh, merciful Saint Anne," Rose said.

Joliffe, likewise hearing Idany's determined tread along the passageway, stood up as hurriedly as Rose did. While she moved toward the hearth as toward a task there, he tried to look, for his part, as if he were just turning from some task to another at the table. Idany, coming in, maybe noted their effort, maybe did not, giving no heed at all to Rose and saying at Joliffe as if he had been hiding from her, "There you are. You're needed to help Mistress Thorncoffyn to Kydd's burial. It's to be in the orchard. Now."

Not troubling for his reply, she turned sharply around and left. Joliffe looked to Rose, who shrugged and shook her head to show she would not tell him what to do. He shrugged back and went. It would probably make less trouble for everyone all around if he did. Besides, he was curious. Had Master Soule given way about the prayers?

It seemed he had not; it was Father Richard at the outer

door of the foreporch, with Mistress Thorncoffyn leaning on one of his arms heavily enough that he had his opposite shoulder braced against the doorframe to hold himself up against her weight. She must be too weak to depend even on her staff today, Joliffe thought, and wondered where Geoffrey was, not to be here helping his grandmother. Come to it, she looked as if she should be in her bed anyway, not bound for the orchard. Besides that she was pasty-faced, her cheeks' and chins' fat flesh was sagging heavily into the folds of her wimple around her face as if the inward force that had kept her round-faced and ruddy was gone out of her. Which it probably was, after her night of sickness, Joliffe thought as he went quickly to take her other arm and some of her weight off the priest.

Father Richard thanked him with deep relief. Mistress Thorncoffyn, her breath wheezing in and out as if driven by a leaky bellows as her lungs labored under the mass of her bosom to draw in sufficient air, wasted none of her strength on thanks, just heaved forward into a determined trudge across the yard, depending on the two men to keep her upright. Behind them, Idany skittered from side to side, wringing her hands and making small, worried sounds. At the yard's end, they levered and steadied Mistress Thorncoffyn through the doorway there and then across the narrow plank bridging the stream there, into the orchard where, thankfully, Geoffrey stood not far away, beside a freshly dug hole and small mound of earth in which a shovel straightly stood. He neither looked pleased nor came to help with his grandmother as Joliffe and Father Richard lurched with her over the uneven ground.

Only after they had shuffled her to a stop beside the hole did Joliffe see the small bundle that must be Kydd lying on the grass nearby in the shadow of one of the trees, wrapped around with a length of white linen that was likely one of Mistress Thorncoffyn's fine linen towels that Emme was expected to wash but never trusted to iron.

Standing spread-legged to keep herself up, Mistress Thorncoffyn shook Joliffe off her one arm and beckoned sharply at
Geoffrey to come to her. Joliffe willingly drew back the three
long steps to the rear a servant should be and took up a waiting stance, supposing he would be needed when time came
to return to the hospital. Idany hovered nearer to her lady,
ready to be what aid she could, while Geoffrey took Joliffe's
place at his grandmother's side, and she withdrew her arm
from Father Richard, saying, "There, Father. Put him in his
grave and begin."

Father Richard, rather than obeying, said, "That is not
my place."

Mistress Thorncoffyn jerked her head around to glare at
him, but before she could do more, Idany said, "I'll do it, my
lady," and went quickly forward, took up the bundle from
the grass, and kneeled to set it gently in the bottom of the
grave. As she stood up and stepped back, Mistress Thorncoffyn swayed, dragging Geoffrey nearly off balance, and said on
a heaving sob, "My poor, brave Kydd!"

Geoffrey, bracing his feet more widely apart, pleaded,
"Grandmother, worse grieving will only make you more ill."

"I can't help it!" She seized the handkerchief that Idany
held out to her and mopped at her face and nose. "He sacri-
ficed himself for me! He ate that ginger to warn me!"

Now standing on the far side of the hole, Father Richard
said curtly, with the deep disgust on his face and in his voice,
"We will pray," and bowed his head.

Mistress Thorncoffyn, Geoffrey, and Idany did likewise.
Joliffe contented himself with wondering which prayers
meant for the passing of human souls Father Richard
meant to use—and whether the use of them this way was
blasphemous.

He did not have to wonder long as Father Richard began,
"Lord of Mercy, grant that our souls—and this woman's
above all—be lightened of the burden of greed for earthly

pleasures, and hers most particularly of its willingness to cruelty for the sake of showing her power over others and her
pride in . . ."

Mistress Thorncoffyn's head snapped up, her mouth working with an outrage seeking for words until she burst out,
"You hedge-bred mamzer! You dare—" She broke off, gasped
for air, then raged onward. ". . . you *dare* say that at me in my
grief, in my . . ."

With scorn and years of in-held fury, Father Richard said
back at her, "Your grief is an offense to God. If no one else
will tell you so, I do! You grieve for that dog instead of for
all the people you've made to suffer from your"—he sought
for the word—"your *monstrous* centering on yourself. Even
your dog's death you use to no better end than seeking other
people's pity for you!"

Mistress Thorncoffyn gaped and gasped with breast-
heaving fury, unable to find words, but Geoffrey said furiously, "You're here to pray what she wants prayed, priest.
You'll pray or . . ."

"I've prayed all the prayers I'm going to pray here! For her
or you or that dead animal there!"

Geoffrey let go his grandmother. Fists clenched, he took a
threatening step forward. "You'll pray what you're told to pray!"

Idany grabbed to steady her mistress. Joliffe stayed where
he was, not minded to get in anyone's way. The two men were
close enough in age and size to maybe make a fairly even
fight between them. Certainly Father Richard was not quail-
ing from Geoffrey's threat, but finding out whether Geoffrey
would have gone so far as to strike a priest was forestalled
by Master Osburne saying, level-voiced and quietly warning,
"Good masters."

Father Richard must have seen the crowner coming. His
fixed gaze on Geoffrey did not waver, but everyone else looked
sharply around to where the crowner stood several trees away,
his clerk behind him.

Mistress Thorncoffyn, unbalanced by her own sudden movement, began to sway perilously. Idany gave a frightened yelp. Geoffrey quickly put her aside and grabbed his grandmother's arm himself as Joliffe sprang to her other side with the sudden horrible thought of the struggle it would be to get Mistress Thorncoffyn up from the ground if she fell. Happily, she did not fall, instead took hard hold on Geoffrey's arm and said fiercely, "He's a priest. Don't touch him." And added with a gimlet stare at Father Richard, "There are other ways."

"All of which you undoubtedly know and have used on others," the priest said back at her, then to Master Osburne, "Do you need me for anything?"

"Not presently. If you want to leave, do."

Father Richard bowed his head in thanks to him, turned, and went away toward the road and the gate there, the shortest way back to his church, while Geoffrey said at Master Osburne, "My grandmother needs to return to her bed."

"Of course," the crowner granted courteously.

Indeed, Mistress Thorncoffyn's moon of a face was gone from pasty to an unhealthy dark red, and as Geoffrey and Joliffe labored to turn her toward the hospital, Geoffrey ordered, "Idany, find Master Hewstere. Let him know she needs him." Idany bobbed a curtsy and scurried away. Geoffrey, giving a nod back at the grave, asked his grandmother, "What of finishing here?"

"You can come back to it," Mistress Thorncoffyn snapped and lumbered onward.

Master Osburne stepped well aside from her way but Joliffe saw him watching her with a look that seemed to Joliffe sharp with more than the plain curiosity her deformity could call forth from any onlooker. What was the crowner thinking? That if he ended by having to charge her with manslaughter, she was going to be unwieldy to take into custody?

That brought a new thought. Despite all her strained centering on herself, Mistress Thorncoffyn was no fool. She had to know what trouble Aylton's death could cause for her. Was she hoping to forestall that trouble by making all this trouble of her own with the poisoned ginger and her violent illness last night?

The supposedly poisoned ginger.

There was an unsettling thought. Some of it was assuredly poisoned, but she had handed that piece to Piers yesterday, and Idany had given Sister Ursula the one that sickened Sister Letice. What if those had been deliberately poisoned toward deceiving . . .

No, because that would mean she had deliberately poisoned Kydd, too, and Joliffe could not see her doing that to one of her dogs.

Or could he? Mistress Thorncoffyn used her wildly swinging humours to keep everyone around her off balance. Would she go so far as to use one of her dogs to the same end? And Kydd may not have been meant to die, only be very ill, like his mistress. After all, Hewstere had been the actual cause of the dog's death, not any poison.

All those thoughts had possibility. And she could have used some safer means than poison to make herself ill last night. The one great stumble in that was that Joliffe could not see her deliberately making herself as ill as she had been last night. Although that could have been a miscalculation on her part.

But there was a second stumble, too. If all this was somehow to turn aside trouble over beating Aylton yesterday, how did she come to have this poison, whatever it was, with her?

No, the best likelihood was that the ginger had been a true and clever attempt by someone to poison her. As Rose had said, the more poisoned ginger she gobbled to settle her stomach, the more ill she would feel and the more ginger she would probably eat, working herself toward what had to have been the desired end—her death.

Except—why do it here, with Hewstere and the sisters so ready to hand to tend her?

Unless Hewstere was working together with whoever meant to have her dead. After all, who better to help her along the way than her physician, able to see to her dying while seeming to seek her healing?

Except Hewstere was unlikely to want Mistress Thorncoffyn dead. Every sign was that she was increasingly, willingly dependent on him, and a wealthy patron was much the same as a goose who gave golden eggs. Dead was the last thing he would want her to be.

Maybe whoever poisoned the ginger did not want her dead, had only wanted her very ill, and therefore had done it here where she would have best help.

But where was the why to any of that? Of that he had no guess at all, and he lost track on his thoughts as he and Geoffrey labored Mistress Thorncoffyn across the stream and into the yard. She gave little help in the struggle except insofar as she did not fall full down. That was help enough, Joliffe supposed, since he was unsure how they would ever have hauled her upright again.

Master Osburne was following them, offering neither help nor comment until they were heaving Mistress Thorncoffyn up the single step to the foreporch. At that probably carefully chosen moment, he said, "I need to ask you more about your gift to your grandmother, Master Thorncoffyn."

Geoffrey snarled, short-breathed, "What? Gift? Oh, the ginger. You've already asked me."

"I'd started. Then I had to tell your grandmother why, you remember, and after that she was so"—Master Osburne seemed to seek the right word—"was so fretted I had to leave. From where did you have the ginger, Master Thorncoffyn?"

Intent on keeping his grandmother on her feet and going forward, Geoffrey panted, "That bastard Aylton got it."

"You don't know where he had it from?"

"He said something a while since about how she favors candied ginger and that I might want to gift her with some. I told him to see to getting me some. He did."

They were in the passage now. Master Osburne went obligingly to open the outer of the doors to Mistress Thorncoffyn's rooms ahead of them and waited until they had maneuvered her through before he said, "So it was Aylton who bought the ginger, not you?"

"I've said," Geoffrey answered through shut teeth.

"I've been told you've said the ginger was brought yesterday by the common carrier."

"Yes."

"The carrier is still in town. I sent to have him asked if that was true. He says he brought nothing for either you or Master Aylton yesterday."

Joliffe would have admired how skillfully Master Osburne timed that goad, except he was suddenly holding up Mistress Thorncoffyn alone as Geoffrey let her go and turned on the crowner, saying furiously, "He says that? I gave Aylton good coins to pay him! One of them is a liar and a cheat, and I'm willing to guess which one it is! If damned Aylton were here for me to get my hands on him . . ."

"But he isn't," Master Osburne said. "Is he?"

That brought Geoffrey to momentary silence, staring at him until Mistress Thorncoffyn, perhaps feeling Joliffe's legs beginning to buckle under her leaning weight, snapped, "Geoffrey!"

Geoffrey whipped around and took hold on her again. Master Osburne again went ahead of them, now to open the bedchamber door. That brought her dogs scurrying from their beds, all trying to be with her at once while Geoffrey cursed at them as he and Joliffe struggled her into the room. From the doorway behind them, Master Osburne said, "I of course will have questions asked about where the ginger came from and about the poison."

"Ask away!" Geoffrey flung back at him. "Get away, you miserable hounds! Aylton had it from somewhere. That's all I know about it."

"Not the bed," Mistress Thorncoffyn gasped. "Chair."

Glad not to face the complicated business of helping her to lie down, Joliffe helped steer her to her chair and, having heaved her around, let her go and stepped well clear as she collapsed backward into it with a groan and a grunt. He noted Geoffrey, too, took care to be well clear. A hand or arm crushed between her and any part of the chair would be no jest.

The dogs immediately clambered and scrambled up her, vying to lick her face in welcome. While she tried to wrap her arms around the wiggling mass of them, Master Osburne asked in the same even way he had been saying everything, "My lady, will you be going to Master Aylton's funeral Mass?"

"No! His soul"—she paused on a gasp for air around thrusting dog-faces—"can't rot fast enough—to suit me." Still struggling with her dogs as much as for breath, she went on, "Geoffrey. I want a letter. To the bishop. Against that priest. Today."

Joliffe, backing away toward the door, intent on escape, marveled despite himself at how much venom she could summon even while ill and distracted as she was. He had played in enough plays where the Sins and Virtues took part by their own names that he had no trouble naming her two greatest sins as Gluttony and Wrath, and could not help wondering which of them would be the one that finally carried her off.

Chapter 20

As Joliffe went along the covered walk toward the kitchen with his hands pressed to the small of his back in apology to his spine, he encountered Master Hewstere going rapidly the other way, trailed by Idany. He stepped aside with a bow of his head, was ignored by them both, and when they were past, went on his own way to the kitchen where he found Rose and all the sisters busy at readying supper. Even Sister Letice was there, albeit only sitting on a stool beside the hearth stirring weakly at something in a pot and looking wan. Although he supposed it was more than time that he do something of his neglected duties, the women had less interest in his help than in why Idany had come in such hurried search of Master Hewstere. That led of course to telling of Kydd's burial, and for the sake of much-needed laughter among the women, he played, in turn, defiant Father Richard, raging Mistress Thorncoffyn, furious Geoffrey, and lurking crowner (which was unjust to Master Osburne who had been quite openly there). He kept a half-eye on Sister Letice, to be sure he did not offend about her brother, but she seemed almost triumphant on Father Richard's behalf, sitting up a little straighter and exclaiming, "Oh, very good for him!"

"So that's why Idany came scurrying in search of Master Hewstere," Sister Ursula said when he had done.

"All angry at us that he wasn't here in the kitchen," said Sister Petronilla. "As if we'd lost him on purpose to spite her."

"He being so often here in the kitchen," Sister Margaret said scornfully. She raised her voice. "And here is Idany *again*."

As if to cue, Idany stalked into the kitchen. Having heard, as she was meant to, she cast a sharp look at Sister Margaret but demanded at Sister Letice, "Master Hewstere wants whatever syrup of poppy you have."

Matching her for curtness, Sister Letice said back at her, "I've none to give."

"*None?*"

"None."

With a glare around at everyone, Idany declared, "This is a very ill-run place," and stalked out.

When she was well gone, Sister Margaret asked, concerned, "Are we truly out of all poppy?"

"No." Sister Letice looked and sounded all weariness again. "We aren't. She asked for *my* syrup of poppy. *I* don't have any. What there is, is the hospital's."

Laughter rippled among the women, but Sister Letice looked to Sister Ursula with sudden guilt and said, "That may have been wrong of me. If Mistress Thorncoffyn needs the syrup to help her rest . . ."

"Then she can send somewhere for some," Sister Ursula said firmly. "It's costly, and she'd give neither thanks nor recompense for ours. We've little enough left as it is until the Michaelmas buying." Meaning the great after-harvest buying of what would be needed through the coming winter months but could not be grown or made close at hand.

With cold satisfaction, Sister Margaret said, "The little we still have should be kept for those who deserve ease from their pain. Let Mistress Thorncoffyn endure her pains with her wits about her. It will give her chance to contemplate her sins."

That was the harshest thing Joliffe had heard any of the sisters ever say, but no one rebuked her. Instead, Sister Petronilla said, a mocking edge to her usually kindly voice, "Sins? She's only ever sinned *against*. The difference is that this time she truly was. Of course that came as no surprise to her. She was already declaring she was poisoned before even anyone knew she was. She was raving at Geoffrey last night that he had to find who had tried it this time."

"This time?" Joliffe echoed. "There've been other times?"

"Every time her inward parts are out of sorts, she declares it's because someone is trying to kill her," Sister Margaret said with the weariness of someone who had heard it too many times. "At her worst, she's even accused Geoffrey. She likes the thought she's so much someone that someone else would take the trouble to kill her."

"Who *doesn't* she accuse?" Joliffe put in. "That will be who's guilty."

As he had meant it to, that sent a ripple of laughter among the sisters, but not from Sister Letice, who said with quiet worry, "The trouble is that this time she was truly poisoned."

A little silence fell until Sister Ursula said slowly, "Nor does Master Osburne seem to think Master Aylton's death was as simple as we thought it was. Not to judge by the questions he's asked us."

"What manner of questions?" Joliffe asked.

The women looked among themselves before Sister Ursula

answered, "He seems to want us to say Master Aylton did eat something here and did not pour the bedtime drink away but drank it."

"He seemed almost to want us to be lying," said Sister Petronilla. "Why would he want us to be lying?"

Joliffe could have answered that, knowing what he did, but he did not and was forestalled from asking any more questions of his own by Rose saying, "Joliffe, I think dinner's bowls are still unwashed in the scullery. We're going to need them shortly."

He had had a vague hope that someone had seen to them as breakfast's had been, but since not, he gave a smile and nod and went. The bowls were indeed unwashed and needed hard scrubbing, but as he set to them, he did not altogether regret a chance alone to think.

The answer to Sister Petronilla's question was that if Master Osburne could satisfy himself that the bread found in Aylton's belly had been eaten here, then his death at the stream stood a good chance of being ruled a plain mischance and the matter closed. Almost as good would be learning Aylton had indeed downed the evening drink instead of pouring it out, because that might give sufficient reason for his collapse at the stream, making it no more than an accident. Unfortunately, that simple end to the matter was blocked by the sisters insisting Aylton had *not* had the drink.

Or Sister Petronilla insisted.

Joliffe was unable to stop that treacherous thought or the one that followed it. She and Daveth had seen to the bed-pots this morning. It was only on her word they thought Aylton had poured out the drink.

Joliffe shook his head at himself. What reason was there to doubt her word? None. Come to it, what reason would she have to lie about it anyway? However—whyever—Aylton had died, she had had no part in it. If it had been a matter of harm coming to either of the boys, Joliffe could see her doing almost anything to protect them, but no matter how afraid Daveth might have been of Aylton, the man had been about to be hauled away from here forever.

Well then, if not for herself, would she lie for someone else? For another of the sisters maybe? But which of them had any more reason than she did to bother with having Aylton dead? They did not even have reason to particularly care if he escaped. Besides, whether Aylton drank the sleeping draught or not, the bread in his belly still needed explanation. The bread more than anything was holding Master Osburne to his questions, because unless someone here could be found to have given it to him, that bread meant Aylton had been somewhere else and come back here and been going away again, to drown the direction he did in the stream.

Joliffe could still not make *that* make sense. But if he did not accept that had been the way of it, it meant someone here was lying. It meant that someone here had fed Aylton and let him leave and now was not admitting to it. Or—someone had fed him, given him a sleeping draught, and taken him out of the hospital to his drowning.

Never mind the *why* of someone doing that. Who *could* have done it? It was one thing to ask who could have given him bread, and something more to ask who could have given him bread *and* drowned him.

To answer who could have fed him, there was, first and most simply, Sister Margaret, taking her turn to sleep in the pantry last night. She might well have been willing to help Aylton flee Mistress Thorncoffyn's wrath but now be lying about it, unwilling to take whatever blame might come her way—or the hospital's—for having unwittingly let him go to his death. That would answer everything. Except that Joliffe could not see her being that much a coward, to keep quiet now when there was so much trouble over Aylton's death.

As for her giving him a sleeping draught for the sake of afterward drowning him—first, why would she, and secondly, how would she have dragged him to the stream without leaving any sign on him of being dragged, since very surely she could not have lifted or carried his far greater size and weight than her own.

So, no, it still came back to Aylton having gone out through the sacristy, unseen and unheard by anyone. Unless . . .

Unless he had gone up to Master Soule's chamber, and for some reason Master Soule had both fed him and let him leave. That would at least give reason for the bread in his belly. But why would Aylton think Master Soule, of all people, would help him, especially knowing what after-wrath would come from Mistress Thorncoffyn? And what reason would Master Soule have to—somehow—render Aylton senseless, then haul him down the stairs and around to the stream to drown him? Let alone why Master Soule, who had nothing to do with giving any medicine to anyone, would have something readily to hand to use on Aylton and afterward manage to haul the larger man down his stairs and as far as the stream without leaving at least bruises on him or at least signs he had been dragged, since surely slight-built Master Soule could no more have carried him than Sister Margaret could have.

No, what made the straightest sense was that Aylton had poured out the sleeping draught and left the hospital by way of the sacristy and asking help of no one.

But then why had he circled around and been going through the kitchen garden? Like the bread in his belly, his being in the garden spoiled all the reasonableness there would otherwise be about his death.

But how reasonable was it to suppose that someone had fed him, given him a sleeping draught without Aylton knowing it (supposing Sister Petronilla was not lying about him having poured out the other), then hauled him senseless to the stream and drowned him in hope it would seem an accident happening as he tried to escape?

Then again, how *un*reasonable was it *not* to consider that possibility?

Of course that brought the matter back to who would have done it.

And why.

And where. Because if Aylton had not eaten that barely digested bread here, then he had to have been somewhere else.

To Father Richard maybe, maybe thinking to take sanctuary in the church? But why would Father Richard want him dead? Not to spare the Thorncoffyns trouble, that was sure. Besides, if the priest was inclined to kill anyone, wouldn't it be Mistress Thorncoffyn, in revenge for the wrong she had forced him to do to his parents? Why do her the favor of killing Aylton? Maybe there was an unknown link between Aylton and the priest that would have given Father Richard reason to kill him, but if so, it would be for Master Osburne to find out, able as he was to ask questions where Joliffe could not.

What of Hewstere? Would Aylton have chanced going to him, maybe in hope of something to control the pain while he made his escape? The physician, at least, would be likely to have had a drug to hand to send Aylton senseless. He also had the size and likely the strength to have carried him to the stream. The gate into the orchard was close enough to his front door to have made very slight his chance of being seen in the black depth of night. And, Joliffe thought triumphantly, they had only Hewstere's word for it that there were no marks on Aylton's body other than from Mistress Thorncoffyn's beating of him.

But all that fell flat, Joliffe realized with a sigh as he started on the last of the bowls, because Hewstere had been with Mistress Thorncoffyn all the night, not at his house to either help or hinder Aylton. And aside from that, there was the same objection as with everyone else: why would he want

Aylton dead? Aylton's secret death would not serve to put him any further into Mistress Thorncoffyn's graces than he already was. What happened to Aylton had nothing to do with him.

The sacristy bell was ringing for Vespers as Joliffe brought the cleaned bowls back to the kitchen. The women's hands paused at their tasks, heads turning toward the hall. Rose, seemingly taking up something said while he was not there, said, "Go if you think it good. There's not much left to do here. Joliffe and I can see to it."

"I think we should," said Sister Ursula. "It's been a disturbed and disturbing day. Our being there may help to settle the men as well as us." She added, as she and the other sisters brushed at their aprons and straightened their headkerchiefs, "We just have to be sure we say nothing about the poisoned ginger where the men can hear us. Master Aylton's death has given them more than enough to talk on. For a wonder, their long ears haven't picked up the word 'poison' in any of this. We should keep it that way if we can."

The other sisters nodded and murmured agreement with that as they left the kitchen. Joliffe looked to Rose, meaning to ask if he should finish the bread, but she had left off setting out the bowls on the table, ready for filling, was looking at him with worry, and said before he could say anything, "Did I do wrong to tell Sister Ursula you had skill at finding out things? Should I have kept quiet about it?"

"Assuredly no," Joliffe said hurriedly, to ease her worry. "It only made easier what I—"

He broke off, seeing her worry shift to silent laughter.

"Only made easier what you would do anyway," she finished for him.

He pulled a mock-shamed face, agreeing with her, and asked, "Shall I finish slicing the bread?"

"I will, if you'll fetch the milk and pour it in the kettle."

The men's supper was always a simpler meal than their

dinner, being usually only toasted, buttered bread soaked
in warm milk, or sometimes gravy if there had been hearty
meat in the mid-day meal, with a cooked or soft fruit when
those were to be had, and weak ale—nothing that would sit
heavily in stomachs and disturb sleep. Rose and Joliffe, familiar at working together after their years of sharing tasks,
easily set to what was left to do, while Master Soule's voice
began in the hall, too faint for the words to matter here but
with the soothe of Vespers' prayers in it, hopefully quieting
the troubled day toward its end.

He was still praying when there was nothing left to do
toward supper except toast the bread before breaking it into the
bowls and, at Vespers' end, swing the kettle of milk over the
fire to warm. Joliffe, setting the gridiron over the coals at the
edge of the low-burned fire, said to Rose, "I can do the rest, if
you want to leave now. You surely want to see how Piers does."

"I went at mid-day. He was better enough then to be
plaguing Ellis." She brought the cutting board with its bread
and set it on the hearth beside the low stool he would sit on
to watch over the toasting. "But, yes, I think I'll go."

She did not, though; instead she stood beside him as he
settled onto the stool, and as he laid the first slices of bread on
the gridiron to toast, said quietly, "Joliffe, I know we aren't
supposed to know much at all about what you did after you
left us."

He kept himself from looking up at her but his voice came
out too flat as he answered, "Either not much or not anything
at all."

"Or anything at all," she accepted. She knelt down beside
him, to bring their heads more level. "Nor where you've been.
But Joliffe—" She laid a hand on his near knee, looking at
him while he went on not looking at her. "Is it well with you?
Or will it be well, if it isn't yet?"

He made himself meet her gaze then and said with what
he meant to be a reassuring smile, "Don't I seem well?"

Rose did not return his smile. "No."

The plainness of her answer stopped him. From the chapel the sound of Master Soule's voice at Vespers hardly touched the silence between them until Joliffe finally said, "Oh." And then, looking back to the bread and turning a piece that did not need turning yet, added, "No, it's not altogether well with me. But it's better. I'm finding my balance again. When that's done, I'll be well enough again."

Rose went on looking at him. He met her gaze again, openly now because he had told her the truth, not a truth-shaded lie. Or at least truth enough to satisfy her because finally she smiled a slight, accepting smile at him, stood up, patted his shoulder like a comforting friend—or mother—who knows they can't do more, and left.

She had had to do a great deal of accepting in her life. Joliffe was sorry to bring more need of it on her, but that was past remedy. He could only ask her to endure it now—until he could make it better, he promised himself. And quickly turned the toasting slices of bread just before too late.

Chapter 21

Supper was done and Joliffe was alone in the scullery, cleaning the bowls yet again, when Sister Margaret came in with the kettle that should be the day's last dirty pot. As she set it down on the board beside him, Joliffe said, "May I ask you something about your son?"

"If you like," she said with neither the rancor nor unease there might have been.

Distracted by that from his intended question, he asked instead, "You truly don't care he helped his grandmother to cheat you out of what should be yours?"

Sister Margaret smiled. "When they cheated me out of what they thought I should want, they gave me chance at my true desire. I'm far happier here than I ever was as wife or mother or, God and all the saints know, daughter-in-law. What about my faithless, foolish son would you like to know?"

"Do you think he could pretend his deep concern for his grandmother while—" Joliffe broke off, not certain he could ask even a mother so openly uncaring: Is your son murderous?

Sister Margaret saved him the trouble. "While trying to kill her? No. He thinks himself subtle, but he's not. It was one of the sorry things about watching him help his grandmother cheat me. She's cunning enough in her low way, but with him I would have had to be a fool absolute not to see what he was at. No, strange though that may be, Geoffrey does truly care about his grandmother. I can see him doing something in a fit of temper, but in some secret, subtle way, with poison, never." She took up some of the cleaned bowls. "Are these ready to be set back on the shelf?" In the warm kitchen where they would dry better than the damp scullery.

Joliffe nodded and she went away with them, a woman calm in her certainty of being where she should be.

All that should have remained to the day was the brief benediction of Compline's prayers and the round of quieting drinks for the night, but while Joliffe was setting out the cups on their tray on the kitchen's worktable, Master Osburne came in from the hallward passageway. Sister Petronilla was gone to see Daveth and Heinrich into bed, so it was Sister Ursula, Sister Margaret, and Sister Letice who paused to look questioningly at the crowner while Joliffe went on setting out the cups as Master Osburne said with what seemed his constant quiet courtesy, "By your leave, I thought I'd watch how matters went as the men are settled for the night, to have some thought of how it was with Master Aylton last night."

Aylton's last night, he did not add, but the words hung there, and Sister Ursula answered, "Of course," as courteously as if she had choice in the matter. "Sister Letice, to begin with, tell him, pray, about the men's drink."

Sister Letice betrayed her unhappiness at that by her voice gone even quieter than usual and her eyes kept steadily down while she told Master Osburne what herbs she made into the syrup that was stirred into the men's evening ale. To the crowner, she probably only seemed shy, but when she had finished, Sister Margaret forestalled what questions Master

Osburne might have asked by suggesting he take a fingertip's taste of the syrup. He did and said, surprised, "It's sweet."

"They drink it the more happily that way," Sister Margaret said. "If we could afford mead, that would go smoothest of all, but we do with sweetening the ale."

"They have this every night?"

"Every night," Sister Ursula agreed. "A supper usually of bread and warmed milk, sometimes with cinnamon in coldest weather to warm the stomach. Then Compline. Then this drink. Which we should be taking to them now."

That was gently said, but with under it a firmness that told the time was come for the women to get on with their evening duties; Master Soule's voice at Compline's prayers had stopped a little time ago. Master Osburne gave a slight bow acknowledging her authority and took himself aside while they finished readying the tray. That done, Sister Ursula said, "Sister Letice goes now, most evenings, to see that all is well in the herb garden while we go to the men. That's what she did last evening. Tonight, though, I think she should go straight to her bed."

Master Osburne gave Sister Letice a smile maybe meant to reassure her. "By all means, yes. She's earned rest."

Sister Letice, with her gaze still lowered, not seeing the smile, bobbed a curtsy toward him, and went away. Joliffe picked up the tray with the men's drinks and followed Sister Ursula and Sister Margaret out of the kitchen. Master Osburne trailed them and in the hall was satisfied simply to stand by the door while the sisters went along the beds, Sister Margaret handing drinks to the men on the left, Sister Ursula to the men on the right, Joliffe keeping to the middle way with the tray. He had expected talk as usual between the men and sisters, and certainly curiosity toward the crowner, but either wariness at the presence of a king's officer or something in the sisters' faces kept them all quiet. Sideways looks went Master Osburne's way but that was all, except that Basset, with his cup in his hand, raised his eyebrows to Joliffe as Sister Margaret turned away. Joliffe could do nothing in answer but lift his own eyebrows in return.

Across from him, John Oxyn, who had been so lost in fever when Joliffe first came, was lately able to sit up a little to drink, but with hands so unsteady with weakness that Sister Ursula paused to hold the cup and help him while Joliffe with the empty tray went up the hall to where Master Osburne waited, leaving Sister Margaret going from bed to bed to speak quietly to each of the men in turn, seeing that they were as comfortable as might be and in need of nothing for the night, then drawing the curtain between each bed as she moved on.

Master Osburne, watching her, asked Joliffe, "You will go where now? Or, rather, where did you go yester night?"

"I'll shortly go to bed, just as I did then. We have long days here and sometimes disturbed nights. It's best to sleep while I can."

"Disturbed nights despite these sleeping draughts for the men?"

"The draughts are usually less strong than they were tonight and last night. Most of our days are not as unsettling as these have been."

Sister Ursula joined them. Master Osburne turned his questioning to her. "Where do you go now?"

"To the dorter, to my bed. We all do at this hour, except for whoever is taking turn at sleeping down here."

"As Sister Margaret did last night."

"And as Sister Petronilla will tonight."

"What about the cups? Do you leave them with the men?"

"We let the men finish drinking at their own pace, yes. Joliffe or one of us gathers them in the morning."

Joliffe wondered if the crowner's thought was the same as his own: that while drawing the curtains along each bed, a sister could make chance to say something privately to any of the men. It was not something he had ever had reason to think of before now.

"You give out the cups the same way each night, you to the right, Sister Margaret to the left?" Master Osburne asked.

"No. We try to change over, evening to evening, lest the men think there are favorites among them."

"But always the two of you, not ever Sister Petronilla or Sister Letice?"

"Always the two of us. Sister Margaret as *medica* must be sure all is as well as may be with each of the men. My duty is to see that all else is as it should be at a day's end. Neither task can be given off to someone else."

"Last night it was you who gave Master Aylton his drink, but Sister Margaret would have spoken to him afterward."

As if she saw nothing in the question, Sister Ursula said simply, "Yes."

Because what *was* there to see in the question, Joliffe thought. Whoever gave him the drink, Aylton had not drunk it.

Because he was warned not to?

The thought jarred as Joliffe remembered how Sister Ursula had bent over Aylton's curled, pain-taut body and spoken to him, telling him this was a drink to ease his pain and help him sleep. Could she then, in what had seemed a pause while she waited for him to answer, have added a very softly-said "Don't drink it," a warning gone easily unheard by anyone more than a few feet away, as Joliffe and the beds to either side had been.

But why would Sister Ursula have any interest in Aylton escaping his earned punishment? Or—Joliffe could not stop the thought—any interest in having him dead, supposing warning him from the drink was intended to lead to that? There seemed no likelihood to any of that, or, come to it, likelihood *any* of the sisters had interest in Aylton beyond caring for his hurts.

Joliffe, watching Sister Margaret as she drew the curtain

beside Ned Knolles' bed, wondered why Aylton had troubled to pour his drink into the bed-pot. No one checked to see if each man had drunk his. But Aylton had no way to know that, did he? So he had done what he could to seem to have drunk it. Because he feared someone—and not simply a sister doing her duty—would check to be sure he slept? Or because he *knew* someone would and wanted to deceive them? Had he been worried Geoffrey might seek him out in the night, not knowing Geoffrey's night had been taken over by his grandmother's illness? Had Aylton even known Mistress Thorncoffyn was ill? Or, if the poisoned ginger was his doing, had he been counting on her being ill and hoped it would give him his chance to flee? Let alone giving him added reason to flee, come to that.

Sister Margaret joined them. Master Osburne asked her and Sister Ursula together, "This is all then? You're done for the night?"

"Unless someone needs us, yes," Sister Margaret answered.

"My thanks for your patience. I've seen what I needed to see. I doubt I'll have more questions this way."

"We'll be here if you do," Sister Ursula replied calmly.

He bowed his head to them both, of course not including Joliffe, he being only a servant here. Sister Ursula and Sister Margaret bowed their heads in return, while Joliffe bowed more deeply, playing the servant and nonetheless aware of a final considering look from the crowner that said he was still part of the man's calculations.

More than that, as the sisters went out the near door, Master Osburne did not. Instead, he went down the hall, and Joliffe, lingering, saw him pause at Basset's bed and seem to say something, then wait as if hearing an answer before finally leaving by way of the door there.

Joliffe went to his own bed, not to settle but to wait until all was quiet, with Sister Petronilla gone to the pallet in the pantry, the other sisters to their dorter. In the silence and shadows then, he rose and went quiet-footed to the hall and in by the door near Basset's bed. Since his duties included greasing door hinges, to make as little noise as might be when he or the sisters came and went in the night, he had little worry about being heard. Once in, he slid silently past the edge of the curtain at the head of Basset's bed. The last lingering twilight through the hall's high windows showed Basset lying full length on his back, hands folded on his chest, head a little raised on the pillow, eyes open and shifting sideways to acknowledge Joliffe was there without need to turn his head. Beyond him, along the hall, there were still restless murmurings and rustlings as some of the men moved about on their beds and talked through the curtains, but the bed beside Basset's was still empty and across the way Oxyn's deep and even breathing told he was already soundly sleeping. This being as alone as he and Basset were likely to get, Joliffe knelt beside the bed and said softly, "What did the crowner want with you?"

Basset made a small sound that might have been smothered mirth. "Good evening to you, too," he mocked back softly. "He asked how Sister Ursula drew the curtains last night. He asked if it was in such a way as gave her chance to say something secretly to Aylton."

"He asked that outright?"

"Outright."

"Did she?"

"I didn't take note of how she was drawing the curtains."

"Is that what you said to him or what you truly noted?"

"Both, you distrustful louter."

"What are the men saying about it all?"

"If they had aught to wager with, they'd be laying it that someone else is going to die soon. Mistress Thorncoffyn most likely. Tonight for choice."

"God's mercy," Joliffe breathed. If he had been elsewhere,

it would have been a loud oath at finding the men's thoughts too near his own. Death came easily and fairly often in this place—the sisters among themselves privately doubted that Deke Credy would last much beyond the start of winter—but that was death in the common way of things, not violent death, not intended death. Those were another kind of death altogether, and once someone began intending deaths, where did it stop? Someone had set to poisoning Mistress Thorncoffyn—Aylton probably but there was no proof of it yet—but before poisoning was even suspected, Aylton himself had died, very possibly by murder. But why? By whom? And without knowing the reason for one murder, what were the chances of forestalling another? *If* Aylton's death had been murder. *If* another was intended. *If* it was not Aylton but someone else who had poisoned the candied ginger.

Meaning Geoffrey. Because no matter what Sister Margaret claimed she believed about her son, Joliffe could imagine more reasons for Geoffrey to want both his grandmother and Aylton dead than could be conjured up for anyone else.

All this was one of the troubles with secret murder, done by cunning instead of in an open moment of rage with everyone to see it. Not knowing who had murdered, or why, made space to doubt almost everyone—what they said, what they did. As witness Master Osburne's continued suspicion of me, Joliffe thought.

Aloud, still softly and not hiding he was frustrated, he said, "I've been watching, listening, asking questions all day, to no use yet. None of what I know goes together. All my thinking is getting me nowhere."

"Happens a lot with folk," Basset said. "Those that trouble with thinking at all."

Joliffe shrugged acknowledgement of that truth but persisted, "The trouble is there's no sense to Aylton being dead. Geoffrey Thorncoffyn is the only one with possible reason to want it, but only if he and Aylton were cheating his grandmother together, and even if they were, he was with her all last night while she was sick, with no chance at Aylton. It would help to find a link between Aylton's death and the ginger. Geoffrey claims he thought of it as a gift to his grandmother because of something Aylton said, and that Aylton got it for him to give to her, with claim the carrier had brought it."

"For all of which, we have only Geoffrey's word, yes?"

"Yes. The crowner says the carrier says he never brought anything for Aylton or Geoffrey, and he has no reason to lie about it."

"So far as we know."

"Don't add to my troubles. But, yes, so far as we know," Joliffe granted. "The one sure point seems to be that Aylton had the ginger before passing it on to Geoffrey. I'm willing to think he poisoned it in hope of being rid of Mistress Thorn-coffyn because he thought that Geoffrey might be easier to work for—and to deceive—than she might be."

"Unless he and Geoffrey were together in deceiving her *and* in trying to poison her."

"Which would at least make sense of Aylton being dead. Except Geoffrey was with his grandmother, giving him no chance at Aylton."

"So far as you know. His grandmother and that woman of hers would almost surely lie for him."

"It would need Master Hewstere's lying, too."

"Always possible," Basset pointed out.

Joliffe sighed. "Always possible. But I think I'd like it best if the ginger could somehow be proved to be all and only Aylton's doing—he had attempted murder but instead died himself trying to escape his other crime. Mistress Thorncof-fyn, at least, would find that a highly satisfying example of God's justice at work in the world. Unfortunately, we're still left with that bothersome bread in Aylton's stomach. Did he get it here or somewhere else? Nobody admits to feeding him here, but if he was somewhere else, why did he come back here? Except, given how he was lying in the stream, he was not coming back here but going away."

Two beds away, Dick Leek called softly, sleepily, "You talking to yourself, Tom Player?"

"Counting over my sins is all, Dick," Basset called as softly back.

"Eh, say 'em louder for us to enjoy 'em with you."

"I'd not dent your innocence that badly."

Since the only chuckle that brought was from Dick, Joliffe guessed the rest of the men were to sleep. For safety's sake, he and Basset sat quietly a while, until an uneven snore suggested Dick had joined the others. By then, the hall was too dark to see each other's faces, and Joliffe, with no new thoughts come to him in the wait and supposing Basset, too, was ready to sleep, made to rise, but Basset, having used the time for his own thoughts and not sounding sleepy at all, said, "What it comes down to is that you *think* there has to be a link between Aylton's death and the fact that someone tried to poison Mistress Thorncoffyn, but all you know for *certain* is that someone poisoned the candied ginger Geoffrey gave to his grandmother and that Aylton ate some bread before he died. There's no proof that Aylton's death was other than accident. If you allow that it was and that Aylton poisoned the ginger, then everything is settled and you can let it go."

"It's the bread," Joliffe whispered glumly.

"Forget the bread and you'll be fine."

Just the way Jack said they should forget the stream. The stream that showed Aylton had been going away from the hospital with bread in his belly that should not have been there.

The stream that he had so conveniently fallen in to drown.

He shook his head despite Basset probably could not see him in the dark and whispered, "There's almost surely someone else in this. Someone who put him into that stream."

"You *think*," Basset said. "You don't *know*. It could be no more than the accident it seems."

"Seems except for the bread."

"Let it go, Joliffe."

"I probably have to. I can hardly set about asking questions of those I most want to. Master Hewstere. Master Soule. Father Richard. Let alone Mistress Thorncoffyn and Geoffrey," he ended dryly, meaning to make a jest of it and leave Basset to a quiet night.

But Basset said, not jesting, "If you can't let it go, you have to consider the sisters, too."

Although he already had, Joliffe said, "No, I don't." Then gave the lie to his denial by adding, "All else aside, I doubt any of them could have carried Aylton to the stream and put him in it, and he assuredly was not dragged there."

Not any one of them, his mind said treacherously—but what of two of them together?

"Supposing he didn't just fall into the stream by *accident*," Basset persisted.

To shove his unwanted thought further off, Joliffe said lightly, "I hate to say you're likely right and it was only accident. Besides, if the sisters were going to trouble with killing someone, it would be Mistress Thorncoffyn. Come to it, if *anyone* was going to trouble with killing someone, that someone would surely be Mistress Thorncoffyn."

"Someone *has* tried," Basset pointed out.

But it was Aylton who was dead. Not Mistress Thorncoffyn.

Yet.

Chapter 22

The night went more quietly than Joliffe had feared it would. He was restless, yes, his sleep uneven and embroidered with senseless fragments of dark dreams, but the men slept steadily. Neither he nor Sister Petronilla had to leave their beds until dawn. Better than that, he thought wryly as the sisters gathered to break their night's fast by candlelight, they had made it to morning with everyone alive. Even Mistress Thorncoffyn.

Or had they?

Hewstere coming all unexpectedly into the kitchen startled them all from their early morning quiet around the kitchen's table. He was never seen at the hospital before late morning unless there were dire cause for it, and Sister Ursula's sharp, "What is it?" reflected all their instant alarm.

"Nothing, nothing," Hewstere assured them with a cheer that, from a man usually grave with his own great dignity, was alarming in a different way. "I was summoned in the night to see to Mistress Thorncoffyn is all. What do you have to break my fast?"

Sister Ursula gestured to the table where the bread loaf and wedge of cheese sat on their boards. He looked on it with disfavor but said, "Well enough, if that's what there is." He made no move to help himself, in clear expectation of being served. Joliffe obliged, less for Hewstere's sake than to save the sisters from the bother, while Sister Ursula asked, "Was she sick in the night again?"

"Not as she was before, no. Her body has purged itself that far. The trouble is in restoring her humours to balance after such affliction. At the best of times that would take much skill and careful judgment. With the planets in their present aspect, the difficulty of it is doubled, and likewise doubly necessary."

With becoming solemnity, Sister Ursula said, "I'm certain it's within your skill."

"It is," he agreed, taking the bread and cheese Joliffe held out to him. He frowned down at it. "You've nothing better?"

"No," Sister Ursula said.

Hewstere made a dismissive and disapproving sound and went away with the bread and cheese and no thanks.

No one said anything, good or ill, when he was gone, their silence sufficient comment on what they were likely thinking among themselves.

Rose, coming in soon afterward, was better welcomed. To Joliffe's question about Piers, she said he was all but well and turned to ask Sister Letice how she was.

"Almost altogether well, too," she said with her quiet smile that went deep in her eyes.

"Nonetheless, it will do you no harm to rest today," Sister Margaret said.

Sister Letice started to protest that with a shake of her head, but was forestalled by Sister Ursula saying, mock-sternly, "What she shall do is spend the day in the garden, doing as little or much as she feels able and strictly charged"—she turned a truly stern look on Sister Letice—"*strictly* charged to sit and rest whenever the need comes on her."

To that, Sister Letice bent her head in acceptance.

From there, the morning went on its usual ways outwardly at least. The men asked some questions about what the crowner had wanted with watching how they were settled for the night but were satisfied with being told Master Osburne was only being thorough about Aylton's last hours. Other than that, having heard no questions about his death or whispers of poison, there was little else to say except what had been said among them yesterday. Nor, so far as Joliffe heard, did the sisters talk of any of it. For them, not knowing of the bread, there was no great question about Aylton's death, and the poisoned ginger had nothing whatever to do with them now that Mistress Thorncoffyn was past the danger of it.

Joliffe, unfortunately, could not keep his mind as inwardly quiet as everyone else outwardly was. Not that he had anything new to think. With nothing added since yesterday to what he knew and guessed at, and Master Osburne failing to show himself at the hospital all morning, his thoughts only went in circles on themselves. He was braced when he took his dinner and Jack's to the gatehouse for whatever questions Jack might have about what was happening beyond sight of the gatehouse windows, only to be greeted by Jack asking merrily, "Has the rejoicing begun yet?"

"About what?" Joliffe asked blankly.

"At Mistress Thorncoffyn leaving!"

"Leaving?" Joliffe said, even more blankly. "She's leaving?"

Jack laughed at him. "You'd not heard?"

"None of us have. You're sure of it?"

"She means to go as soon as her carriage can rumble here from her near manor. The soonest it can be here is tomorrow sometime, I would guess, but yes, she means to be away as soon as may be. Unless she's changed her mind in the past half of an hour or so."

"You're *sure* of it?" Joliffe repeated, not yet willing to give way to the rise of his spirits at the very thought of her, her dogs, Geoffrey, and Idany being gone.

"If Geoffrey swearing to himself as he went out and in and out again this morning is anything to go by, yes. From what Simms at the inn says, she's going to be out of this 'house of death and sickness' as soon as may be. She's not told the sisters yet?"

"No. Which is maybe just as well. Seeing them sing and dance at the news might set her to choler again, and Hewstere would hardly approve of that."

Jack laughed. "Your Master Hewstere . . ."

"He's not mine." Joliffe caught at a new hope that shoved his spirits another notch higher. "He's going, too, isn't he? That's what you're going to tell me. That he's going with the Thorncoffyns."

"Seems so. Simms says he's hired a pack-pony for tomorrow. My guess is he's going with his golden goose."

So she looked that way to Jack, too. Joliffe gave a single, sharp, triumphant clap of his hands. "I *knew* it! He's surely got her believing her life depends on him and she isn't willing to leave him behind."

"He knows a richer pot when he sees it, that's certain," Jack said. "But if you've not heard about even that, what about this apothecary the crowner has sent for?"

"What apothecary?"

"Some apothecary he particularly trusts, I gather. He wants more confirmation of the poison, I'd guess. Besides what Sister Letice told him. Showed him."

"How do you know about that?" Joliffe asked in surprise.

"Amice," Jack said, sounding very satisfied with himself. "Last night."

"Ah."

"All night," Jack added.

"And maybe the night before, too?" Joliffe tried, matching Jack's light-heartedness but curious for another reason.

"The night before, too," Jack said readily. "Luckily enough, given Master Osburne was here asking if there was anyone besides myself could swear Aylton didn't leave or come back this way that night."

That Amice *could* swear on Jack's behalf would have relieved Joliffe's mind of the small shadow of suspicion about Jack that Basset had planted there, except he himself had told Jack about the bread in Aylton's stomach and the questions it raised. Had that warned Jack he should have ready a safe account of himself for that night should the crowner ask?

There was no way to know now, and he covered his discomfiture by asking jibingly, "Does Father Richard know about this between you and Amice?"

"It's Master Borton finding out that we worry on. There'll be a fine to pay if he finds out before we wed."

"It's going to come to wedding then?"

"We mean for it to. About Martinmas, we think."

"My best wishes for you both," Joliffe said, meaning it fully. "But how do you know about this sent-for apothecary when no one else here does? You didn't have *that* from Amice."

"Simms at the stable again."

"Who is this talkative Simms?"

"A friend from grammar school days. He comes by now and again to see if there's anything I can't limp to get for myself, and when he fetches me the occasional pottle of wine from the tavern, we share a cup and talk." Jack grinned. "As we did this morning, with him wanting to hear what I could tell him about matters here and him telling me all he was hearing."

That was one of the advantages of being familiar in a place, instead of only a stranger passing through, Joliffe thought: you could have friends who told you things you'd not hear otherwise. Come to it, being friends with Jack was now doing the same for him as Jack went on, "Seems, from a guess made from something Simms half overheard, the crowner wants this apothecary of his to look through the hospital's medicines and all." Jack looked suddenly worried. "Although maybe this is something that shouldn't be passed on to the sisters, nobody supposedly knowing about it save the crowner."

"You're likely right," Joliffe agreed slowly. "I'll say nothing." Little though he liked leaving Sister Letice to whatever suspicions Master Osburne must have about what she claimed about the poisoned ginger. Or maybe he was simply unwilling to settle for one person's word about something if he could have two person's, and one of them no part of this mess here. He was thorough at his work, was Master Osburne.

More than that, by all Joliffe had seen so far he was evenminded, too, looking for right answers rather than merely quick ones. Besides, what would be the point of warning the sisters about the apothecary coming? Anyone who had used anything here against Mistress Thorncoffyn—whether Sister Letice or someone else—had surely had sense enough to be rid of it, now that the crowner was involved.

Or if someone here *had* poisoned the ginger, then best they were found out.

To the good, Joliffe saw no way any of the sisters could have come at the ginger to poison it. The guilt surely had to lie somewhere between Aylton, Geoffrey, and Idany. Or all of them together. That was the comforting thought he took with him as he crossed the yard back to the hospital after leaving Jack. To have the three of them guilty together—or just Aylton and Geoffrey—would very satisfactorily link together Aylton's murder and the attempt on Mistress Thorncoffyn. It would all be so straightly forward if Aylton and Geoffrey had intended Mistress Thorncoffyn's death, and then Geoffrey had seen and taken his chance to be rid of Aylton who could be nothing but a danger to him from that point on.

Except Geoffrey had apparently worked as hard as anyone to keep his grandmother alive that night. That was the fact that Joliffe kept coming up against. Geoffrey might have briefly gone out, but hardly for long enough to have chance at Aylton. Surely not long enough to feed him, drug him, and drown him.

Damn.

He inwardly grabbed his mind and shook it. He was becoming as addled as a drunken egg, he thought. He was *not* going to think about any of it any more. Not unless he could find out something new that would make it worth his while to think about it rather than circling and circling pointlessly, conjuring phantoms out of nothing.

Passing along the covered walk toward the kitchen now, he raised a hand in greeting to Sister Petronilla and Daveth sitting on the garth's grass rolling a red-painted wooden ball back and forth between them, with Sister Petronilla gently urging Heinrich to watch the ball, see the ball, catch the ball, none of which Heinrich did, only sat swaying softly forward and back, staring into nowhere in front of him or at somewhere no one around him could see. Daveth waved to Joliffe, though, and Sister Petronilla smiled and nodded.

He came into the kitchen to find no one there but Rose, scrubbing the tabletop. Without pausing at her work, she asked, "How goes it? Are you any further with any of it?"

"Who says I'm thinking about *it* at all?" he lightly jibed.

"Anyone who knows you."

"Then, no," he admitted, letting his regret show. "I'm as good as flat-faced against a wall and getting nowhere."

"Ah well." She did not sound overly concerned. "There's work in the scullery to keep you busy for now."

Not finding himself ready yet to share what Jack had told him and be forced to talk about it, he went to the scullery and indeed found work there, and a bucket of warm water sitting ready, too, so he need not return to the kitchen even for that, just set straight to the washing—and to his thinking again, unable to stop himself.

It all came back to Geoffrey, didn't it? Leaving aside how easily he could have dealt with poisoning his grandmother, was he truly as innocent of Aylton's dealings as he claimed? If he were not, he had reason to have Aylton dead and would have had the necessary chance to kill him under guise of helping him escape, the escape being Aylton's price for keeping silence about their mutual cheating of her. They could have been together in poisoning Mistress Thorncoffyn. Or not. If Geoffrey was indeed involved in the extortions, he had nearly as much reason as Aylton to have his grandmother dead before she found out. She was unlikely to have set the law on him as she had threatened to do to Aylton, but she surely would have made his life hell for a long while to come.

All that, however appealing it was, all fell apart, though, on the two-pronged trouble that, first, there was no proof that Geoffrey had known of Aylton's extortions and, second, he had been trapped all that night by his grandmother's illness. Unless Idany was lying for him. That was the other appealing possibility—that he and Idany were together in this. But that could be something impossible to prove if they held to lying for one another.

Could Geoffrey have been working with someone other than Idany—someone free to see to Aylton for him? Who? Perhaps Hewstere, as part of a plan to get Mistress Thorncoffyn into their shared control? That had possibilities, because after all Hewstere's word that Geoffrey had been all night with his grandmother was needed as much as Idany's. Yes. Hewstere's cooperation was needed if either Geoffrey or Idany had seen to Aylton. So it had to be all three of them. Or none.

Joliffe rubbed at his forehead that was beginning to ache,

forgetting his hands were wet and somewhat gritted with the scrubbing sand. As he paused to wipe his face dry, he admitted to himself that in trying to see all three of them guilty together he was stretching almost as far as wondering about, say, Sister Petronilla. If he was going to stretch his imaginings that far, why not consider Master Soule more closely? He was a man who kept himself to himself. Who knew what secrets he held while seeming apart and above all the common fray? And if Master Soule, why not Jack, who could be lying about not seeing Aylton that night? Of course Amice would have to join in Jack's lie, but who knew what a woman would do for love?

Of course among the things Joliffe did not know was what possible reason either Jack or Amice would have for bothering to have Aylton dead.

Wryly, he wondered whether there was anyone else in the hospital he had yet to suspect. Someone among the patients? Such as were not bedridden. After all, they had had closest chance at Aylton that night. And why not Daveth and Heinrich, too, while he was at it? Well, not Heinrich—but Daveth? Had he been enough afraid of Aylton to want him dead?

He put a stop to all that far-stretched thinking and brought his thought around to the poisoned candied ginger. No one of the hospital had had chance to poison it. Yet to poison her here, where skilled help was so immediately to hand, argued the poisoning had to have been by someone who would not have other chance at her. *That* argued against it being Geoffrey or Idany or Aylton.

Still, Joliffe could not make it likely that Mistress Thorncoffyn's poisoning was not linked to Aylton's death, any more than he could make himself believe there was only chance in Aylton dying as he had. The two things simply could *not* stand separate from one another. They *had* to be linked. But how?

His certainty held that somewhere there was a missing piece whose shape he could not see, could not yet guess at or even guess whether it had to do with something he already knew but so far failed to understand, or with something not yet found out at all—something that would bring all the pieces together into a clear answer.

He found that he had been scouring a single cup until now it was almost shining, not an easy accomplishment since it was of wood. Impatiently, he sloshed it in the rinse water, set it aside, and reached for another, wishing his thoughts could be as readily set aside.

Chapter 23

He did not have to give the sisters the news of the coming departures. Sister Ursula, summoned to Mistress Thorncoffyn, had it from her directly and shared it with the other sisters, Rose, and Joliffe in the kitchen, causing thereby a rejoicing not much tempered by the word they were losing their physician, too. In truth, none of them seemed uneased by that at all, Sister Margaret saying, openly pleased, "We can call on Master Benedict at the other end of town if there's need of a physician until we have another. He'll come gladly."

Master Osburne's apothecary arrived late in the afternoon. Joliffe, not entirely by chance, was near to hand when Master Osburne brought him into the hospital and explained to Sister Ursula the why of Master Goldin's being there. She took it quietly, only saying respectfully, "Whatever you deem needful, Master Osburne, surely. I can't agree, though, that he be in the stillroom and among our medicines without Sister Letice there."

"I'd not have it otherwise," Master Goldin said for himself.

He was of late middle years and middle build, soberly dressed as suited his work, with a not unpleasant face and mild eyes.

Sister Ursula smiled on him. "She's there now, I think. I'll take you. Master Osburne, will you come, too, or would you care for a cup of ale while you wait?"

"I doubt Master Goldin needs me watching over his shoulder."

"I do not," Master Golden confirmed.

"Then I would indeed be glad of ale, and will sit on that bench in the rear-yard, to be out of your way here in the kitchen."

"Joliffe will bring out your ale. Master Goldin, if you'll come this way."

Joliffe poured a cupful of ale and followed Master Osburne out the rear door, finding him sitting on the bench there, head leaned back against the wall, eyes closed. He opened them as Joliffe stopped beside him, straightened to take the cup, thanked him, and said, "You are someone from outside this place. I gather from what the sister has said that you have no intent to stay but mean to leave when you can, yes?"

"Yes."

"Then, as someone from outside, what can you say about what you see among these folk, day by day? Is there anything that rises to—" He paused, maybe seeking the best way to say what he wanted.

"Murder?" Joliffe supplied.

"Murder," Master Osburne agreed.

"No."

With a tilt of his head and an inquiring look, Master Osburne asked for more without giving away what that more might be.

Joliffe, trying for honesty beyond the swirl of his mostly rootless suspicions, said, "Not even of Mistress Thorncoffyn. She makes almost constant trouble for the sisters while she's here. No one welcomes her coming. But everyone knows she'll go away again. No one is going to kill because of an itch that's going to go away."

"She has been more than an itch to Sister Margaret, as I hear."

"You'll also hear that Sister Margaret was glad to escape her and is more than content in her life here. She has no interest in revenge on Mistress Thorncoffyn."

"So it is said. Is it true?"

"From all I've seen of her at her work, yes. The skill to heal isn't only in her head. It's in her heart and her hands. I can't see her ever using it to murder. It would be a betrayal of who she is."

"What of this Sister Letice and her brother the priest? They have to be bitter against Mistress Thorncoffyn. Could he have urged his sister to use her skill with herbs to take revenge by poisoning the candied ginger? Or could she have chosen to do it on her own?"

Plainly, Master Osburne had been very thorough in his time here, and Joliffe granted, "It's possible, but I haven't thought of how either of them could have come at the ginger to poison it. Or how Sister Margaret could. Mistress Thorncoffyn never lets her close."

"Sister Petronilla?"

"She has the least of anyone to do with the Thorncoffyns and no more chance at the ginger than the other sisters. Her concern is mostly the children, and she shows completely happy at that."

"What of Sister Ursula? Since every problem with Mistress Thorncoffyn's being here comes to her, soon or late, could she come to the point of thinking murder a way of simply easing things once and for all?"

"It would take something far greater than simply easing her life to bring her to murder, I think," Joliffe said. "Supposing she could be brought to it at all. I don't know that she could."

"But if need were great enough?"

"I don't see being rid of Mistress Thorncoffyn, even on her worst days, as need enough." Uncomfortable with the crowner's questioning, Joliffe gave way to a deliberate grin and added, "And even then it would be murder done in the moment, not planned as the poisoned ginger had to be. I'd say we must grant the poisoned ginger to Master Aylton. But then, who killed *him*? None of the sisters, surely. They would have no reason."

Master Osburne did not join his smile. "No reason we yet know," he said, his gaze fixed on Joliffe's face.

Joliffe lost his grin, abruptly aware that he had spoken too openly, unwarily. Not like a servant being questioned. "No reason we know," he agreed.

The crowner kept his look fixed on him. "You have thought much on all of this."

That probe was careful, inviting him to say more. Joliffe, since his seeming of a servant was already so deeply dented, gave in and went on, "If I were to lay a wager on who had best reason to have Aylton dead, it would have to be on Geoffrey Thorncoffyn, on the likelihood they were together in thieving from Mistress Thorncoffyn. The trouble there is that he was with his grandmother all that night." He paused, then could not help adding, hoping for something back from Master Osburne, "At least no one has said otherwise, I gather."

"No one has," Master Osburne agreed. "Not her woman or the sisters or Master Hewstere for such of the time he was there."

Joliffe snatched at that. "Such of the time? He wasn't there all the while?"

"He went home for a time to compound a medicine for her, since she would take only what came from his hands, nothing any of the sisters might have tainted here. No one is sure of the hour he went or for how long. 'Not long' he says.

'Too long' the woman Idany says. 'I don't know' says Master Thorncoffyn."

Joliffe's mind leaped to the possibilities that opened and again forgot to curb his tongue. "The last thing Master Hewstere is likely to want is Mistress Thorncoffyn dead. She's worth too much to him. If he had come to think the ginger was poisoned, then encountered Aylton escaping in the night, he maybe killed him in revenge for nearly ruining his chance to make his fortune with Mistress Thorncoffyn." Joliffe's excitement abruptly faded. More flatly, he said, "Except why take the risk and trouble of murder when simply giving Aylton over to the law would have been more than revenge enough?"

"More than that, Master Hewstere had no thought it was poison working in Mistress Thorncoffyn. He even dismissed it as a possibility when I told him what Sister Letice had learned."

"Did you tell him how she had learned it?" Joliffe asked, instantly angry on Sister Letice's behalf.

"He claimed her belief the ginger would make her sick caused her to be so," Master Osburne said evenly, not giving away his own thought on the matter. He held out the empty cup. "Thank Sister Ursula for me. When Master Goldin finishes, tell him that I'm here."

Knowing dismissal when he heard it and suspecting the crowner had timed his drinking to end with his questioning, Joliffe took the cup, slightly bowed, and had taken his first step away when Master Osburne said, still even-voiced, "You, of course, never knew Aylton, never had anything to do with him until here, did you?"

Joliffe paused for a startled moment, then said, "No. Never."

He waited for what more the crowner might ask. When there was nothing, he finished leaving. In the kitchen Rose and the sisters, except for Sister Letice, were readying the men's supper. As he came in, they paused their work to look at him, intent with unasked questions while leaving it to Sister Ursula to say, restrainedly, "He kept you in talk."

"He wanted a servant's eye view of the Thorncoffyns and the hospital."

"Of us," Sister Margaret said, more bluntly.

"Of me, too," Joliffe quickly added.

"Did he say anything about this apothecary?" Sister Ursula asked.

"Nothing."

"He's a long while with Sister Letice," Sister Petronilla said, and worried looks passed among them all, but Sister Ursula said, "There's nothing we can do about it. So best we get on with supper."

The bell was just being rung for Vespers when Sister Letice and Master Goldin at last came into the kitchen together, showing none of the unease the sisters had been suffering. Instead, they were in earnest, eager, smiling talk together, apparently about whether thyme compounded with vinegar or thyme compounded with burnt salt was better against headache, sounding like two people sharing an interest and even a respect for one another's skill. Certainly Master Goldin did not sound as if he were condescending to her, and when he had paused to ask after Master Osburne and been told where he was, he and Sister Letice went instantly back to their talk and out the rear door together.

"Well," said Sister Ursula with some degree of surprise when they were gone.

Master Osburne shortly came into the kitchen, gave Sister Ursula thanks for her patience and the ale, said that Master Goldin and Sister Letice were gone to see the garden, and went on his own way.

"Well," said Sister Ursula again.

"Very well indeed," Sister Petronilla said, widely smiling.

Rose was gone, Vespers was done, the men had their suppers, and the women and Joliffe were gathered around the table for their own before Sister Letice returned, now alone.

Sister Margaret immediately asked, with everyone else's curiosity, "This Master Goldin found nothing that troubled him?"

"No. He approved of everything." Sister Letice's voice and face were alight with unfamiliar happiness. "He told me things, too. He's promised to send a distillation that he says works well against some high fevers."

"What about the poison?" Sister Margaret asked.

"Arsenic."

In the utter silence that answered the blunt word, Sister Letice, surprised, looked around at everyone's startled stares fixed on her. "Well, it had to be something," she said, then went on eagerly, "He says it's surely arsenic. He says it can be had as a powder that can be mixed into a sugar syrup and the ginger then soaked in it. If the ginger was already candied, doing that would make it even sweeter and the more likely someone would be to eat all the more of it."

"The more likely Mistress Thorncoffyn would, for a certainty," Sister Margaret said.

"That's what I said to him," Sister Letice agreed happily.

"Where would someone come by arsenic?" Joliffe asked at the same moment Sister Ursula asked, "What *is* arsenic?"

With the same gladness of knowing something new, Sister Letice said, "Master Goldin says it's some sort of a mineral and has to be dug out of the ground. He says it's not found here or even much seen."

With none of Sister Letice's gladness, Sister Petronilla said, "It's had from the East but is become more used here of late." She had been a merchant's wife, Joliffe remembered. "Taken slightly, it serves to whiten a woman's skin. Beyond that, it's good only for poisoning."

"That's what Master Goldin said," Sister Letice said. "He

said, too, it isn't readily come by and he couldn't guess who beyond an apothecary would have it anywhere here. Oh, and he said it could be stirred into a drink, too, he supposed, but beyond doubt the ginger was poisoned."

"What did he say of you trying it yourself?" Sister Ursula asked.

Sister Letice ducked her head to and said in a rush that did not hide her pleasure, "He said it was foolishly done but very likely what he would have tried himself."

Sister Petronilla put an arm around her shoulders in a quick, approving embrace, smiling, while Sister Margaret declared, "Foolish, yes, but courageous, too," and Sister Ursula said, more soberly, "So he's done what Master Osburne wanted of him," sharing a look with Joliffe that said she was wondering what came next.

Since he was wondering the same, he had no answer for her.

When Jack had said Mistress Thorncoffyn's carriage would come sometime on the morrow, he had probably not meant *dawn* on the morrow, but that was when it rumbled up to the hospital gates with tired horses and a pair of drivers who had made use of clear moonlight to drive all night under the goad of whatever sharp order Mistress Thorncoffyn had sent.

The sisters and Joliffe knew of it when Idany came into the kitchen soon thereafter to demand Joliffe's help in loading Mistress Thorncoffyn's belongings into it. Sister Ursula refused, saying he was the hospital's servant, not Mistress Thorncoffyn's, and had too many duties at this hour to be spared. Idany left in high displeasure. Sister Ursula hummed a little, happily.

There was no keeping from the men in the hall the scuff and thudding of things being moved through the foreporch that began while they were breaking their fast. Told what was happening, they took more interest in looking at Mistress Thorncoffyn and Idany when they came to Mass than in the Mass itself. Joliffe took interest in the fact that Geoffrey was not let off seeing things into the carriage even for Mass. It seemed Mistress Thorncoffyn was *very* determined to be away as soon as might be.

Of Master Hewstere in the midst of all that there was no sign.

After Mass, the boy Will came to tell Sister Ursula that Master Soule wished to see her. She went, and all the sisters and Joliffe lingered in the kitchen with Rose instead of getting on with their morning tasks, to hear what Master Soule had wanted. She came back very shortly to say Master Soule was in great displeasure, having had a message from Master Hewstere brought to him just before Mass, to say the physician was resigning from the hospital to accompany Mistress Thorncoffyn in her need.

"Master Soule is not best pleased," Sister Ursula said, "despite I assured him that we shall do well enough until someone else can be found."

"Or even better," Sister Margaret said, low-voiced. No one said otherwise.

But still they were not done with Mistress Thorncoffyn. At mid-morning, as Joliffe was stacking firewood beside the rear door, Idany came into the kitchen and declared at Sister Ursula, "My lady is ready to leave now. You're to come bid her farewell for courtesy's sake. All of you," she added at the other sisters, dropped her gaze to Heinrich under the table, and amended coldly, "Nearly all."

Coldly in return, Sister Ursula said, "Such of us as are free to come will do so."

Idany looked on the verge of challenging that, then must have thought better and settled for a sharp nod before leaving.

Sister Ursula looked around. Everyone looked back from their various tasks and made no move, until Joliffe said cheerfully, "I'll come, if you like."

"That should do very well to show our courtesy," Sister Ursula said. "Come. We wouldn't want to miss seeing her leave."

Even so, they were too late to bid her a direct farewell. By the time they came, in no great haste, to the foreporch, Mistress Thorncoffyn was already in the yard, crossing toward her carriage, held up by Geoffrey on one side and stabbing her staff into the yard's dust on her other. The carriage was perhaps three times the length of the players' cart, with high wooden sides and a tall canvas tilt curved over it on half-hoops. The thing had been turned, undoubtedly very awkwardly in the narrowness of the yard, so it and its four horses were facing toward the gate, its open rear toward Mistress Thorncoffyn as she stomped toward it. From what Joliffe could see of the shadowed inside, more than half the carriage was crammed with chests and bags, with Mistress Thorncoffyn's chair last, facing the carriage's rear. Willow hampers set on cushions were strapped to the carriage's sides the remaining length, the yapping from them telling where Mistress Thorncoffyn's dogs were. Idany stood between them, at the top of the steep steps from the ground to the carriage.

So only Mistress Thorncoffyn remained to be loaded, and Joliffe was more than glad that task was Geoffrey's and the man waiting at the foot of the steps, one of the drivers, Joliffe supposed. Mistress Thorncoffyn gave them small help, lifting one foot enough to stomp it onto the bottom step herself but depending on Geoffrey and the man to heave her up sufficiently for her other foot to join it. They had to repeat the effort step by step, with the men's gasping for breath and occasional grunt almost lost under Mistress Thorncoffyn's own bellows-breathing. When she was at the last step, Idany reached out to take hold on her out-held hands and hauled her forward as the men gave a final heave upward. With that, she was into the carriage, and while the driver dropped down from the steps and made for the front of the carriage, Geoffrey kept at his grandmother's side, helping Idany take her forward, turn her, and loose her to drop into her chair.

Joliffe hoped all her long, intense indulgence in too much food was worth the trouble and humiliation her body was now become to her and everyone around her.

Geoffrey came out of the carriage and went to his horse tied close by, while Idany set to being sure her mistress was comfortable. Her own place was probably the pile of cushions on the floor beside the chair. Mistress Thorncoffyn, for her part, glared out of the carriage's shadows at Sister Ursula and Joliffe but offered no more of thanks or good-bye to them than they did to her as the driver cracked a whip over the horses. They leaned into their harness and the carriage rolled ponderously forward. Beyond the gateway, the turn into the road seemed to take forever but was done at last. Then, as the carriage rolled from sight and Jack began to swing the gate shut, Master Hewstere rode past, leading a pack-pony. He did not look aside but simply went.

So they were gone. All of them. Mistress Thorncoffyn, her dogs, Idany, Geoffrey, Master Hewstere. Joliffe wondered if it was only in his imagination that a relieved peace was already settling over everything almost as quickly as the dust raised by their going had settled in the yard behind them. The gate thudded shut.

"There," said Sister Ursula, as if at a task well done, and turned away.

Turning with her, Joliffe saw Sister Margaret had joined them after all. Or not quite joined them but stayed well back in the shadows of the foreporch, able to see but probably unseen. Which Joliffe guessed meant she was not as indifferent to her son and erstwhile mother-in-law as she chose to seem, and as she joined them in going back into the hospital, Sister

Ursula asked her, not altogether lightly, "Are you wishing she ends up in a ditch with a broken wheel and has to spend a night in a hedge?"

Not lightly at all but with an underlay of sadness that took Joliffe by surprise, Sister Margaret said, "I don't wish anything at her. With all the harm she's done to herself, what would be the point in harming *my*self by wishing more on her? What's hard is knowing she's out there in the world again, monsterful and cruel and never believing anything but good of herself."

It was not Joliffe's place, as a servant, to answer something not said to him, but Sister Ursula made no reply either. Perhaps she felt as Joliffe did—that Sister Margaret's words were a very serviceable epitaph for a woman still alive but already dead in so many ways.

The tray Joliffe carried up to Master Soule a while later had only the one meal on it. That had happened a few times since Joliffe had come, when the physician had been elsewhere for a day or sometimes two. This time, though, was different: Master Hewstere would not be coming back.

Unless, of course, he fell out with Mistress Thorncoffyn and returned.

Supposing someone else had not been found for his place before then.

Joliffe scratched at the open door and at Master Soule's summons went into the room. The master was standing at the open window through which a warm breeze was wafting, a book open in his hand. From all Joliffe had seen of him— or, rather, from how little Joliffe had seen of him—he was a solitary man, not much given to a need for company beyond his mid-day talk with Master Hewstere, but today perhaps he was feeling the first loss of even that little, because as Joliffe

set the tray on the table, the master said, "Jack tells me you
are well-read. That you even read Latin."

"Sir," Joliffe said with a slight bow and a servant's voice,
surprised into wariness.

"Did you at some time study to be a priest?"

"A clerk, sir. I at one time thought to be a clerk." Which
was not altogether a lie. One bitter winter, when he and his
brothers were too much outside and too often chilled to the
bones while his father's clerk sat inside with a brazier beside him to keep the ink and his fingers supple, Joliffe had
strongly thought about the benefits of being a clerk. He had
been about age nine, he thought, and the ambition had died
with the first spring weather, but he had had it.

"How did you come from that to being a player?"

Since a servant's place gave him no space to say that was
none of Master Soule's business, Joliffe said in his same
servant-voice that mingled respect and nothing forthcoming
that could be helped, "I found that hours of ink and pen and
sitting in one place didn't suit me, sir." Something that was
as true now as it had been at age nine. But if Master Soule
wanted to talk, he was willing and deliberately brightened
his voice to add, "I did like the reading, though. Have kept
that up. As Jack told you. We have good talks together, Jack
and I."

"He should have been a clerk himself, except his back is so
bad," Master Soule said. "It's kept him penned here when he
might have gone elsewhere." Was there a shade of longing in
Master Soule's voice for some lost chance of his own?

Trying for just the right note of a servant making cheery
but still respectful talk, Joliffe offered, "He sees a lot of the
world, though, right there at the gate. He likes that part of it
all. I warrant he was as glad as the rest of us to see the last of
Mistress Thorncoffyn this morning."

As he hoped, Master Soule rose to that bait, saying with

unchecked disgust, "So are we all. An odious woman who
sees no reason for God and all the earth to exist except to
feed her appetites. Our good fortune would be she's been so
offended she never returns."

"We were all surprised, though, the crowner let her go,"
Joliffe tried. "What with everything and all."

Master Soule came to the table, took a spoon, and began
pushing at the meat pottage in the bowl without sitting
down or showing much desire to eat. "If it comes to charging
her with manslaughter in Aylton's death, she can be found as
readily at one of her manors as here."

"It's pity she took Master Hewstere with her," Joliffe ventured. "It's that put out the sisters are about it."

That was a more outright lie than his claim to have wanted
to be a clerk, but it proved a very serviceable one as Master
Soule threw down the spoon and said, "It would seem we're
well-rid of him, too. He always seemed a man of reason, but
I have to doubt that now he's chosen to become her dog. In
place of the dead one, as it were. He could at least have lingered to be at Master Aylton's funeral."

That was to be this afternoon, Joliffe knew. There had
been talk among the sisters which of them should go, but
there had been no mention of Master Soule attending at
all and, curious why Master Hewstere's failure to be there
seemed so particular an offense to him, Joliffe asked, "Will
you be going then, sir?"

"No." Master Soule took up the spoon again, sat down. "I
have my duties here and did not know the man. It was Master
Hewstere knew him. They were even friends upon a time, I
gather, if not so much of late."

Joliffe echoed sharply, "Master Hewstere knew him?"

"As I understand it, it was Master Hewstere helped him
into Mistress Thorncoffyn's service." Spoon filled and on its
way to his mouth, Master Soule added, "Recommended him
to Geoffrey, I believe."

While Joliffe was gathering his wits around that, Master Soule gave a sideways nod of dismissal at him. Joliffe willingly accepted it, bowed, and escaped from the room and down the stairs, to come to a stop in the sacristy, staring out the window opposite him with a whirl of shifting possibilities in his head.

That Aylton and Hewstere had known each other before here, before Aylton's service to Mistress Thorncoffyn, changed the balance of several things. For one, it made more possible that Aylton would have sought Hewstere's help in escaping that night. More than that, Hewstere, when first tending Aylton after the beating, had had excellent chance to offer his help in Aylton escaping and warn him against the sleeping draught. Or turn it another way: when Hewstere was first tending Aylton after the beating, *Aylton* had had the chance to ask for Hewstere's help.

Either way, Mistress Thorncoffyn's unexpected "illness" had not interfered. Hewstere had simply made a reason to leave the hospital for a time in the night.

Or was Mistress Thorncoffyn's "illness" after all unexpected? Not by Aylton, surely, if it was granted he had poisoned the ginger. In fact, knowing she was going to be ill and, hopefully die, it had surely added to his urgent need to escape, lest suspicion after all rouse and turn his way.

Again there was the question of why poison her here, where the best of help to cure her could be counted on. Unless help *not* to cure her was precisely on what Aylton had been depending. More than that, a physician could know about poisons as readily as an apothecary. Could have arsenic on hand or know how to get it.

But Hewstere had helped to keep Mistress Thorncoffyn alive.

After Aylton was dead.

Or after Hewstere had been certain Aylton would *be* dead.

After all, Mistress Thorncoffyn had all along been worth more to Hewstere alive. Worth far more than Aylton was, that was a certainty.

But then why would he have helped Aylton poison the ginger at all before Aylton gave it to Geoffrey for his grandmother?

Unless—Joliffe's mind jerked and shifted among possibilities—unless there was something Aylton knew about Hewstere that Hewstere did not want known by anyone else. Something Aylton could use as a threat to force Hewstere to help with the poison. So Hewstere had helped him—until chance came to be rid of Aylton and whatever extortion Aylton was using on him, and win himself even deeper into Mistress Thorncoffyn's favor.

Whosever's thought it had been for Aylton to escape the hospital—Aylton's or Hewstere's—the rest would have been easy. Aylton would have gone to Hewstere's house, would have waited there until Hewstere came, and never questioned when Hewstere did come and gave him food and drink and very probably something to ease the pain of the beating— something that had instead sent him senseless. That done, Hewstere, a well-sized man, could have carried Aylton the short way from his house into the orchard and to the stream beside the garden, and laid him there, his head in the water to drown, looking like he had been coming from the hospital when he fell.

Joliffe jerked from his frozen stare out the sacristy window, swung his head side to side as he tried to decide which way to go next, then made up his mind and went out the sacristy's rear door, taking the way Aylton had probably gone that night, through the small garden and around to the road in front of the hospital that would have been in deep darkness then. Under Jack's window he called up to him, and when Jack put his head out, asked, "Is the crowner still in town, do you know? There was mention made he might stay for Aylton's funeral."

"You're on the wrong side of the gate, you know, and where's my dinner?" Jack said back good-humouredly. "So far as I've heard, he's still in town, probably at the inn, or they'll know where he's gone." And added as Joliffe started away, "Hai! My dinner?"

Joliffe waved and kept going.

Master Osburne proved easy to find. As Joliffe neared the inn, the crowner came out its front door and stood regarding the sky as if wondering why it was so clear. He shifted his heed to Joliffe readily enough as Joliffe came to him and asked, as Joliffe bowed to him, "What is it?"

Just as abruptly, Joliffe said, "Master Soule said just now that Master Hewstere and Aylton knew one another before Aylton came into Mistress Thorncoffyn's service. That Master Hewstere knew him well enough to recommend him to the Thorncoffyns. Did you know that?"

Master Osburne, his brows drawing down in thought as he took that in, shook his head slowly. "No, I did not know that. Assuredly Master Hewstere never said anything about it. He has gone with Mistress Thorncoffyn, yes?"

"Yes. My thought is that if he and Aylton knew one another longer than either said, better than anyone has thought, then parts of all this that haven't made sense go together better."

He went from there with what else he had thought, and Master Osburne began to nod while he talked and said when Joliffe finished, "As you say, things go together better, knowing they knew each other well." He stopped nodding and fixed a sharp look on Joliffe. "What needs knowing is what Aylton might have known against Hewstere that was worth killing to keep secret. Since you seem to have a great many thoughts beyond the ordinary in this matter, have you any thoughts that way?"

Joliffe had not gone that far with his thinking yet and said, "No. No thought at all. I had little chance to see them with each other, but in the little that I did, I would never have thought they more than barely knew each other."

"Yet Master Soule seemed to think they were friends. I wonder why?"

"He and Master Hewstere spent much time in talk together. They had to have talked of *something* besides the stars and courses of the planets and mankind's unsettled humours. Or it may be something Master Soule only gathered in passing."

"I shall surely shortly be asking Master Soule about it."

Joliffe could not hold back from asking, "And then?"

"Then I shall likely go looking for what there might have been that might have made Master Hewstere willing to help Aylton poison Mistress Thorncoffyn. Of course the poisoning may have been meant merely to make her ill enough to value and depend on Master Hewstere's care forever after . . ."

"There have to be safer ways of making her ill than arsenic."

The crowner nodded agreement to that. "No, it was death they were after," he said.

"But that had to be Aylton's desire more than Hewstere's," Joliffe said, wanting to be certain that was clear. "Because when the chance came to be rid of Aylton, it seems Hewstere took it with no pause at all."

"No pause at all," Master Osburne agreed. "I think I will not linger to see who does what at Aylton's funeral after all." Staring away along the road, he seemed now to be thinking aloud to himself. "Master Thorncoffyn has told me where Aylton came from. I've sent a man to find out if he has family who should know he is dead. Now there are questions I want asked there, too. Master Soule will likely be able to tell me from where Master Hewstere came to here. I can have questions asked that way, too." His gaze came suddenly back to Joliffe. "You have my thanks," he said. But there was speculation in that thanks and in his look, and Joliffe, aware that in his eagerness he had let go all of a servant's manners, gave an over-deep bow, said humbly and quickly, "I pray I've been of service, sir," bowed deeply again, and retreated even while Master Osburne was saying, "You have been. Most assuredly, you have been."

Chapter 24

Through the following few days, the hospital's life settled back into quiet and commonplaces. Surprisingly quickly and with a welcome ease, the troubles raised by Mistress Thorncoffyn and by Aylton's death smoothed out of the hospital's life like water settling to calm on a briefly troubled pond. That the crowner simply left meant that those who knew no better went on thinking Aylton's death had been because of Mistress Thorncoffyn's beating, and while talk of murder would have been more diverting among the men in the hospital's hall, the other made pleasant talk enough until newer, nearer matter came with tired-looking Agnes Kemp bringing in her aged and tottering grandfather. Both he and she seemed relieved to have him there, she parting from him with a kiss on his forehead and promise to return on Sunday to see how he did, he settling down onto his mattress declaring it was softer lying than he had had in many a moon and neither was there anything so bad about being soaked clean from head to foot all at one time either. Within two days he was as familiar with the hospital's ways as if he had been there a month, cheerfully at ease, and all the more welcomed by the other men for wanting to hear everything they had to tell of the Thorncoffyns and that of Master Aylton.

Oddly, Master Hewstere seemed no more missed than Mistress Thorncoffyn and all of hers. The town's other physician sent word he would come when needed, and the sisters supposed among themselves that Master Soule would sometime stir himself to find someone else, but in the meanwhile no one was displeased with Sister Margaret's care.

All of that might have been sufficient reason for Sister Letice's raised spirits, her more often smiling and sometimes laughter, but when Joliffe said something of it to Rose, she said with one of those smiles that women use to puzzle men, "She's had that distillation from Master Goldin, as he promised. He's also written to her that he hopes to be here again about Saint Edward's day." When Joliffe showed his uncertainty of what that had to do with anything, Rose added pointedly, "He's a widower. And the sisters here are nursing sisters. They've no nuns' vows to hold them here."

Finally seeing, Joliffe said, "Oh."

"Oh," Rose agreed, smiling

So in some ways nothing here was changed and yet everything was changing. The old men went on as they had been, with maybe nobody but the sisters seeing how Deke Credy was fading day by day. Adam Morys of the broken leg was able to leave his bed and walk a little, held up between Sister Petronilla and Joliffe while he rediscovered his balance but with promise of crutches to come and Sister Margaret's assurance that his leg had mended so straight he would likely have no limp at all. Iankyn Tanner's bouts of struggling to breathe became fewer; he had hope of going home at cider-making time. John Oxyn's fever finally fully freed him, leaving him weak but no longer wildly restless for hours on end. And Basset was able to bear being on his feet and, with the help of a staff, was walking, at first for only little whiles and unsteadily but better every day, to the point where Sister Ursula told him, "We'll not have you here much longer." And cast a look at Joliffe as she added, "Which means we lose you, too, I suppose."

Joliffe spread his hands to show it was not his fault.

"Still," she said, "harvest is coming to an end, and that will likely bring Ivo back to us. Hopefully before you leave."

She included Basset and Joliffe together in that, and now it was Basset who spread his hands, saying, "You'll have to blame Sister Margaret and Sister Letice for our loss. It's their good care has made me better."

"I shall make certain to chastise them for their carelessness in that," she said and went away, smiling.

Basset and Joliffe looked at one another, and Basset asked, "You're ready to leave, aren't you?"

"Whenever you're able to," Joliffe said and did not add, "Soon, I hope," although he wanted to, because although time to move on was not just yet, he felt it coming. The familiar restless urge to be somewhere else had begun to rouse in him again these past few days. He hoped it was because his healing time here now had him well enough to take up his life again. If nothing else, the nightmares came less often, were less fierce than they had been. Knowing the uselessness of fleeing what was in his own mind, he had never tried to deny them, never tried to run from where they came. He doubted he would ever be fully free of them but hoped now that maybe they were behind him, following, instead of something he stumbled over at almost every forward step.

For one forward step, there was the matter of another horse for the company. The end of harvest meant a less pressing need for horses, making it a good time for buying—or as good a time as any. Joliffe had never enjoyed the challenge of horse-dealing, having been told all too often in his younger days that he was no judge of horseflesh. "You'd buy for liking of the beast," his father had told him, disgustedly. "Not for the likelihood it's any good."

So after talk with Basset, he set Ellis to the business. Once Ellis understood what it was about and what he might spend, he gladly undertook it, saying, "There's a good little bay gelding I wouldn't mind us having. He's pulled a few times in team with Tisbe and they got on. That's to the good." Then he fixed an acidly questioning gaze on Joliffe and said, "Whatever you've been at, it must have paid beyond ordinary well."

"Well enough for a new horse and the harness to go with it," Joliffe answered blandly. "Yet here I am again. Unable to stay away."

"Yes. Here you are again," Ellis agreed, not sounding as if he thought that made the matter any better. But he was able to buy the bay gelding and the harness and have money left over, and when he brought the gelding to the hospital's rear-yard along with Gil and Piers, to show the new member of their company to Basset, Basset was able to walk out leaning only on a staff and no one's arm.

Joliffe had thought to bring some bread with him, and while he stood at the gelding's head, stroking him and feeding him the bread, the others—after Basset had approved him—set about considering what his name should be, since his present one of Nodkin appealed to none of them.

"If we still had Hero," said Piers, remembering the company's horse before Tisbe, "we could call him Leander."

"Then we'd have to worry every time we crossed a ford," said Gil, "for fear he'd take after his namesake." Piers made a face at him.

"Much though I hate to suggest the straightest way," Basset said, "don't we have to call him Pyramus, to go with Tisbe?"

"We could change Tisbe's name," Joliffe suggested. That

earned the expected glare from everyone before they ignored him and went on.

Of course at the end the choice did come down to Pyramus, but Joliffe could see nothing of the tragic lover about the horse and whispered in his ear, "You're just Ramus, aren't you?"

By the twitch and bob of his head, Ramus seemed to agree, and swung his head sideways to butt Joliffe firmly in the chest as if to confirm it.

Joliffe gave him over to Piers then, stood with Basset to watch horse, Piers, Gil, and Ellis leave the yard, and went on standing there a moment longer after they were gone, hearing the dry clop of Ramus' hoofs along the cart track, before Basset said, very quietly, "A few more days. Once they've had harvest-home, then it will be time to go."

Joliffe nodded, his agreement no less deep for being silent. If he looked on his while here as a healing time for him as much as for Basset, then like Basset he was well enough to be on his way.

And yet . . .

There were several parts to that "and yet." One was his unwillingness to leave the sisters short of his help. The other was regret at not knowing what had come of the crowner's search away from here. Willing though he always was to go on, sometimes there were things hard to leave behind undone.

Some of his unwillingness was solved that afternoon's end. While he and Rose and all the sisters were readying the trays with the men's suppers, someone loomed into the kitchen's rear doorway. The sudden blocking of the light turning everyone's head that way, and even before Sister Ursula said, somewhere between disgust and welcome, "So you're back," Joliffe guessed the wide, stoop-shouldered man was the wandering Ivo.

"I'm back," Ivo agreed. He beckoned his head at Joliffe. "Who's he then?"

"The fellow who saw to it we've missed you not at all," Sister Ursula said tartly. "Nor are you having him out of his bed just because you've showed yourself again."

From where she was warming the milk at the hearth, Rose said, even-voiced, "But he'll be gone in a few days, so nobody need fret about it."

Everyone—not least Joliffe—changed their heed sharply to her. She looked away from the milk to Joliffe and added, still evenly, "We all will, I suppose, now that Basset is so well and everything."

"Yes," said Joliffe slowly; and to Sister Ursula, "I suppose we will be."

The rest of his unwillingness was taken care of the next afternoon. He was sitting on the grass in the garth, giving Daveth a lesson on the lute, Sister Petronilla sitting close by with Heinrich on her lap and clapping his hands for him to match the music, no matter that he seemed not to hear it at all. Daveth, on the contrary, was showing a true ear and deft fingers, and Joliffe was just deciding that when time came to leave, he would gift him with the lute and get another for himself somewhere along the way, when Jack came limping along the walk to say the crowner was at the gate and wanted to see him. Sister Petronilla immediately looked alarmed, but Jack said, "Nay, it's not trouble for Joliffe. Master Osburne just wants to tell him something, he says. He's waiting outside the gate. Said he'd not come in."

Joliffe got up, told Daveth trying to hand him the lute, "No, I trust you with it. Go on playing," and joined Jack, only with difficulty matching his slow walk when what his curiosity wanted was for him to break into a run.

Jack, likely knowing that, said at the outer doorway, "You go ahead. It's you the crowner wants to see. Best not to keep him waiting."

"I'll tell you what I can about it afterward," Joliffe promised and lengthened his stride.

Master Osburne and half a dozen of his men were waiting on horseback outside the gate. They were dusty with travel and sat their horses as if they would be traveling more, and Master Osburne said, without troubling over greetings, "We're on our way to Mistress Thorncoffyn's to arrest Hewstere."

"You found out what you needed."

"I found it. About both him and Aylton. I followed both their trails back, past where they crossed and parted and crossed again, until I found people who knew them both, knew things about them that neither man would have been happy to have told here *and* gave the reason Hewstere would prefer Aylton dead to Aylton alive. It seems Hewstere is a physician only because he says he is. He never trained to be more than a poorly skilled apothecary. He and Aylton grew up in the same place, knew each other from their young days. Aylton went off and became steward to a gentry family two shires away and sometime recommended Hewstere as a physician to them and the neighborhood. How the two of them came to decide to do that, I don't know, but it got Hewstere out of being an apothecary and into being a physician. That was eight years ago and their paths twined and untwined afterward, neither man staying long anywhere, until Hewstere had chance to recommend Aylton to Geoffrey Thorncoffyn after Aylton had had a falling out with the last man he worked for. The man did not want the bother of setting the law on him, so turned him loose without a recommendation instead."

"I don't suppose Aylton was above putting threat on Hewstere to give him away if he didn't help him to a place with the Thorncoffyns," Joliffe said.

"I don't suppose so, either. Then of course they both had to keep quiet about the other, since one couldn't give the other away without giving himself."

"So when Aylton wanted to be rid of Mistress Thorncoffyn in favor of the more easily deceived Geoffrey, he could force Hewstere to help him under threat that he would take Hewstere down if he went down. Hewstere, being an apothecary, would know how to go about poisoning the candied ginger."

"Just so."

"And all that," Joliffe summed up triumphantly, "would be why Aylton would go to Hewstere, confident of help in escaping, *and* why Hewstere would be happier simply to have him dead."

"That is how it will be put to the jury, yes."

Master Osburne sounded grimly satisfied it would suffice. He and Joliffe regarded each other in a momentary silence, Joliffe not knowing what else was in the crowner's mind but with a sharp awareness in his own of how Hewstere's and Aylton's lives, seemingly made up entirely of selfish choices, had been crowned by a final, mutual ugliness.

Then Master Osburne gave a curt nod as if to acknowledge it was finished and said, "Tell Master Soule. Give my apology I didn't tell him myself but I wanted no more than to pause. This is something best done as soon as may be."

Joliffe could not hold in a smile. "Mistress Thorncoffyn won't be best pleased."

"Nor will Hewstere," Master Osburne said, not smiling, "if I decide to let her have at him before I take him into custody."

He gathered his reins, turned his horse, and rode away, his men with him. Joliffe, watching them leave, was aware feelings were mixed in him. On one side, it was hard not to be in at the end of the thing, hard to watch the men ride away to settle it and know he would know no more about it. But then again, on another side, he had a kind of relief that the ugliness was going to happen far away from him, where he would have no part in it since after all, given choice and on the whole, far away from him was how he would like all ugliness to happen.

Three days later, under a sky that looked like it might turn to rain—but no one caring, now harvest was done—Ellis, Gil, and Piers brought Tisbe, Pyramus, and the cart with its red and yellow tilt to a stop outside the hospital's foregate where Basset, Rose, and Joliffe waited, Joliffe with his sack over his shoulder, Rose with a bundle in her arms that smelled of fresh baking that was the sisters' farewell gift, Basset leaning on his staff. With no immediate need for words among them, Joliffe took Rose's bundle to stow in the rear of the cart along with his sack—smaller by the lack of the lute he had left with Daveth—while Piers stayed at Tisbe's head, and Ellis and Gil helped Basset climb into the forward seat.

Having slid his staff to lie at his feet, Basset straightened, looked all around, and declared, "I feel a king." He patted the seat beside him. "Rose, come you and sit, too."

Rose began a refusing shake of her head, but Ellis took her by an elbow and half-lifted her to step up onto the wheel and from there sit beside her father. Looking caught between pleased and uncertain, she smiled down at Ellis, who smiled back at her even while he caught Piers by the belt to forestall him clambering up, too, saying, "You walk with the rest of us, youngling. Give the new horse a chance."

Joliffe, already gone to Tisbe's head, clucked her forward on the road to who-knew-where-next, deep in the contentment of being where he chose to be.

Author's Note

So many clichés about the Middle Ages are based on Victorian notions of the "Gothick" and are derived not from actual medieval circumstances but from a later time in English history, when societal and economic changes contributed to the over-population and decay of the towns, a slump in the general quality of life for ordinary people, and the destruction of long-established systems of charity for the needy. (I shall not resist the urge to insert a snippy and ironic "Well done, Tudors," here.)

In the case of medieval English hospitals, the clichés are particularly unfair. To learn more about these hospitals and the people who worked in them, some reasonably easily available books are *The Medieval Hospitals of England* by R. M. Clay, *The English Hospital, 1070-1570* by Nicholas Orme, and *Medicine and Society in Later Medieval England* by Carole Rawcliffe. The bibliographies in the latter two especially will show the way to extensive other reading.

As for the level of the medical treatment patients might receive in one of these establishments, one should rightly suppose there was the same variation of good to bad that one may receive in the modern health care system. Physicians acted then with the same combination of knowledge and guesswork, care and carelessness, as their modern counterparts do, and like their modern counterparts, used the best techniques available to them. Or not, of course, depending—

then as now—on the individual physician. That six hundred years of scientific knowledge had not yet happened for medieval physicians is hardly their fault, and it may be salutary to consider what will be said about our present medical care six hundred years from now.

A great many treatises and books were available regarding medicines and care of the sick. Somewhere like St. Giles in this story would almost surely have been gifted at some point with at least one volume, to be used by those involved in the care of the ill and aged. A number of these books have been reprinted and are available. One specific to the time of this story is *Healing and Society in Medieval England*, edited by Faye Marie Getz. That it is in Middle English adds to its delights.

The Seven Corporeal Acts of Mercy mentioned in Chapter 2 were an integral part of medieval religious life. They are: to feed the hungry, give drink to the thirsty, clothe the naked, bury the dead, shelter the traveler (today shifted from travelers to the homeless), comfort the sick, and free the imprisoned (today changed to visit them). In medieval England, the belief that performing these acts of mercy can lead to the soul's salvation—and their neglect to damnation—led to the founding of many charitable institutions and bequests, most of which—being usually affiliated with religious establishments—were dissolved or seized in the Tudors' Reformation.

The seven-paneled painting *Works of Mercy* by the Master of Alkmaar depicts them in a medieval context, albeit far more elaborately than would be found on the chapel walls of a small country hospital.

6/12